Praise for Mary Robison

"There is much to be gained from her lean, deeply felt fiction. Bearing as her tools the best ear for English since James, a sense of pacing that is nothing less than perfect, and an intensely accurate feel for American life."
David Leavitt

"Robison has a poet's eye for the unconscious surrealism of commercial America. . . . And she has a playwright's ear for American speech, the things one hears people say all the time but rarely sees written down."
Katha Pollitt, *The New York Times Book Review*

"Mary Robison's short stories are short, subtle, and substantial . . . her ironic sense of detail bursts from every sentence."
Vogue

"Mary Robison's hard-edged, fine-tooled, enigmatic super-realism is a joy."
John Barth

"[Robison] is a master of line and texture who gets maximum information out of the glittering and intentionally deceptive surfaces of our image-dominated culture. Robison raises sitcom wit to the level of real emotional situations, real comedy as real art."
Joseph Coates, *Chicago Tribune*

"There isn't a writer working today who sees the world, or hears it, or tastes it, or inhabits it more fearlessly than Mary Robison."
Frederick Barthelme

Praise for Believe Them

"Sorrow and pain are underground messages in these finely made stories. . . . Robison uses a minimalist discipline and barely ruffled surfaces, but her hidden pictures of childhood and other states of vulnerability can be boundless in their emotion."
Richard Eder, *Los Angeles Times Book Review*

"Robison's methods allow the careful reader an honest perspective into lives usually dealt with either melodramatically or contemptuously by other authors."
Larry McCaffery, *The New York Times Book Review*

"Terrific . . . full and resonant and packed with feeling. Her verbal energy is just astonishing."
   Bobbie Ann Mason

"Full of observations that stay in the mind long after reading. . . . Readers may begin to feel that Robison is writing directly to them, telling secrets to them and no one else."
   San Francisco Chronicle

Praise for *An Amateur's Guide to the Night*

"No American short story writer speaks to our time more urgently or fondly than Robison. Word for fucking word, her work demands our attention."
   David Leavitt, *The Village Voice*

"Like Raymond Carver and Ann Beattie, whose fictional territory closely resembles her own, Miss Robison has achieved in one novel and two short-story collections a style perfectly adapted to delineating these attenuated lives."
   Michiko Kakutani, *New York Times*

"The writing is cool and detached, controlling a breathtaking compassion . . . [A]n intimate, enriching experience."
   San Francisco Chronicle

Praise for *Days*

"There is an almost incredible purity of line and texture in these stories. Every phrase is lucid, every character comes alive, and every sentence suggests a calm, wise, heartbroken version of the world. Robison writes like an avenging angel, and I think she may be a genius."
   Richard Yates

"[These] are not so much stories as splinters of contemporary life, set under a microscope . . . there is humor here, as well as a deadpan exactitude . . . Mary Robison's style at its best [is] stripped, incisive, clear as a piece of glass held up to the light."
   Ann Tyler

Tell Me

Also by Mary Robison

Tell Me
30 Stories
Mary Robison

COUNTERPOINT
WASHINGTON, D.C.
NEW YORK, N.Y.

Author's Note: Several of the stories in this volume appear as they did originally in *The New Yorker* and are in slightly different form from the versions collected in *Days* and *An Amateur's Guide to the Night*. The author is most grateful to the magazine and especially to Roger Angell.

"Coach," "Smoke," "In the Woods," "The Help," "I Get By," "Daughters," "Seizing Control," "Kite and Paint," "Trying," "Pretty Ice," "While Home," "In Jewel," "I Am Twenty-One," "Independence Day," "For Real," "May Queen," "The Wellman Twins," "Mirror," "Doctor's Sons," "What I Hear," "Smart," "Sisters," and "Yours" appeared in *The New Yorker;* "Likely Lake" appeared in *The Paris Review;* "Happy Boy, Allen" appeared in the *Mississippi Review;* "An Amateur's Guide to the Night" appeared in *Seventeen;* and "Your Errant Mom" appeared in *Gentleman's Quarterly*.

Library of Congress Cataloging-in-Publication Data
Robison, Mary.
  Tell me : 30 stories / Mary Robison.
    p. cm.
  ISBN 1-58243-258-9 (pbk.)
  I. Title.
  PS3568.O317 T45 2002
  813'.54--dc21
                                    2002008499
FIRST PRINTING

Text design by Trish Wilkinson

Printed in the United States of America on acid-free paper that meets the American National Standards Institute Z39-48 standard

COUNTERPOINT
387 Park Avenue South
New York, NY 10016-8810.

Counterpoint is a member of the Perseus Books Group.

10   9   8   7   6   5   4   3   2   1

with affection,
for my stepfather, Robert Reiss,
and for Dr. F. Elizabeth Reiss, my brilliant mother

Contents

I

Coach

1

THE AUGUST TWO-A-DAY practice sessions were just sixty-seven days away, Coach calculated. He was drying breakfast dishes. He swabbed a coffee cup and made himself listen to his wife, Sherry, who was across the kitchen, sponging the stove's burner coils.

"I know I'm no Renoir, but I have so much damn fun trying, and this little studio, that one room, we can afford," Sherry said. "I could get out of your way by going there, and get you and Daphne out of my way. No offense."

"I'm thinking," Coach said.

Sherry coasted from appliance to appliance. She swiped the face of the oven clock with her sponge. "You're thinking too slow," she said. "Your reporter's coming at nine, and it's way after eight. Should I give them a deposit on the studio, or not? Yes or no?"

Coach was staring at the sink, at a thread of water that came from one of the taps. He thought of a lake place where they used to go, in Pennsylvania. He saw green water being thickly sliced by a power boat—the boat towing Sherry, who was blond and laughing on her skis, her back rounded and strong, her suit shining red.

"Of course, of course. Give them the money," he said.

Their daughter, Daphne, wandered into the kitchen. She was a dark-haired girl, lazy-looking, fifteen; her eyes lost behind her bangs. She drew open the enormous refrigerator door.

"Don't lean on that," her mother said.

"And what are you after?" Coach asked.

"Food, mainly," Daphne said.

Coach's wife went away, to the little sun patio off the kitchen. He pushed the glass door after her, and it smacked shut.

"Eat and run," he said to Daphne. "I've got a reporter coming in short order. Get dressed." He spoke firmly, but in the smaller voice he always used for his child.

"Yes, sir," Daphne said. She opened the freezer compartment and ducked to let its gate pass over her head. "Looks bad. Nothing in here but Eggos," she said.

"Have Eggos. I did. Just hustle up," Coach said.

"Can't I be here for this guy?" Daphne asked.

"Who guy? The reporter? Uh-uh. He's just from the college, Daph. Coming to see if the new freshmen coach has two heads or none."

"Hey, lookit," Daphne said. She blew a breath in front of the freezer compartment and it made a short jet of mist.

Coach remembered a fall night, a Friday game night long ago, when he had put Daphne on the playing field. It was during the pre-game ceremonies before his unbeaten squad had taken on Ignatius South High. Parents' Night. He had laced shoulder pads on Daphne, and draped the trainer's gag jersey—No. ½—over her, and placed Tim . . . somebody's enormous helmet over her eight-year-old head. She was lost in the getup—a small pile of equipment out on the fifty, from which warm wisps of air trailed now and then.

She had applauded when the loudspeaker announced her name, and the P.A. voice, garbled by amplification and echo, rang out, "Daughter of our coach Harry Noonan and his lovely wife: Number One-Half—Daphne Noonan!"

She had stood in the bath of floodlights as the players and their folks walked by when they were introduced—the players grim in their war gear, the parents looking tiny and apologetic in everyday clothes. The co-captain of the team, awesome in his pads and cleats and steaming from warmup running, had playfully palmed Daphne's big helmet and twisted it sideways.

From behind, Coach had heard a great "Haaa!" from the home stands as Daphne turned in circles, trying to right the helmet. Her left eye had twinkled out through one earhole, Coach remembered. "God, that's funny," the crowd said. And "Coach's kid."

᠍

On the sun porch now, his wife was doing a set of tennis exercises. Framed by the glass doors, she twisted her torso from one side to the other between Coach and the morning sunlight. Through the weave of her caftan, he could make out the white image left by her swimsuit.

"I knew you wouldn't let me," Daphne said. She had poured a glass of chocolate milk. She pulled open a chilled banana. "I bet Mom gets to be here."

"Daph, this isn't a big deal. We've been through it all before," Coach said.

"Not for a college paper," Daphne said. "Wait a minute, I'll be right back." She left the kitchen.

"I'll hold my breath and count the heartbeats," Coach said.

They were new to the little town, new to Ohio. Coach was assuming charge of the freshman squad; it was a league where freshmen weren't eligible for the varsity. He had taken the job not sure if it was a step up for him or a risky career move. The money was so-so. But he wanted the college setting for his family—especially for Daphne. She had seemed to begin to lose interest in the small celebrity they achieved in high-school towns.

She looked bored at the Noonans' Sunday spaghetti dinners for standout players. She had stopped fetching plates of food for the boys, some of whom were still game-sore. She had even stopped wearing the charm bracelet her parents had put together for her—a silver bracelet with a tiny megaphone, the numerals 68 (a league championship year) and, of course, a miniature football.

Coach took a seat at the kitchen table. He ate grapes from a bowl. He spilled bottled wheat germ into his palm. On the table were four chunky ring binders, their black Leatherette covers printed with the college seal, which still looked strange to him. They were his playbooks, and he was having trouble getting the tactics of the new system into his head. "Will you turn off the radio?" he yelled.

The bleat from Daphne's upstairs bedroom ceased. A minute later, she was back down in the kitchen. She had a cardboard folder and some textbooks with her. "Later on, would you look at this stuff and help me?" she asked Coach. "Can you do these?"

He glanced over one of her papers. It was pencilled with algebra equations, smutty with erasures and scribbled-out parts. "I'd have to see the book, but no anyway. Not now, not later. I don't want to and I don't have time."

"That's just great," Daphne said. "And Mrs. Math Genius told me 'Do it yourself.' Well, I can't."

"Your mother and I got our algebra homework done already, Daph. We turned ours in. That was in 1956. She got an A and I got a C."

"Mom!" Daphne called, pushing aside the glass door.

"Forget it, if it's the homework you want," Sherry said.

"Don't give in to her," Coach said. "I know you. The last time, you did everything but go there and take the tests for her, and she still flunked. This is summer school, and she's on her own."

"But I can't do it," Daphne said.

"Besides, I've got my own homework," Coach said, and frowned at his playbooks.

2

Toby, the boy sent from *The Rooter* to interview Coach, was un-shaven and bleary-eyed. He wore a rumpled cerise polo shirt and faded jeans. He asked his questions wearily, dragging his words. Twice, he yawned during Coach's answers. He took no notes.

"You getting this, now?" Coach said at last.

"Oh, yeah, it's writing itself. I'm a pro," Toby said, and Coach was not certain if the boy was kidding. "So you've been here just a little while then. Lucky you," Toby said. "Less than a month."

"Is that like a question? It *seems* less than a month—less than a week. Seems like a day and a half," Coach said. For the interview, he had put on white sports slacks and a maroon pullover with a gold collar—the school's colors. He had bought the pullover at Campus World. The clothes had a snug fit that flattered Coach and showed off his straight stomach and heavy shoulders. He and Toby were on either end of the sofa in the living room.

"And you bought this house—right?" Toby said. He stood up. "Well, believe it or not, I've got enough for a couple sticks," he said. "That's two columns, among us press men. If you're going to be home tomorrow, there's a girl who'll come and take your picture. Marcia. She's a drag, I warn you."

"One thing about this town, there aren't any damn side-walks and the cars don't give you much room if you're jogging," Coach said, getting up, too.

"When I'm hitching, I wear a safety orange poncho and carry a red flag and paint a big 'X' on my back," Toby said. "Of course, I realize I'm just making a better target for the speeders."

"I run down at the track now. It's a great facility, compara-ble to a Big Ten's. I like the layout," Coach said.

"O.K., but the interview's over," Toby said.

"Well, I came from high schools, remember. In Indiana and Pennsylvania—good schools with good budgets, but high schools nonetheless."

"Yeah, I got where you're coming from," Toby said.

"Did you need to know what courses I'll be handling? Fall quarter, they've got me lined up for two. 'The Atlantic World' and 'Colloquium on European Industrial Development,' I think it is. Before, I always taught world history. P.O.D. once or twice."

"That 381 you're going to teach is a gut course, in case no one's informed you. It's what we call 'lunch,'" Toby said.

"It's in the nature of a refresher course," Coach said.

Daphne suddenly came into the room from the long hall. Her dark hair was brushed and lifting with static. Her eyes seemed larger than usual to Coach, and a little sooty around the lashes.

"You're just leaving, aren't you, Buster?" Coach said to her.

"Retrieving a pencil," Daphne said.

"Is your name really Buster?" Toby asked.

"Get your pencil and scoot. This is Toby, here. Toby, this is Daphne," Coach said.

"Nice to meet you," Daphne said. She slid into a deep chair at the far corner of the living room.

"Can she hear us over in that county?" Toby said. "Do you read me?" he shouted.

Daphne smiled. Coach saw bangs and her very white teeth. "Come on, Daph, hit the trail," he said.

"I've got a joke for her first," Toby said. "What's green and moves very fast?"

"Frog in a blender," Daphne said. "Dad? Some friends asked me to go swimming with them at the Natatorium. May I?"

"You must see the Nat. It's the best thing," Toby said.

"What about your class, though? She's in makeup school here, Toby, catching up on some algebra that didn't take the first time around."

Toby wrinkled his nose at Daphne. "Algebra? Blah! At first, I thought you meant makeup school. Like lipstick and rouge."

"I wish," Daphne said. She slipped her left foot from her leather sandal and casually stroked the toes.

"She's a nut for swimming," Coach said.

"You'll be *so* bored here," Toby said to her. "Most nights, your options are ordering a pizza or slashing your wrists. Those are the choices of what there is to do."

"Yes, sure," she said, disbelievingly.

"Take it from Toby," he said, waving goodbye.

Coach let Toby out through the front door and watched until he was down the street.

"He was nice," Daphne said.

"Aw, Daph. That's what you say about everybody. There's a lot better things you could say—more on-the-beam things."

"I guess you're mad," she said.

Coach went to the kitchen, back to his playbooks.

Daphne came after him. "Aren't you?" she said.

"I guess you thought he was cute," Coach said. He flipped through some mimeographed pages, turning them on the notebook's silver rings. "I don't mean to shock you about it, but you'd be wasting your time there. You'd be trying to start a fire with a limp wet match."

Daphne stared at her father. "That's sick!" she said.

"I'm not criticizing him for it. I'm just telling you," Coach said.

3

"This is completely wrong," Coach said sadly. He read further. "Oh, no," he said. He drowned the newspaper in his bathwater and flung the wet pages over into a corner.

His wife handed him a dry copy, one of the ten or twelve *Rooters* Daphne had brought home. Sherry was sitting parallel to Coach on the edge of the tub, with her back braced against the tiled wall. "Oh, cheer up," she said. "Probably nobody reads a free newspaper."

Coach folded the dry new *Rooter* into an oblong around Toby's article. "O.K., I wasn't head coach at Elmgrove, and I sure wasn't Phi Beta Kappa. Ugly, ugly picture," Coach said.

"Your head looks huge."

"You were never at Mt. Holyoke. Where did he get that one? I didn't bitch about the sidewalks this much."

"You didn't? That's almost too bad. I thought it was the best part of the article," Sherry said.

Coach slipped deeper into the warm water, until it came up to his chin. He kept the newspaper aloft. "Oh, come on, give me some credit here!" he cried. "Don't they have any supervision over in Journalism? I don't see how he could get away with this. It's an unbelievably sloppy job."

"It's just a dinky article in a handout paper, Coach," Sherry said. "What do you care? It wouldn't matter if he said we were a bright-orange family with scales," Sherry said.

"He didn't think of that or he would have. This breaks my heart," Coach said.

"Daph liked it," Sherry said.

Coach wearily chopped at the bathwater with the side of his hand. They read this in the football office. I'll spend my first year here explaining how none of it's true."

"Lie," his wife advised him. "Who'll know?"

"And sure Daphne like it. She was called 'pretty' or whatever. The pretty Noonan daughter who'll be attending Flippo High School in the fall," Coach said.

"'Petite,' actually. 'The petite brunette,'" Sherry corrected.

"Daphne's not that small," Coach said.

"I just think the person who's going to come out of this looking bad is that reporter, finally," Sherry said.

"I could kill him," Coach said. "Then he'd look bad."

4

Now Coach had a little more than a month before the start of the two-a-days. He was seated awkwardly on an iron stool at a white table on the patio of the Dairy Frost. Daphne was beside him, fighting the early-evening heat for her mocha-fudge ice-cream cone. She tilted her head at the cone, lapping at it.

"You aren't saying anything," Coach said.

"Wait," Daphne said. She worked on the cone.

"I've been waiting."

"If you two want to separate, it's none of my business," she said.

Out in the parking lot, a new powder-blue Pontiac turned off the highway, glided easily onto the gravel, and took the parking slot by the door. The boy in the driver's seat looked familiar to Coach. Good-looking shoulders. The couple in the back—the boy's parents, Coach thought—were both talking at once.

"Have I been wasting my breath for nothing?" Coach said. "*Not* a separation. Not anything like it."

"All right, *not*," Daphne said. She stopped her attack on the cone long enough to watch the Pontiac boy step out. A blob of ice cream streamed between her knuckles and down the inside of her wrist.

"You're losing it, Champ," Coach said.

Daphne dabbed around the cone and her hand, making repairs.

"Hell, real trouble—your father wouldn't tell you about at a Dairy Frost," Coach said. "This apartment your mom found is like an office or something. A place for her to go and get away every now and then. That kid's in my backfield. What the *hell's* his name?"

They watched as the young man took orders from his parents, then came into the Dairy Frost. He looked both wider and taller than the other patrons—out of their scale. His rump and haunches were thick with muscle.

"Bobby Stark!" Coach said, and smiled very quickly at the Pontiac. He turned back to his daughter.

"She wants to get away from us," Daphne said.

"Definitely not. She gave me a list, is how this started. She's got things she wants to do, and you with your school problems and me with the team, we're too much for her. She could spend her whole day on us, if you think about it, and never have a second for herself. If you think about it fairly, you'll see."

"That guy looks dumb. One of the truly dumb," Daphne said.

"My halfback? He's not. He was his class salutatorian," Coach said.

"He doesn't know *you.*"

"Just embarrassed. Can't we stick to the point, Daphne?"

She gave a sigh and marched over to a trash can to deposit her slumping cone. She washed up after at a child's drinking fountain. When she came back to the table, Coach had finished his Brown Cow, but he kept the plastic spoon in his mouth.

"What was on this list of Mom's?" Daphne asked.

"Adult stuff, Daphne."

"Just give me an example," she said.

Coach removed the spoon and cracked it in half.

"Dad!" Daphne said.

"I always do that. Your mother's list is for five years. In that time, she wants to be living differently. She wants to be speaking French, regularly. She wants to follow up on her printmaking, and we both know she's got talent there, with her lithographs and all."

"This is adult stuff?" Daphne said.

Coach raised a hand to Bobby Stark. Stark had three malt cups in a cardboard carrier and he was moving toward his car. "Hey, those all for you?" Coach said cheerfully.

"I still got a month to get fat, Coach. Then you'll have five months to beat it off me."

Some of the people at the tables around Coach's lit up with smiles at the conversation. Stark's parents were grinning.

"Every hit of that junk takes a second off your time in the forty," Coach said.

Stark pretended to hide the malts behind his arm. He was blushing.

"Duh," Daphne said in a hoarse voice. "Which way to duh door, Coach?"

"He can hear you," Coach said.

"Duh, kin I have a candy bar, Coach?" she said. "Kin I? Kin I?"

They watched Stark get into the Pontiac. He slammed the door and threw Daphne a wink so dazzling that she went silent.

5

Coach was in the basement laundry room, both arms busy hugging a bundle of jogging clothes. He was waiting for Sherry to unload her clothes from the washer.

"The Dallas Cowboys are soaking their players in a sense-deprivation tub of warm salt water," she said.

"We know," Coach said.

"If Dallas is doing it, I just thought you might like to consider it."

"We have. Hustle up a little with your stuff," Coach said.

"It's like my apartment," Sherry said. "A place apart."

Coach cut her off. "Don't go on about how much you love your apartment."

"I wasn't," Sherry said. She slung her wet slacks and blouses into the dryer.

Coach had two weeks before the start of the heavy practices. His team would have him then, he knew, almost straight through to the Christmas holidays. "You already spend half your time there," he said.

A little later, Coach and his wife were on the side patio together, sharing a Tab. They could hear the hum and tick of the dryer indoors.

"You know what's odd? Daphne's popularity here," Sherry said. "I don't mean it's *odd*." She was taking sun on her back, adding to her tan.

"No, that isn't new. She's always done terrific with people," Coach said.

"Your people, though. These are hers," Sherry said. "The phone hardly ever stops."

"Well, she's out of math trouble, I guess," Coach said. "And you have your apartment hideout, and you're adjusted here. Now, if only I can have the season I want."

"I love it with her and that reporter," Sherry said.

Daphne had become tight friends with Toby after she telephoned her gratitude for what he had written about her in *The Rooter*.

"Yeah, they're like sisters," Coach said.

"You're still bitter?"

"I'm really not," Coach said. "I live one careful day at a time now. No looking back for a second. Fear motivates me."

"You're fearful," Sherry said.

"Shaking with it," Coach said.

6

It was eight days before the two-a-day practice sessions would begin. The sky was colorless and glazed, like milk glass. When Coach flicked a glance at the sun, his eyes ached as if he were seeing molten steel. He had run some wind sprints on the stadium field, and now he was doing an easy lap on the track. A stopwatch on a noose of ribbon swung against his chest. He cut through the goalposts and trotted for the sidelines, where he had dumped his clipboard and a towel.

Bobby Stark came out from under the stands. His football shoes were laced together and draped around his neck. He was in cutoff shorts and a midriff-cut T-shirt. He walked gingerly in white wool socks. "Did everybody go, or am I the first one here?" he called to Coach.

"'Bout a half hour," Coach said, heaving.

Stark sat down to untangle his shoes, and Coach, sweating, stood over him. Coach spat. He folded his arms in a way that pushed out his muscles. He sniffed to clear his lungs, twisting his whole nose and mouth to one side. "You know, Stark, I heard you were salutatorian for your class," he said.

"High school," the boy said. He grinned up at Coach, an eye pinched against the glare.

"That counts, believe me. Maybe we can use you to help some of our slower players along—some of the linemen."

"What do you mean—tutor?" Stark said.

"Naw. Teach them to eat without biting off their fingers. How to tie a necktie. Teach them some of your style," Coach said, and Stark bobbed his head.

Stark settled the fit of his right shoe. He said, "But there aren't really any dumb ones on the squad, because they just flunk out here. Recruiters won't touch them in this league."

Coach planted his feet on either side of a furrow of lime-eaten grass. Above the open end of the stadium, the enormous

library building was shimmering and uncertain behind sheets of
heat that rose from the empty parking area.

Stark got up and watched his shoes as he jogged in place.
He danced twenty yards down the field; loped back. Other
players were arriving for the informal session. Coach meant to
time them in the mile and in some dashes.

Stark looked jittery. He walked in semicircles, crowding
Coach.

"You worried about something?" Coach asked him. "Girl
problems? You pull a muscle already?"

Stark glanced quickly around them. He said, "I've lived all
my life two doors down from Coach Burton's house. My mom
and Burton's wife are the best of friends, so I always know
what's really going on. You probably know about it already,
anyway," Stark said. "Do you?"

"What the hell are you talking about, Stark?"

"Oh, so you don't. Typical. Burton's leaving, see, like the end
of this year. His wife wants him out real bad, and the alumni want
him out, because they're tired of losing seasons. They're tired of
finishing third in the league, at best. Everybody says he should go
to Athletic Director, instead. So what I heard was that you were
brought in because of it, and if we do well this season—because
people think you're a winner and pretty young—like, *you'll* be
our varsity coach next year."

"That's conjecture," Coach said. But his voice sounded
strange to him.

"We could go through four years together. I respect Coach
Burton, but I don't see why in four years *we'd* ever have to lose
a single game," Stark said. He toook a stance, his body pushing
forward.

"Ho!" Coach barked, and Stark lunged out.

"See me after this practice!" Coach called to him.

↜

It was three o'clock, still hot. Coach was moving along a sidewalk with Stark, who was balanced on a racing bike, moving just enough to keep the machine upright.

"Three things," Coach said. "I've seen all the game films from last year, and I came here personally and witnessed the Tech game. No one lost because of the coaching. A coach can work miracles with a good team, but he's helpless if his folks don't want it bad enough. That's the worst thing about running a team—you can't climb down into your people's hearts and change them."

Some college girls in a large car passed and shrieked and whistled at Bobby Stark. "Lifeguards at the pool," he explained.

"I don't know if Burton's leaving or not, but if his wife wants him to, he'll probably go," Coach said. "If you're ever thinking about a career in coaching someday, Bob, think about that. Your family's either with you or you've had it. You drag them all over hell—one town to another—and bury them, and whether you stay anywhere or not depends on a bunch of *kids,* really. I swear, I'd give up a leg for a chance to get in a game myself—just one play, with what I now know."

"I wish you could," Stark said. He swerved his bike's front tire and let it plunk off the curb into a crosswalk. He stood on the pedals for the jolt of the rear tire.

"The last thing is, don't mention the varsity-coach thing to anybody, and I mean anybody. Do you read me?"

Stark nodded. They went on a block, and he said, "I turn here. You going to tell your beautiful daughter about it?"

"My daughter. You want a kitten? Because when I tell her, she's going to have kittens," Coach said.

No one was home. A plastic lady-bug magnet held a note to the face of the refrigerator. The note read; "Noonan, I'm at my place. Daph's with Toby K. somewhere, fooling around. Be good now. Sherry Baby."

"Dope," Coach said, smiling. He felt very good.

He took a beer upstairs and drank it while he showered. He cinched on a pair of sweat pants and went back down and fetched another beer. He watched some of a baseball game on cable television. He thought over the things he had told Bobby Stark.

"Boy, is that true!" Coach said, and then wasn't sure why he had said it.

He frowned, remembering that in his second year of college, the only year he had been on the varsity team, he had proved an indifferent player.

"Not now," he whispered. He squeezed his beer can out of shape and stood it on top of the TV.

꙳

There was a thump over his head. The ceiling creaked. Someone had come home while he was in the shower. He took the stairs in three leaps and strode into the bedroom, saying, "Sherry?"

The dark figure in the room surprised him. "Hey!" He yelled.

Daphne was dancing in front of the full-length mirror on Sherry's closet door. She had improvised a look—sweeping her hair over her right ear and stretching the neck of her shirt until her right shoulder was bared. A fast Commodores song thumped from her transistor radio.

"Nothing," she said.

"You're not home. Aren't you with Whoosis? You're supposed to be out. You are *beet* red," Coach said.

Daphne lowered her head and squared her shirt, which bagged around her small torso. "O.K., Dad," she said.

"No, but how did your audience like the show? I bet they loved it," Coach said. He smiled at himself in the mirror. "I'm just kidding you. You looked great."

"Come *on*, Dad," Daphne said, and tried to pass.

He chimed in with the radio song. He shuffled his feet. "Hey, Daph. You know what time it is?"

"Let me out, please," she said.

"It's Monkey time!" Coach did a jerky turn, keeping in the way of the exit door. "Do the Shing-a-Ling. Do the Daphne." He rolled his shoulder vampishly. He kissed his own hand. He sang along.

"Thanks a lot," Daphne said. She gave up trying to get around him. She leaned over and snapped off the radio. "You've got to use a mirror, so you don't look stupid on the dance floor. Everybody does," she said.

"I really was kidding you. Seriously. I know dancing is important," Coach said.

"May I go now? I've got algebra," Daphne said. She brought her hair from behind her ear, which was burning pink.

"Before that, you have to hear the news," Coach said. "Here's a news bulletin, flash extra."

"You're drunk. You and Mom are going to live in different cities. Somebody shot somebody," Daphne said.

"No, this is good news. There's a chance I'll be head coach here, of the varsity. The varsity coach. Me." Coach pointed to his chest.

"Let me out, please," Daphne said.

Coach let her pass. He followed her down the thin hallway to her bedroom. "More money. I'll even be on TV. I'll have my own local show on Sundays. And I'll get written up in the press all the time, by real reporters. Daphne?"

She closed her door, and, from the sound, Coach thought she must have leaned against it.

"What's going on? Tell me, why am I standing here yelling at wood?" he said.

8

By dusk, Coach was drunk at the kitchen table. He was enjoying the largeness of the room, and he was making out a roster for his dream team. He had put the best kids from his fifteen years of coaching in the positions they had played for him. He was puzzling over the tight-end spot. "Jim Wyckoff or Jerry Kinney? Kinny got that tryout with the Broncos later," he said out loud. He pencilled "Kinney" onto his diagram.

He heard Daphne on the stairs, and it occurred to him to clear the beer cans from the table. Instead, he snapped open a fresh can. "Daphne?" he said.

"Wait a second. What?" she said from the living room.

"Just wondered who else was alive besides me. I know your mom's still out."

Daphne entered the kitchen.

"You're sorry you were rude before?" Coach said. "That's O.K. Daph, just forget it."

Daphne made the slightest nod. "You drank all those?" she said.

"Hold still. What've you got on?" Coach asked. He hauled his chair about so he could see Daphne, who had gone behind him.

"Two, four, five," Daphne said, counting the cans. She wore one of the fan shirts that Coach had seen on a few summer co-eds. On the front of the shirt, against a maroon field, were the golden letters "GO." Across the back was "GRIFFINS!"

"Now you're talking," Coach said.

"It was free. This guy I met—well, these two guys, really, who work at Campus World gave it to me. But, I don't know, I thought I'd wear it. I wanted you to see that I care if you get that big job. I do care. I want to stay here. Do you think we can? Do your people look any good this year?"

"Winners," Coach said.

"Yeah, but you always say that," Daphne said.

Coach skidded his chair forward. "Have a beer. Sit down and let me show you on paper the material they've given me to work with."

Daphne took the can Coach offered, sipped at it, shook her head, and said, "Ooh, it burns. No wonder people burp."

"These guys are fast and big, for once. I'm not overestimating them, either. I've seen what I've seen," Coach said.

A car swept into the drive, and then its engine noise filled the garage. Coach and Daphne were quiet until Sherry bustled down the short hall that connected the garage with the kitchen.

"Really late, sorry, sorry," she said.

"It's a party, I warn you," Coach said to her.

"So I noticed." Sherry was carrying a grocery sack, not very full. There were bright streaks of paint on her brown arms. Daphne got up and plucked a bag of Oreo cookies from the groceries.

"Shoot me one of those," Coach said.

"Any beer left for me?" Sherry said. "I want to drown my disappointment. I can't paint!"

"You can paint," Coach said.

"Ugh. My ocean today looked like wavy cement. My rocks looked like big dirty marshmallows." She put her sack down on the kitchen counter.

"Tell Dad he's got to do well so we can stay here," Daphne said to her mother.

Coach said, "Man, Daphne! I hope somebody finds your 'off' switch." He told his wife, "Plant your behind in that chair, Picasso. Let me tell you how we're moving up in the world."

"Every August," Sherry said, "Coach wants us to get packed up for a trip to the moon."

2

An Amateur's Guide to the Night

S TARS WERE SOMETHING, SINCE I'd found out which was which. I was smiling at Epsilon Lyrae through the front windshield of my date's Honda Civic—my date, a much older man who, I would've bet, had washed his curly hair with Herbal Essence. Behind us, in the little back seat, my date's friend was kissing my mom.

I could see Epsilon, and two weeks before, when I biked all the way to a veterans' cemetery outside Terre Haute, I had been able to separate Epsilon's quadruple stars—the yellows and the blues—with just my binoculars. I had been way up on the hill there, making a smeary-red glow in the night with my flashlight. The beam had red cellophane taped on it, so I wouldn't desensitize my night vision, which always took an hour to get working well. My star chart and the sky had made sense entirely then, and though it was stinging cold for late spring, I stayed a while.

It was cold now, or our dates would have walked us away from the car for some privacy.

Mom was with the cuter guy, Kevin. She always got the lookers, even though she was just five feet tall. She wore platform shoes all the time because of it. That was her answer.

My problem was my hair. It was so stick-straight that I had had it cut like the model Esmé—a bad mistake.

I could hear Mom telling her date, "I woke up this morning and the car was gone."

"Sounds like a blues song," he said.

And now she was saying, "It's time for our beddy-bye. Sis has classes tomorrow."

❦

Mom and I passed for sisters. We did it all the time. I was an old seventeen. She was young for thirty-five. We would double-date—not just with these two. We saw all kinds of men. Never for very long, though. Three dates was about the record, because Mom would decide by the second evening out that there was something fishy—that her fellow was married, or running from somebody.

So it was perfectly fine with me. But I knew she hadn't pulled the plug on the evening because of my school, or the hour. I was late for school almost every day. Mom would say, "Why don't you wait and go in at noon? That would look better, not like we overslept, but more like you were ill. I'll write a note that says so."

As for studying, it was my practice to wait until the night before a test to read the books I was supposed to have read.

And I was used to a late schedule because of my waitress job, and the stars, and the late movies. If there was a scary movie on, one with a mummy or a prowler, say, Mom had to watch it, and she made me stay up to watch it with her.

❦

"Thanks for the Greek food and for riding us around. Thank you for the beer," we said to our dates. We had been let out on our front sidewalk.

"Next time we won't take you to such a dive," said one of the men.

"Adios!" I called to them. I threw an arm around Mom.

"Until never," she said, as she waved.

We lived about ten miles north of Terre Haute—me, my mom, and my grandfather. We rented a stone house that was a regular Indiana-type house, on Burnside Boulevard, in a town called Phoenicia.

"Greater Metropolitan Phoenicia," my grandfather liked to say, the joke being that the whole town was really just two rows of shopping blocks on either side of 188.

Grandpa was up, in the living room. We were all night owls. He was having tea, and he had on the robe that was embroidered with dandelions, in honor of spring, I suppose.

"Girls," he greeted us. "Something called *The Creeper* on Channel Nine. Starring an Onslow Stevens. Nineteen forty-eight. Sounds like your sort of poison."

"Did you tell Lindy about our croquettes?" Mom asked him, and laughed. She tossed her handbag onto the couch and pushed up the sleeves of her sweater.

"I forgot all about telling Lindy about the croquettes. That totally slipped from my mind," Grandpa said.

"Well, honey, they poisoned Pop's chicken croquettes. They got his *dinner,*" Mom said to me.

"A narrow escape," Grandpa said.

Lately it had been poison Mom talked about, and who knew if she was kidding? She also talked about "light pills" a great deal.

"This *Creeper* that's on—it says in the *Messenger*—he's half man, half cat-beast," Grandpa said.

"Ooh," Mom said, interested.

I asked them, "Would you like to go out in the back yard with me? I'll set up my telescope and show you some stuff."

I had a Frankus reflector telescope I bought with my waitress money. It wasn't perfect. I got it cheap. It did have motor drive, however, and a stabile equatorial mount, cradle rings, and engraved setting circles.

Mom and Grandpa said no, as always. Not that they could have told the difference between Ursa Minor and Hunting Dogs, but I wanted them, just once, to see how I could pull down Jupiter.

❧

It was late the next night, Friday. I was in my uniform and shoes, just off from work. The big concern, whenever someone giant-stepped over my legs, which were propped up on the coffee table, was to protect my expensive support hose.

The job I had was on the dinner shift, five to eleven, at the Steak Chateau, Friday and Saturday evenings. Waitressing and busing tables—I did both—could really wear you down. That evening I had been stiffed by a group of five adult people. That means no tip; a lot of juggling and running for nothing. Also, I had forgotten to charge one man for his chef's salad, and guess who got to pay for it.

Allen Tashman and Jay Gordon, accountants, were there at our place for popcorn and the Friday-night movie—one called *White Zombie*. They were there when I got home. Allen, the wimpy one, natch, I managed to talk into the back yard.

"Over that mass of shrubs by the garage. See?"

"I see," he said.

"The big Joe is Capella, eye of the Charioteer. And the Pleiades is hanging around somewhere in the same vicinity—there you go. Six little clots."

"Whoopee," he said.

But I loved telling them that stuff, although sometimes I was guessing, or making it up. I was just a C student in school.

"Hey, Lindy, by the way," Allen said, "are people stealing cars, that you know of?"

"Sis?" I asked. Mom and I were pretending to be sisters again.

"Yeah, she told me she thinks there's a car-theft ring in Phoenicia going on."

"Maybe there is," I said.

"She told me to park deep in the driveway and not out by the curb. Have you heard about it? A bunch of cars missing, from this neighborhood, way out here?"

"It's strange," I said, as if it could have been possible.

"I think your sister's crazy sometimes," Allen said:

I didn't bother to get the telescope. Oddly enough, on a *clear* night such as that, a star would have "boiled" in the view-finder. The stars were too bright, was the problem. They were swimming in their own illumination.

ↆ

We were talking about breakfast, which nobody wanted to fix. The weekend was over and it was Monday morning, getting on toward nine o'clock. I had intended to shake out of bed early, to see Venus in the west as a morning star. But Mom did something to my alarm clock.

She had been sleeping with me, the nights she got to sleep, in the same room, in the same bed.

She may have bashed my clock.

She probably reached over me and cuffed it.

So we were running behind. But I knew if I didn't eat breakfast I'd get queasy. "Make me an egg, please, Grandpa?"

"Poof, you're an egg. *I* made the coffee," he said.

"Mom, then. Please?"

She said, "Lindy, I can't, honey. I've got to look for my pills. Have either of you seen them anywhere, I wonder?"

"Not I, said the pig," said my grandfather.

"Sorry," I said.

"That's peculiar. Didn't I leave them with the vitamins?" Mom said. "This is important, you two."

"Nobody's got your medicine. Your medicine's not here," Grandpa said, causing Mom to be defensive.

"Never mind. I remember where they are," she said.

I doubted it, I really did. I doubted such things as "light pills" existed. Whenever she brought them up, I pictured something like a planet, boiling white—a radiant pill. I pictured Mom swallowing those! At the pharmacy, when she was haunting them, fretting around the prescription desk, they told her they didn't know what she was talking about, but if they did have such pills, she'd need a doctor's order.

"Just eat a banana. You'll be tardy again, Lindy," Grandpa said to me. "Harriet, they're going to fire you so fast if you waltz in late."

"I quit, Pop. They didn't like me there, so I quit," Mom said. That was the first we had heard of it.

Mom was a comptometer operator, and even though her mind was usually wandering over in Andromeda, she was one of the fastest operators in the state. She could get another job.

Grandpa had enough money for us, so that wasn't the worry. He had been a successful tailor, had even had his own shop. His only fault had been that he sometimes forgot to tie off his threads—so eventually, some of the clothes he made fell apart a little bit, or so he said.

The problem I saw was that Mom really needed to keep occupied.

Grandpa and she were still debating over who was going to fix breakfast when I stuffed my backpack and left for school.

Our landlady—she was nice—was on the cement porch steps next door where she lived. "Hey, Carl Sagan! Give me a minute!" she called, and I obliged. She said, "A Mrs. H. of Phoenicia asks: 'Why was there a ring around the moon last night?'"

"Ice crystals," I told her, thinking that was probably wrong.

"Goodness, I didn't realize it was that chilly," she said.

"Very high up," I said, still guessing.

It wasn't just our landlady. A lot of the neighbors knew me, and knew what a star fiend I was. They'd stop me and ask questions, like, "When is it we're getting Halley's Comet again?" Or, "What'd you make of the Saturn pictures?"

I never had to worry about security. When I was younger, for instance, when my mom wanted to go out, she would drop me way down the street at the movie theater. Then, a few times, either because I had sat through a second showing in order to resee my favorite parts, or because Mom accidentally forgot and didn't pick me up, I had to walk home in the dark. I didn't think a thing of it. There were these chummy neighbors all along the way.

⌥

"Can't we get out of here? When can we go?" Mom was asking me.

It was a couple days later, a Wednesday afternoon. I had been extended on the sofa, my head sandwiched between throw pillows so I wouldn't have to hear her carp. Our ironing board was set up—a nosy storky bird—aimed at me and waiting for me to press my uniform and something to wear to school the next day.

"Come on, Lindy," Mom urged me. "I need for you to explain to them."

She meant at the pharmacy.

Her good looks were going, I decided. Her brown hair was faded, and since she had quit work, she hadn't been changing her clothes often enough. I planned to iron a fresh something for her, and see if she'd wear it.

"Do you have to do that? Before we can leave?" she said, whining almost. I was testing the nozzle of the spray-starch can.

"What would happen if you didn't get some pills?" I asked her.

"I'd run out," she said, and shrugged.

First I did the collar on my uniform, which was a gingham check and not French-looking, as it ought to have been for a place called the anything "Chateau."

"And then what would happen? After you ran out," I asked Mom.

"Honey," she said, and with a sigh, "I just should have told you. I should've told you *and* Pop. I have a little tumor. Like a tumor, and it's high up in my brain. I can't sleep well because of it, and I need sleep, or it'll worsen and be too diminishing, you see. But the pills fix me right up, is all they do. They give me a recharge. That's how you can think of it. So I don't need to sleep as much."

I finished ironing my uniform. I folded it and put it into a shopping bag so I could take it to school with me on Friday and keep it in my locker. Friday was going to be hell, I knew. There was a school tea planned for the morning, and in the afternoon I would graduate. Friday evening, the Steak Chateau was expecting to get crowds and crowds of seniors and their families.

Grandpa came in from the kitchen. His glasses were on from reading his newspaper. He wiggled a hand through the wrinkled clothes in my laundry basket, which rested on the couch.

"Tell him about your brain tumor, Mom," I said.

"Yeah, brain tumor," Grandpa said. "It's sinusitis. It's just from goldenrod."

It was like him to say that. If I ever had a headache, I got it from combing my hair too roughly, or parting it on the wrong side, according to him. He sat down in his chair. It was a maize color, and had heavy arms. "How does one called *The Magician* sound? It's the Fright Theatre feature this weekend."

I was thinking that Grandpa was a happier man when my father was around. I could completely forget about my father these days, unless I was reminded. He had moved to Toledo, several years before, with his company. He had remarried. When he was still with us, though, he and my grandfather would trade jokes, and they'd make the *telling* of the joke last a long, long time, which was the funniest part. Springs and summers, they would take Mom to the trotting races over at Geronimo Downs. They'd go almost nightly, in a white-and-red convertible they had between them.

It was Thursday, the morning before graduation. I was cutting school, since it was nothing, just a rehearsal, and getting class rings and individual awards at an assembly—class artist, class-reunion secretary—not anything that involved me. I planned to show up after lunch and maybe pick up my cap and gown.

Mom and I were on the Shopper's Special, a bus that ran from Phoenicia to Terre Haute on weekdays. I hoped Mom was going to get her hair done, or buy an outfit for tomorrow, but she hadn't said she would. The other shoppers on the Special were a couple of lumpy women and a leather man in golfing clothes, and a guy in a maroon suit who had Mom's whole attention.

The bus shuddered at a light. Its engine noise and the tremor in the hard seat and the clear early sun were all getting to me, making me drowsy.

The maroon suit was behind a Chicago newspaper. Mom glanced back at him. "What do you think *he* does?" she asked me.

"Could be anything," I said.

"No, kiddo. That's a plainclothesman. You can tell."

"He could be," I said.

"He is. I believe he's on here for us."

I was very used to this talk, but today I didn't feel like hearing it. "Please," I said to Mom.

"Forget it," she said.

She looked young again. "Don't act up, girls," the bus driver had teased us when we got on in Phoenicia.

"I can do something," I said to Mom. "I can name the fifteen brightest stars. Want me to? I can give them in order of brightness."

Mom seemed stunned by the offer and her face slackened. The concern went out of her eyes. She looked twelve. "Can you do something like that? Did you have to learn it in school, or on your own?"

"*I* did it. Here we go. They are Sirius, Canopus, Alpha Centauri, Arcturus, Vega," I told her, and right on through to old reddish Antares.

Mom was both smiling and grave, like a person hearing a favorite poem.

"Mom," I said, after a minute, "before commencement tomorrow, there's the Senior Tea. It's just cookies and junk, but I told them maybe you'd help serve. They wanted parents to be guards for the tables, just so nobody takes a hundred cookies instead of one or two."

She was surprised, I could tell. I wondered if she was flattered that I wanted her to be there.

"Honey, I couldn't do *that*," she said, as though I had asked her to leap over our garage, or jog to Kansas. "I couldn't do that."

The trip to Terre Haute was all the way beside a river. Sometimes, the river was just a large ditch and sometimes it was an actual wild river. Today, it was full to the banks, and we were rolling along in the bus at the same rate as the current.

In the corner of my sight, I saw Mom fussing with the jumbo purse she had brought. I peeked down into it, and there were her toothbrush and plastic soap box and her cloth hair-curlers. So I knew she was thinking of getting off at Platte and seeing if they had a bed for her at the Institute there. I thought maybe Dr. Goff, whom she saw, had decided she ought to check in for a bit again. Or, more probably it was her idea.

~

The hospital *was* Mom's idea, I finally learned from Grandpa, but it turned out they didn't have space for her, or they didn't think she needed to get in right then.

She wasn't at my graduation ceremony, which was just as well, in one way—I didn't do a great job, since I had missed rehearsal. During the sitting moments, I wondered about her, though, and I decided that graduation had been one of the chief things upsetting her. She was scared of the "going forward into the world" parts of the commencement speeches.

Grandpa lied to me. He said he was certain Mom was there, just back in one of the cooler seats, under the buckeye trees. Graduation was outside, see. He said Mom wanted shade.

~

Late that night, we were all three watching the Fright Theatre feature. A girl in the movie was married to a man who changed into a werewolf and attacked people. Sooner or later, you knew he was going to go after the girl.

"That poor woman," Mom kept saying.

"She's got it tough, all right," Grandpa said. "Trying to keep her husband in Alpo."

I was exhausted from work. I was nibbling the black kernels and oily salt from the bottom of the popcorn bowl.

"She has to make sure he's got all his shots. He's got to be wormed. Here she comes now, going to give him a flea collar," Grandpa said.

I liked being as dragged out as I was. My new apricot robe that Grandpa had made for me was across my legs, keeping them warm. My other graduation gifts, from Mom—really Grandpa—were all telescope related.

There was a pause in the movie for a commercial. "Take a reading on this," Grandpa said. He flipped a big white card to me. The card said, "Happy Graduation, Good Luck in Your Future." It had come from my dad.

I was still looking at the signature, *Your father,* when the movie started back up again. "What if Dad were back living with us?" I asked Grandpa and Mom.

"It would cut down on your mom's dating," Grandpa said.

Mom, concentrating on the television, said, "Uh-oh, full moon!"

"But just suppose Dad were to somehow come back here and live with us," I said to Mom. I had put down the card and was pulling on my short hair a little.

"He better not," she said.

"You're damn right, he better not," Grandpa said.

I was surprised. He even sounded angry. I guessed I had been wrong, thinking Grandpa missed having Dad as a crony so much.

I stuffed a pillow behind my head and sat back and listened to the creepy music from the television and to a moth that was stupidly banging on the window screen. It would take a lot for my dad to understand us, and the way we three did things, I thought. He would have to do some thinking.

"Ah, this couch feels good!" I said. "I could lie here forever."

I didn't know whether or not Mom had heard me. But she was beaming, either way. She pointed to the TV screen, where the werewolf lay under a bush, becoming a person again. She said, "Shh."

3

Smoke

MARTY ELBER FOLLOWED HIS mother's green sports car through Beverly Hills, but she was too good a driver for Marty to stay close, even on his motorcycle. The recently remarried Mrs. Audrey Elber Sharon caught the next-to-last corner before her new home at about sixty at the apex of the curve, tires twisting, exhaust pipes firing like pistol shots.

She was laughing, leaning out of the open driver's door of her car and brushing grains of sand from her bare feet, when Marty drove his bike onto the blacktop turnaround. He dropped his kickstand, sat back sideways on the bike saddle, and lighted a cigarette. He was wearing Levis, with suspenders and no shirt, and linesman's boots. He was twenty-six.

"I won," his mother said. "You couldn't catch me, and you had all the way from Santa Monica."

"All the way from Malibu," Marty said. "I saw you leaving the Mayfair Market. You made every single light, though. I had to stop a lot."

Audrey Sharon picked up a paper sack of groceries and a cluster of iced-tea cans from the passenger seat of her car. She cradled the groceries in her arm, hooked the cans with her free fingers, used her knee to slam the car door, and came toward Marty. "Give us a puff," she said.

Marty put his cigarette between his mother's lips. "I need to borrow a great deal of money," he said while Audrey inhaled. "Before the weekend."

"Don't talk to me," she said, "talk to Hoyt."

Marty wiggled his jaw and yanked his chin strap loose. He lifted off his motorcycle helmet. "I can't talk to Hoyt," he said.

Hoyt Sharon came around the corner from the side lawn, carrying a 9-iron and a perforated plastic golf ball. His white hair was cut to a fine bristle, and he wore a long-billed fishing cap and what looked to Marty like a crimson spacesuit— one-piece, with its Velcro closing straps undone from his throat to his belly.

"Marty! Great! Come in, come in," Hoyt said.

"Hey," Marty said, "how's the honeymoon?"

Hoyt had planted himself over the golf ball. He rolled his shoulders and swung the club. The ball clicked and flew up onto the slate-shingled garage roof. "So much for that soldier," Hoyt said. He came up behind Audrey and tried to take the groceries away from her.

"Will you please calm down?" she said to him. "Look at how much you're sweating."

"O.K. Sorry," Hoyt said.

"If you want to help me carry, get the food cooler and beach umbrella from the trunk," Audrey said.

"Remember to talk to him for me," Marty whispered to his mother as they trailed Hoyt across the lawn.

Hoyt dumped the umbrella and golf club he was carrying and opened the front door for Audrey and Marty. They entered a paneled foyer cluttered with plants and bright oil paintings of sinewy cowboys. Audrey went up three carpeted steps and through a swinging saloon door that led to the kitchen.

Hoyt led Marty through another foyer, which was being repapered with flocked maroon sheets; through the shadowy game room, where an old-fashioned dark-green billiard table stood on an emerald carpet; and into the library, which was two stories tall. Two of the library walls were glass, with louvered double doors, and in front of a third wall was a row of plush-covered theater seats, bolted to the floor. Above these, a mural depicted a cattle stampede and a cowboy being flung from the saddle of a panicky-looking horse.

Marty sat down in a large wooden armchair decorated with old cattle brands. Hoyt threw himself into the sofa, which was as long and deep as a rowboat.

"Your mom tell you about Henry Kissinger?" Hoyt said, clasping his hands behind his head. "It's the damnedest thing. She tell you? You won't believe it."

"I don't think so," Marty said. "No."

"Ben Deverow and his wife—you don't know them—go into the Derby for lunch and there he is, Henry Kissinger."

"Really?" Marty said.

"Yeah, having shrimp or something," Hoyt said. "Only, you won't believe this, but he's in drag. He's dressed up like a woman."

"Oh, come on," Marty said, reaching across the coffee table for a copy of *Sports Illustrated*.

"No. He's really Kissinger, but he's got a . . . a whatchamacallit. . . ." Hoyt pointed to the swordfish stitched on his cap.

"A wig?"

"No, he didn't even have a wig. He had a little . . . like a hat thing, you know? With a little lace veil?"

Marty said, "He couldn't do that. Everyone would know if he dressed up like a woman and went out in public."

"That's what you'd think," Hoyt said. "It's what I'd think, isn't it? But it was him. I swear it."

"You weren't even there," Marty said.

"You're too quick for me," Hoyt said. "I was lying. It wasn't Kissinger at all. It was Ronald Reagan."

"He give you the Kissinger thing?" Audrey said as she padded into the room. "Isn't that incredible?" She had put on a pair of jeans and combed her hair in a ponytail.

Hoyt took a red tablet from his shirt pocket. He put the pill on his tongue, hopped up from the couch, crossed the room, and gulped water from a cut-glass pitcher on the bar. "Forgot my Stresstab," he said apologetically.

Marty cleared his throat three or four times, turning the pages of his magazine.

"Marty needs money for his business, Hoyt," Audrey said.

"Why the hell didn't he come to me before?" Hoyt said. He slapped his palms on the seat of his spacesuit.

"He didn't need money before," Audrey said.

"Look," Hoyt said, "I get a kick out of helping young people. You know who helped me when I was stalled? Forty years ago, when Anaheim was just a crop of orange trees?"

"Gene Autry," Audrey said.

"Gene Autry is who," Hoyt said. "That's right, honey." He turned to Marty and said, "No, I don't see any problem here. What are we playing with? Land?"

"Smoke detectors," Marty said. "I can get in on a pretty safe operation, Hoyt. Some friends in Sacramento tell me they're thinking about making detectors mandatory in the next couple of years."

"Besides which, I believe in the damn things," Hoyt said. "They're like little alarms? You bet I do. They save lives. Friends of mine lost a kid in a fire once. I say 'a kid,' but I mean *infant*. You should have seen it." He parted his hands. "They had a teeny-tiny casket only this big."

Audrey switched on the television, and a local charity telethon appeared on the screen. A high-school orchestra was playing "High Hopes." Audrey sat down on the carpet in front of the set, and Hoyt leaned over and kissed one of her ears as they both watched the screen.

"Can I neck with you for a second?" the show's master of ceremonies said to a five-year-old girl whose legs were strapped into metal braces. The child had on a party dress. "Why can't I?" he said. "Are you married?" He dropped on one knee before the girl and squinted at her suspiciously.

"No, I'm too little," the child said.

"You aren't too little," the M.C. told her and the audience. "You're one of the very biggest people on this planet, because your heart is full of courage and hope."

Marty went over and pulled open the double glass doors. They moved easily on their runners. There was the smell of cut grass, the knock of a carpenter's hammer, the hiss of lawn sprinklers.

Hoyt turned abruptly and came across the room. He sprang back and forth on the balls of his feet, shooting fists in combinations like a prizefighter. "O.K., buddy," he said to Marty. "Your turn. Waltz with me a few rounds."

"I really can't, Hoyt," Marty said.

"You want a grubstake," Hoyt said. "You got to do a little dancing." He moved easily, but his face was red. He jabbed wide of Marty's throat, delicately pointing the knuckles of his half-closed fingers.

Audrey turned off the television set and watched the two men with her arms folded.

Hoyt stopped moving. Marty stood before him, flat-footed, with his arms half raised.

"The old monkey," Hoyt said. He swung a clowning round-house right that smashed into Marty's left temple.

"Jesus, Hoyt," Marty said. The blow had knocked him onto the carpet, where he lay on one elbow and hip.

"He's all right," Hoyt said to Audrey.

"I'm all right," Marty said, getting to his feet.

Hoyt danced toward him. "Cover up," Hoyt said, and Marty crouched and crossed his arms over his face.

"Breadbasket," Hoyt said and whipped his left fist at Marty's bare stomach. Marty walked away with his hands on his hips, trying to take a breath. He bent over and went into a squat.

"Leave him alone," Audrey said. "Poor Marty."

"Christ, Hoyt," Marty said.

"Woozy?" Audrey asked him. She pushed Marty forward until he went onto all fours, and then found a metal wastepaper basket, which she put down under his face.

"I'm sorry, Marty," Hoyt said. "That was nuts of me. Just wanted to get the blood running back to the pump, you know? Those weren't supposed to land."

"You didn't have to put his eye out," Audrey said.

"I think he did," Marty said. "I can't see out of it."

"Look at me," Audrey said, taking Marty's chin in her hand. "No. All it is is a little sliver-cut at the edge of the brow. You'll have a mouse that may close your eye a bit. I'll get you a cup of coffee." She left the room.

Marty sat on the couch. Hoyt paced in front of him. "Forget it, Marty, really," he said. "I didn't mean for those to land. You're a great kid for not hauling off and plastering me right back."

Marty said, "I wouldn't mess with you."

"What'd you say you'd need to get in on those alarm systems? Did you say three or four thousand?"

"Really, three thousand is more than it would take," Marty said. "Three thousand is great, sir."

"Not 'sir.' Don't call me 'sir.'" Hoyt went over to the door and took some deep breaths. He pounded his chest a few times. He put a finger on the side of his nose, closing off the nostril, and breathed deeply five or six more times. "Listen, though," he said. "Don't those fire alarms sometimes go off when there's no fire?"

"They're working on that," Marty said.

"Your mother's so mad at me," Hoyt said.

"I'll tell her everything's O.K.," Marty said.

When Audrey came back into the room, she was carrying a full cup of coffee for Marty. "Everything's all right here," Hoyt said. She and Marty smiled at each other. When Marty glanced over at Hoyt, he saw that Hoyt was grinning, too.

"We're in business," Hoyt said. "My father told me the only things you got to worry about are sex, death, and money. And he told me if you've got the right family you'll never have to worry about two of them. That just leaves death. Bear that in mind, friends."

4

In the Woods

HORSES, GOES THE RAP, are skittish and unpredictable and dangerous, but one I knew I got to love, although he was all those things. Sunny, the horse, lived with my sister and brother-in-law on their Indiana farm. A thousand-pound horse of the Tennessee Walking breed, Sunny was a strawberry roan, fifteen hands high. He would let me ride him around the periphery of Kenneth and Barbara's considerable acreage there—hours of riding, every day—and I could safely keep my mind on that, and on Sunny. And I was grateful, because my marriage and most of the rest of me had recently splintered.

It's hard work to ride, and it was usually thick hot weather that summer, yet I never missed a day. I'd gear up in tall black boots, canvas trousers, a velvet helmet. Wearing these clothes every day assured something in me, they were such a treat to wear. From the corrugated-fiberglass stable, we'd go first across a meadow that my brother-in-law, Kenneth, kept mowed. It was washboard earth, ridged and baked hard, and so I'd let Sunny amble. Next we would tour a lane of shade trees and then turn into a careful path that invaded the woods. Along here we'd often get up speed, with the thud of hoof and jingle of bridle and, after a bit, Sunny's rasping huge breath. Deep in, there was a ravine. I liked to rein up on its high side, admiring the frightening detail of full-blown summer. Weed wands would bow to me. Flower spokes would wag, and tree boughs, hideously muscled, would reach for me or shrug indifferently. There were mosses, bright green, and freckled toadstools layered like spills of pancakes against the trunks of trees. Sometimes, over the gabbing and ticking of bugs, I would listen to a tractor's thin ringing. Its noise pulsed every other second, saying nothing, which was best, for there weren't any *words* I wanted to hear.

We'd go on to the open fields, into amazing heat. There were graded and scraped paths there, so Sunny's cannons were safe. I could let him lope. Starting from points between my shoulder blades and breasts, the heat would hold me with its dullness and anger. My focus would soften.

Sunny's scent, I thought, was a regal one—leathery and old. And the heat would draw out other smells around us: cucumber, weeds, and dust. I'd dismount to eat wild scallions, but the blackberry canes that lined one pasture—like rows of spectators for Sunny and me—were so tall that I could pick from them while still in the saddle. Once, while I sat scrunched in the saddle eating berries out of my juice-stained fingers, there was a weird, thrilling thing. The miserly breeze gave up. I saw total stillness, as in a freeze-frame. It was as though the world had died but not quite yet bothered to topple. Blades of grass, bugs, blank sky, even Sunny, were all cast in glass. I was alone in it and feeling suddenly afloat, as if I had bolted a lot of champagne.

In the weeks before my stay at the farm, I had been awake too much. Whenever I did sleep, what ugly dreams! One I remember was of me roller-skating down cement hill after hill, no way to stop. Marcus, my husband, and I lived in a three bedroom, all-electric condominium north of Chicago. Marcus, an architect with a pretty good downtown firm, looked as if he could have been my dad or even my grandfather, with his prematurely white hair and silvery beard. Whenever we were in a place where someone might see us together—even if we just stepped out onto our second-floor balcony for a whiff of the morning—Marcus had to have his arm low on the back of my waist, or his hand on the back of my neck, almost in a chokehold, announcing to everyone that I was in fact his. To me, that was sadder and a bigger problem than his skirt-chasing.

Evenings on the farm, Kenneth would grill steaks or chops outside and my sister and I would do the salad, sometimes corn. We'd open wine. We would cut up muskmelon. After eating, we'd sit on the long flagstone patio, with its view of yard and pond, and maybe drink a Scotch. One night, we finally talked about Marcus and me.

"You're doing everything wrong," Barbara said, as if she had been holding back for a long time.

"For what it's worth, I agree," Kenneth said.

"You broke a window? You phoned one of these women? Those were stupid moves, honey," my sister said.

"The surest way to drive him off forever," Kenneth said.

"While making anybody else look good," Barbara added.

So I had all that, their opinions, to consider, one afternoon while I was brushing Sunny down, pushing the curry brush along his flanks. Sunny started, kicked back, twisted his great neck, and bit me. Kenneth heard my yelp. He came from the tack room—authoritative in jeans, Dingo boots, a white shirt with pearl snap buttons—and scolded me. "Tie up his lead, for heaven's sake. Get his head up. He doesn't know enough not to hurt you. That's a horse you're playing with, not a puppy dog." And he went on and said I might do well to learn a bit more about barn etiquette before I slapped on Barbara's equestrian clothes and rode out "like Princess Di or somebody."

A week or so before, at the aluminum water trough, I had surprised Kenneth when he wasn't wearing his dentures. Of course I knew Kenneth had been stuck with a removable upper plate for many years, although he was only just over fifty. A truck wreck had knocked most of the teeth out of his teenaged smile. He faced me there at the trough with an unusual gentleness. And then he winked. I made no mention of this to Barbara. Kenneth impatient or Kenneth embarrassed could lose no grace by me—he was tops. He deserved every minute of Barbara, to my mind. He deserved his smart wife and his good farm. Self-absorbed as I was, I had watched him going about the chores of his farmer's life—some piddling, some awful, duties. He labored with a kind of patriotism, as though finishing things and doing them well meant the health of his home, his country.

At the tail of August came a series of savage thunderstorms. The rain flailed in the woods and made Amanda Creek wide. Thunder rolled through the afternoon skies, and lightning whitened the world in strobe flashes. Riding was out. I was talking to Marcus long-distance, in daily sessions—five minutes, then fifteen, finally half an hour—and in our pauses I could hear the crackle of electricity in the lines. When I rang off, I would go stand out in the soupy yard, unsheltered, getting soaked sometimes.

The storms ended in fiery, poignant sunsets. In the blush of one of these, with the frogs and crickets ratcheting away down by the pond, Barbara talked to me. She said, "You know, it's all work. Marriage, money, property—the big things. It's not your fault you're too young to know if it's worth it—seeing to all the details. You've got to—you've got to *insist*."

She was riding in the giant doughnut hole of a tractor tire. The tire was roped to a monster willow, off on the side lawn.

"Or maybe you think there's a simpler way to be. All by yourself." Barbara was turning the swing in circles, winding up the hemp. "I hear you sobbing into the phone. I know what Marcus is like."

Five days of not riding and I was feeling flabby and earth-bound. In the mirror in the mornings, my hair was very tired, my sunburn drying away and peeling off beneath my eyes.

"Kenneth's cheated on me. I've done it to him. It's terrible," Barbara said. "But being so selfish and wrong often brings with it a sort of strength. You know?"

I knew. That was the look I'd seen in Kenneth's face when I'd seen him with his teeth out. He didn't care.

She raised her anchor foot and let the tire spin. I was dizzy for her. Whatever that moment was in the woods, I wanted it back. I wanted Barbara to stop revolving, and the rain to end, and the summer to start over—for everything to just hold off until I could catch up.

5

The Help

"I'LL NEED A TON of things if you want me to do this right," Lola said. She pressed her hands on her waist—a pretty, brown-skinned woman in her middle thirties. "Rug shampoo, more steel wool, cleanser, a new mop. I'm not going to clean floors with a sponge. A new mop and some window cleaner. I think I need a professional window cleaner."

"Sit down, darling," Mr. Cleveland said. "We'll hash it out."

"I don't want to sit down. I want to get rolling on the cleaning so I can get it over with," Lola said. She moved from the kitchen doorway into the tile-floored breakfast room, where Mr. Cleveland sat over plates of melon and ham-and-eggs.

He pinned an English muffin with his fork and knifed off a bite. He was sixty-seven, a Texan long ago transplanted to Indiana. He wore an old-fashioned dressing gown with padded shoulders and wide velvet lapels.

"Anyhow, I thought a cleaning person was responsible for furnishing the tools of her trade," he said. He gave her a sweet, closemouthed smile.

"I'm not a cleaning woman. I'm a cook and a maid," Lola said.

"My Lord, call the lawyers. I didn't read the fine print on your labor contract," Cleveland said. "No, you have Howdy drive you to the Fairway, and charge up whatever you need. Only don't charge an electric garage-door opener or a rotisserie barbecue grill. And don't buy a set of drill bits."

"No drill bits," Lola said.

Mr. Cleveland was retired, but he owned most of a company that bottled eighteen varieties of soda pop. He lived in a big Tudor-style home, in a little woods bordering a country club.

"Look who's up from the dead," Lola said.

Cleveland's son, Howdy, came into the dining room and flopped into a chair. He was a tall young man, with a strong jaw, rusty hair like his father's, and clear blue eyes under white lashes.

"Walk on tiptoe," Cleveland said to his son. "Lola's on a human-rights campaign this morning. She'll bite off your head."

"Morning, Lola," Howdy said.

"*Ms.* Turtledge," Cleveland said.

"Coffee's on the counter," Lola said.

Howdy poured some coffee and stared sleepily at the vase of day lilies in the middle of the table.

"Damn teeth," Cleveland said. He had paused, with a forkful of eggs in midair.

"Now you have another toothache," Lola said.

"Aspirin," he said.

"Aspirin is horrible for your stomach," Howdy said. He yawned.

"Last time your dad took aspirin, we heard about it all day and all that night," Lola said.

"You're a lovely woman and a very bright one," Mr. Cleveland said, putting down his fork. "You and Howdy would do well in medical school. Dr. Lola and Dr. Howdy."

"Right," Lola said.

"I'd like to shoot you both in the heart," Mr. Cleveland said. "Only you don't have hearts. Lola, you're fired."

"Sure I am," Lola said. "Again. Good."

"I'll hire you back," Howdy said. "At least long enough to fix me some of those eggs."

"He'll pay you in original art work," Cleveland said. "An original Howdy oil painting each month, and some charcoal studies of naked people for your extra change."

Lola brought a swatch of cloth from the pocket of the smock she wore over her Levis and began dusting the leaves of a potted palm that stood in a cement urn before the diamond-paned windows. "Spring cleaning has officially begun," she said. "In the eggs-and-aspirin department, you can both just forage for yourselves."

"Get me the Yellow Pages, Howdy," Mr. Cleveland said. "I want the phone number of a good employment agency."

❦

Howdy was taking Lola to the store in his M.G. Midget, to get her cleaning supplies. He was driving too fast down a winding graveled road. He wore wraparound sunglasses and white perforated gloves.

"My mother did paintings!" he shouted at Lola. "She won some prizes at a few county fairs. Landscapes."

Lola was gripping her seat and the door of the rattling M.G. They bucketed over a deep pothole.

"She was Irish and very moody," Howdy said. "Her pictures are typically Irish. It was always raining and there were no people in them."

"Maybe she couldn't draw people," Lola said, also shouting over the noise of the car and the wind.

"Maybe," Howdy said. "Anyhow, she divorced Daddy and went back to Dublin. I was ten or so."

"So you told me," Lola said. "Your father told me, too. Could you slow down?"

"Don't think about it," he said, and twisted the wheel. "How're your classes?"

"Poor," Lola said. "I don't have time to do all the reading."

"*What?*" Howdy said.

"The *reading!*" Lola shouted. "It's slow going. I don't have the time to concentrate."

She and Howdy were both going to the local university. He had started in economics and dropped out. Now he was back, as a fine-arts major. Lola was studying sociology, in night school. This was her fifth year there.

"Yeah, me, too," Howdy said. "One thing I found out, though. I don't want to be an artist anymore. That's all a racket, and you have to kiss somebody's behind to have your work taken. Besides, nobody looks at paintings anymore unless they can't help it."

The top of the car was down, and it was hot. Howdy stuck out his left hand and let it ride on the air current. "Guess what," he said.

"Don't make me guess," Lola said.

"I took a drama class as an elective—" Howdy said.

"Uh-oh," Lola said.

"And you know, I'm good? For my first project, I did Tom's opening speech from *The Glass Menagerie*. I got an A-plus— *plus*."

"They don't have those plus jobs in the Sociology Department," Lola said.

"Don't tell Daddy, but I'm also painting the scenery for the Midsummer Fête. It's a musical, written by some senior drama students. I'm in the chorus, too, believe it or not."

"You'll *sing* in it?" Lola said.

Howdy worked the clutch and yanked the gearshift for a sharp corner. "It's a musical comedy about Stalin and Marilyn Monroe," he said.

"What?" Lola said.

"It's *satire!*"

"Your father will like that," said Lola.

Howdy laughed and banged the steering wheel with the heel of his hand. "Won't he? He won't see the humor, of course."

"I'm not sure *I* do," Lola said.

"Come on, Lola. Stalin really gets his in this musical. In fact, it has a very sad ending—sort of powerful. That's a break-through, to me. Traditionally, the Fête is gay and frivolous."

"Not this year," Lola said.

"Right," Howdy said. "I'm really thinking I was born for the stage."

◞

Lola trundled her cart up and down the wide, bright aisles of ath-letic equipment, toys, cameras, fabrics, pyramids of cut-rate mo-tor oil, TVs, hammocks, shoes. Howdy followed her, singing along with the Muzak: "'Ahhh, look at all the lonely people. . . .'"

A man in plaid pants stared at Howdy. Howdy sang louder, watching the man.

"Cool down," Lola said.

"I'll tell you," Howdy said. "Most people are prisoners in their own flesh."

He went off, saying he was going to inspect the art supplies. Lola rolled the cart around the housewares department until her basket was full, and then she pushed up to the checkout coun-ters. She stood away from the lines, waiting for Howdy, who had the charge card.

After twenty minutes, she left the cart and went to hunt for him. She finally spotted him in men's sportswear. He was posing in front of a triptych of mirrors, in a white jumpsuit.

"Where have you been? I was about to report a lost child," Lola said.

"Right here," Howdy said. "Ray? This is Lola." He gestured toward a chunky salesman, who was standing beside him. "This is . . . Ray?" he said, and the salesman nodded.

"Don't you love this coverall?" Ray said.

"What are all the zippers for?" she asked.

"Whatever," Ray said.

"I can see his underpants through that material," Lola said.

"I have complete movement," Howdy said. He did a knee bend.

"I think it's for girls," Lola said. "Can we please go?"

"Men are wearing these, actually," Ray said to Howdy. "You'll see a lot of them this season."

"Well, don't bring that playsuit to me on washday," Lola said. "It'll have to be washed in its own machine, with four or five quarts of bleach."

"It's new and it takes getting used to," the salesman said. "I think your wife here will get to like it, though."

"His wife?" Lola said.

Howdy looked pleased. "Well, I'll take it," he said. "You can bag my old clothes."

The carry-out boy stacked Lola's sacks in the trunk of the M.G. Howdy slammed the trunk lid and said, "Now lunch. How about the lunchroom right across the way?"

"I should be home—I left the dishwasher running," Lola said. "It's broken, and the only way it'll stop is if somebody yanks the door open."

"Daddy'll figure it out," Howdy said.

Inside, they climbed onto revolving stools at the soda fountain. They gave their orders to a girl wearing a paper waitress hat. "I want my coffee right away," Howdy said.

They didn't say anything while they waited. Howdy slowly rotated on his stool. Lola was thinking about her Statistics test, the next week. When her order came—a banana split on an oblong dish—she pushed the whipped cream to one side and then took a careful spoonful of strawberry and chocolate ice cream, mixed.

Howdy swore suddenly and put down his coffee cup. Coffee had dribbled all down the front of his new outfit.

"Well, you can wear it to wash the car in," Lola said. "That's probably what it was made for anyway."

Howdy scrubbed at the stains with a napkin. "This'll come out, won't it?" he said.

"Nope. But I could make enough coffee to fill your bathtub, and you could put it in and then the suit would be all coffee color."

Howdy shrugged. "How many years have I known you?" he said.

"Four, about. Why? Are you going to ask me for a date?" Lola said, and hacked up her banana.

"Not a date, exactly. I was going to ask you to come and see me in a play."

"Oh, of course I'll do that. I'd enjoy that," Lola said.

"I don't know hardly anybody to ask, after all the rehearsing I'm doing. Daddy wouldn't like it, for sure."

"No," Lola said. "So I'll come. But you'll have a lot of people watching. A whole audience."

"All strangers," Howdy said.

Lola said. "I'd be nervous with family or friends out there."

Howdy said, "But you wouldn't do it to begin with."

❧

Mr. Cleveland swung his slippered feet down from the davenport. "Great to see you-all," he said to Lola and Howdy. "You have a good vacation in Jamaica, or what? You've got some explaining to do to the police, the both of you, because I called them after Lola wasn't back in time for *Another World*. I explained how you must have been captured by the P.L.O., or something." He'd been watching television in the den, drinking a Scotch-and-water.

Howdy helped Lola carry the sacks into the kitchen, and then went back out to the M.G. for the last of the supplies. Lola yanked open the dishwasher, and steam billowed out. She cleared some space in the floor cabinets and put away the cleaning equipment. "I suppose you're starving," she called out to Mr. Cleveland. "I'll make a chef's salad and soup."

She dried her hands and walked back to the den. "You must be drunk, Mr. Cleveland. I didn't hear you comment on Howdy's new suit."

"Where is he?" Cleveland said.

Lola put her index finger up to signal quiet. Howdy came by the den door, struggling with a bucket and a couple of brooms.

Mr. Cleveland looked him up and down. "That's terrible," he said.

"So what's going on here?" Lola said, pointing to the television.

Cleveland said, "That boy, Willis, is back in the soup with his wife. And that other boy, with the dark hair, is upset about his mama."

"Umm. Same as yesterday," Lola said.

❧

Lola worked the rest of the afternoon. She took down the drapes, all over the house, and boxed them for the dry cleaner. She washed the insides of the windows. She carried a plastic transistor radio from room to room, tuned to a classical station. She checked in to the kitchen, at intervals, to tend a pot of fish chowder and some chicken breasts she was getting ready for the broiler.

Howdy had gone to his afternoon classes. Mr. Cleveland was asleep on the davenport.

At six, Lola stood on the kitchen counter, cleaning the top shelf of a high cabinet. The overhead lights snapped on.

"You'll ruin your eyes," Mr. Cleveland said. He had changed from his robe to a V-necked sweater and chinos.

Lola jumped down and switched off her little radio.

"You look beat," Cleveland said. The front-door chimes sounded. "Sit still," he said, but Lola followed him to the entrance hall.

They opened the door to a slender girl wearing rawhide work gloves and a pair of men's pants. She was leaning on a shovel. "Howdy in there?" she said.

"Howdy, out there," Mr. Cleveland said, and laughed. It was an old joke.

"Howdy's not home," Lola said.

"I just need my pay," the girl said.

"Pay? For what?" Lola said.

"For raking down the ravine," the girl said. "And hauling off all the bottles and trash there. For getting the rest of the fence out, and digging up the posts. For rolling the barbed wire, and turning the earth over in the side garden back of the garage, and putting down the Vigorow." She sounded tired and a little angry.

"I don't get it," Mr. Cleveland said. "I pay a man for my gardening."

"You pay my father," she said. "He had the chills and fever today and couldn't do his work, so I did it."

"You're Jack's daughter?" Cleveland said.

"Stephanie," the girl said, nodding. She took off a glove and stuck it over the top of the shovel. "Howdy said start wherever Dad had quit. I did a lot, if you want to come and look at it."

"Lord, no," Cleveland said. "You wait there, sweetheart." He motioned for Lola to follow him back away from the door.

"Her dad's a drinker. I bet he's home with the d.t.'s," Cleveland whispered.

"You pay him to do the gardening, you don't expect his children to do it," Lola said.

"Well, maybe it's all right for today. Today it was just the heavy work. I'll sign a check for you to fill out, for whatever Howdy promised. But you tell her this is the only time. I don't want an amateur trying to trim hedges or grow azaleas. That's landscaping, and that's why I pay Jack."

The M.G. revved in the driveway as Lola and Cleveland returned to the door. Howdy jumped out. He had colored paint all over his new jumpsuit and on the tops of his sneakers.

"I'm glad you're still here, Steph," he said. He put his arm around the gardener's daughter. "You're staying for supper."

"I got to go," the girl said.

"No, you don't. You pay her yet, Daddy?"

"We had it in mind," Cleveland said.

"Good. Come on in, Steph. Let me show you around."

"O.K.," Stephanie said. "Let me get these boots off." She got down on one knee and worked the knot in her shoelace.

❧

Lola shook garlic croutons onto a bowl of salad. At the dining table, she put down the salad, along with a bottle of lo-cal dressing she had carried in the pocket of her dinner smock.

Howdy was saying, "So they asked the actor, who was impoverished, why he stayed in the best hotels, and ate only the most expensive food, and the poor actor said, 'My body's my business. I treat it as I'd treat a thoroughbred horse.'"

"This soup tasted too good to be any good for me," Cleveland said to Lola.

"Nothing in it to hurt you," murmured Lola.

"If an actor gets sick—" Howdy continued.

"Why on earth won't you join us, Lola?" Cleveland said.

Lola clattered the soup plates, stacking them. Stephanie had been using her soup plate for an ashtray. "Who'd bring in the food?" Lola said.

"Where I was raised, we had a custom called buffet. Even polite people occasionally did buffet," Cleveland said.

"When the actor gets sick, he's out of business. It's his duty to stay healthy," Howdy said to Stephanie.

"I can see that," Stephanie said.

"You don't pay me to sit and eat soup," Lola said.

Howdy scooped salad into Stephanie's bowl. "Put a lot of salt and pepper on it, Steph. Lola doesn't salt anything, because of Dad's diet, so it all tastes bland until you get used to spicing it yourself. Everything's done for him around here."

"Sure," Stephanie said.

"You'll get used to it," Howdy said.

"Excuse me," Cleveland said. He rose from the table and helped Lola carry plates into the kitchen. "What is Howdy talking about? What's going on in there?" he said. "And what's biting *you*? If you don't come and eat with us, Lola, I really will fire you. I mean it."

"You might," Lola said.

Cleveland glared at Lola, who was using a fork to put tuna salad on a sesame roll. She folded the bread, bit into it, and munched furiously.

"Howdy's got a girl, that's all," she said when she finished chewing. "He mentioned something about her on the way home from the store today. I just forgot about it. As for me, nothing is wrong except I've got too much to do. Cleaning, cooking meals, reading, and now I'm serving food to a dinner guest."

"Then sit down and eat with us and take a load off, and you can help me deal with my son," Cleveland said. "He's twenty-four years old and still three feet off the ground. He doesn't know what he's doing, or what he's *going* to do, and this artist junk is fine, but it won't take him anywhere. You've seen his paintings. And now he's got a girl. Just thinking about it all makes my blood boil at his damned Irish mother for leaving us high and dry."

Lola was sitting on the counter. She sipped coffee from a mug and gently kicked her heels against the cupboard below her.

"He's not ready to take on a girl, even part time," Cleveland said.

"You make it sound like he's hiring her."

"Listen, Howdy doesn't realize how attractive he could be to some people, and thank the Lord. Because of his money. You can't tell looking at Howdy or listening to him that he's a rich kid. He doesn't know it himself, bless him, so he's never used it to—to cure his loneliness."

"That's true," Lola said.

"He's been very lonely, and it's his own fault. He drives girls away with his dumb clothes and his chatter, before they can find out about his dough. *My* dough, I mean."

Lola was nodding and sipping coffee. "He's not so bad," she said.

"Oh, yes he is," Cleveland said, "but it's not his fault. I feel sorry for the poor wretch."

"Give him a chance," Lola said.

"I will, but not with Jack the gardener's goddamn daughter."

Lola put down her coffee mug and jumped off the kitchen counter. She opened the broiler door and, using a dish towel, pulled out a long pan. She fanned away smoke, and scowled at two rows of burned chicken breasts.

"Well, that's a first," she said, sighing. "It's been a long day."

"Does Howdy look to you like he's thinking of marriage?" Cleveland said. "I need to know."

"It beats me, Mr. Cleveland," Lola said wearily.

"I think he told me he doesn't believe in marriage. He says it's 'stultifying.' Can you believe it? That's his screwball mama talking."

Lola put the blackened pieces of chicken onto a platter and took some rolls out of a bun-warmer. She and Cleveland carried the food into the dining room. Lola took off her smock and sat down at the table next to Stephanie.

"For this fall, I'm thinking about Europe," Howdy said. "Neither Steph nor I have been."

"Nor have I, since the war. It was a very untidy continent then," Mr. Cleveland said. "Anyway, what about your classes?"

"What war?" Stephanie said.

"Think about it," Lola said.

"Oh," Stephanie said.

"Europe costs a fortune," Mr. Cleveland said. "Dan and Billy Willinger just got back, and Dan told me they paid eight dollars for a sweet roll and a Coke in Paris."

"God," Stephanie said.

"Dan Willinger's head of quality control for me," Cleveland said.

"We'd bicycle and backpack and stay in youth hostels. We wouldn't go to Paris," Howdy said.

"Still, it would be a little money, wouldn't it? Your fares over and back, and so forth," Mr. Cleveland said.

"You could work all year, save your money, and go in the spring," Lola said. "Work nights, even."

"Oh, sure," Howdy said. "That's one way. Steph can do lots of things. I heard about a good job I can get reading best-sellers onto tapes for the blind."

"Perfect," Lola said, and looked at Mr. Cleveland. He was chewing slowly, with his elbows on the table and a piece of chicken in his hands. He looked at her over the chicken.

"I'd like to go, too," she said.

"To be sure," Cleveland said. "They'll need somebody to see to their clothes, and secure their reservations, and shop those markets over there without getting robbed, and to put some decent meals together at roadside after the long days of bicycling in the Alps, and to figure out that foreign money. It'd be good for you, Lola—chuck your college degree. Who wants to be a sociologist?"

"I can't go yet," Stephanie said. "Maybe not for a long time. Somebody's got to take care of my dad, see?"

"Well, that's a shame," Cleveland said.

"Scratch Europe," Howdy said cheerfully.

"It's a dirty shame," Cleveland said. "I was getting all excited about going along myself. I know just where my passport is. I'd only have to collect my luggage and oil up my bicycle."

"You'd *have* to go, if Lola went," Howdy said. "You couldn't make out here without her. In fact, after all this time, I don't know if *I* could."

Lola had torn a roll in half and was beginning to spread it with butter. "I think you're both beginning to learn," she said.

6

I Get By

RIGHT AFTER THE WINDUP of the memorial service in the hospital chapel that evening in February, the principal of the elementary school where my husband, Kit, had taught approached me. Enough of a crowd had gathered and passed that I had to inch over and strain to hear him, because the chapel doors had opened. From down the hall there were metal bed and tray noises, buzzers and dings, and doctor-paging voices, as my husband's mourners made their exit.

My mother-in-law, Rennie, still sat in the pew behind me, arm-rocking the baby, who was sounding little pleas. The principal was talking to me. "I think I've found a replacement for Kit," he said.

I had to let that remark hang there for a beat. He meant another teacher. He was either too cruel or too vacant a person to have prefaced what he'd said in some way. He told me, "Her name's Andrea Dennis. Came down from Danbury for interviews this afternoon. Knocked us sideways, actually. You two might get in touch."

I said, "Isn't that nice."

My kids, Ben and Bibi, helped me up from the pew. The principal mentioned he'd tried to call with his condolences. Possibly he had; I had unplugged all three of our phones.

↜

After we got home, Ben and Bibi lingered in the backyard. It was snowing by now—a friendly snow, scurrying in the floodlights behind the house. Rennie took over the couch. She had the baby and our whole stack of pastel sympathy cards. "Going to *read* these," she said, as though someone ought to do more than open the envelopes and nod, acknowledging the signatures.

I warmed a bottle of formula in hot tap water, and watched my children through the window over the sinks. Bibi had fitted into the tire swing somehow. She is broad-bottomed at eighteen. The swing's rope, knotted around a limb of the weeping willow tree, was stiff with ice.

Ben was only a few feet away, urinating onto a bump of snow. I had to look twice, to be sure. He was eleven, *almost* eleven, and peeing in view of his sister.

Bibi had just colored her hair, but I wasn't ready to accept her as a champagne blonde yet. She looks *familiar*, I'd think, whenever I happened onto her.

The Saturday morning we learned about Kit, the Old Hadham police visited. So did two station wagons from television news teams. I took a confirming call from the idiot aircraft-company people who'd rented Kit the light plane in which he died. After the call, I snapped the telephones out of their plastic jacks, and Bibi chain-locked the door of the upstairs bathroom and stripped away the hair color nature had given her.

↜

I met Andrea Dennis. I was at the school, sorting through two decades' worth of teacher paraphernalia, looking for anything personal in classroom cupboards and in Kit's mammoth oak-wood desk. I found a comb, his reading glasses, a Swiss Army knife, and a hardback copy of *Smiley's People,* bookmarked halfway. This was on a school day, but after classes had adjourned. Andrea pushed open the heavy door and found me. She introduced herself in an inquiring way: "I'm Andrea?"

We talked some. We didn't say anything I thought to commit to memory. I spilled Elmer's Glue-All all over. The white glue moved thickly across the desk blotter. "I'd better take care of that," Andrea said. "Let me fetch a sponge or something from the lounge."

I used to be entirely comfortable in the staff and faculty lounge.

Old Hadham Elementary had gone up in '64. Inside and out, the building was an architectural oddity. Kit's classroom (he'd had half of sixth grade), for instance, was in the shape of a semicircle. His huge desk and his roller chair faced out from the straight wall. The room had three rising rows of student chairs with attached laminated writing arms. The floor was covered with jewel-blue linoleum. The curved wall wore a band of pale corkboard.

In the couple of weeks Andrea Dennis had been teaching, she'd tacked up stuff for the lull between Valentine's Day and St. Patrick's Day. There were pen-and-ink drawings that looked like student self-portraits to me. Some printed quotes were pinned up—sayings of statesmen and explorers. There were two science charts: one explaining the pollination of a flower, the other an illustration of polar and equatorial weather movements. Left over from Kit's days here were the usual flags—Old Glory and the Connecticut state flag—and some empty hamster cages

with empty water fonts and play wheels. I planned to leave all
those behind, of course, as well as Kit's globe, showing the con-
tinents and oceans in their proper cloudy colors. Kit hated
globes with countries done in pink or purple.

I had to admit Andrea Dennis was an appealing woman. She
had clearly put a lot of clever thought and effort into presenting
herself at her best. She had on a touch-me-please cashmere
sweater and a soft wool-blend skirt with a lining that rustled.
Her sheer nylons gleamed. She had hair long enough to toss.

I had noticed something about us. Whenever I mentioned
Kit, I nodded at his desk. When Andrea referred to him once,
she gestured north. Toward the forest where the plane fell?

I hung around for fifteen minutes. Andrea didn't return
with the sponge. Anyway, the glue had hardened by now. I pictured her yakking away with young Mr. Mankiewicz or flirting
with old Mr. Sonner.

I packed Kit's things into a blue nylon gym bag. I bundled
up and walked home—a matter of a mile or so—in the road. My
part of Connecticut has no proper sidewalks. I kept stumbling.
Ever since the baby, and then especially after what happened to
Kit, I had been sleeping sporadically and then only in short
spurts. That was part of the reason I'd been so clumsy and had
flubbed with the glue. My getup was pretty cockeyed too. I
had forgotten to wear socks, and yet the shoelaces on my Nikes
were triple-bow-tied. Beneath my parka, my sweater was lumpy
and had the smell of Johnson's baby products, as did the whole
interior of our beautiful saltbox house when I got there—baby
oil, baby powder, baby's softened-fabric bunting.

Everywhere I looked was bright with baby things, baby
artifacts.

I went into the kitchen, grateful for Rennie, who'd tidied
up. Rennie had almost never stayed with us when Kit was alive.
We'd seldom gone to see her. She lived alone on what once had

been an apple orchard, near Darien. She cared for the big central house there, and there were two barns and two brown outbuildings on the land.

Her husband had long ago put himself into a VA hospital. He was a troubled, haunted man. I had witnessed some behavior. He'd sit for long afternoons with his head in his hands. He would roam searchingly over the yards and meadows. He'd seem to hide beside the shadowy brown barns. Other times, he'd pitch and splatter hard apples furiously against the fallen-in stone walls around the borders of the orchard.

Thinking of him, I made a bet with myself I hoped I wouldn't win. I bet that Rennie connected Kit's accident with his father's illness. That would have been unfair.

🙰

March came. We'd get a couple more snowstorms in Old Hadham, I suspected. Spring wouldn't arrive in any decided way for weeks and weeks. But I was seeing new grass and there was dry pavement. April would be breathtaking along our road. There'd be arbutus, hepaticas, downy yellow violets. In the living room, Rennie had sections of the local evening newspaper strewn around. The baby was in the playpen, wadding and tearing a Super Duper coupon page.

"Where's the baby's dolly?" I asked Rennie.

She said, "Ask Ben."

"Ben? Ben has Susie Soft Sounds?" But I didn't call up to Ben. Every day, it seemed, there was more about him and Bibi that I didn't care to know.

They had identical rooms, across the hall from each other—identical except that Bibi's wallpaper showed jazz dancers against a mint-green background, whereas Ben's had ponies grazing in a field. The night before, I had happened past the rooms and heard

Bibi say, from behind Ben's door, "I am safely buzzed." Next I heard the pop-tab of what I assumed was a beer can.

"That's your *third!*" Ben had whispered.

Another curious moment was when I noticed something in among Bibi's hand laundry; she had borrowed my push-up bra.

Bibi talked a lot about Andrea Dennis these days. Andrea, it turned out, sometimes snacked after school at the Nutmeg Tea and Sandwich Shop, where Bibi waited tables. It seemed as if Andrea was always with someone I knew well, or had known. I could never resist saying, "Really? What did she have on? Did she look tired? Who picked up the check? Did they have desserts or entrees? Did she have that fruit cup?"

꙳

I was driving home with Rennie and the baby. We'd been to the lawyers'. The airplane company's insurance people had investigated and decided to settle some money on me. I liked it about the money, but what I wanted just now was my bed, pillows, the electric blanket. For three days, a quiet sleet had been falling on Old Hadham.

The car's windshield wiper on my side suddenly locked taut on a diagonal. A film formed immediately on the glass. I tried the squirters, but all I got was blue fluid congealing with the ice at the base of the windshield. I maneuvered down Willow, on Old Hadham's steepest hill—a plunger, which had been only cursorily sanded. There was a car not far ahead, and a truck on my tail, no shoulder. I had to tip my head out the driver's window to see. Meanwhile, Rennie was smiling, half asleep. The baby said a noise very much like "Why?" I had something close to nausea suddenly: suddenly missing Kit.

꙳

The baby woke me. It was an April morning, predawn. I was groggy, but I had a sweet dream still playing in my head—some of the dream's color and its melody—as I heated water for the formula and started coffee. "Here we come!" Rennie said, and drove the baby's castered crib into the kitchen. Rennie was oddly cheerful, giddy. Her taffeta robe was on inside out. She sat down and swayed the crib and sang some ballad about whaling boats and messmates, with a line about the lowland sea.

To distract the baby, Rennie had dropped a fat nest of pink excelsior into the crib—a leftover from Easter baskets. I was a little afraid the baby would eat the pink cellophane, so I intended to snatch it away. But for now the excelsior ball rolled back and forth with the crib's movement, and with Rennie's song and what rhythms there were of my lingering dream.

When the baby was asleep, we two sipped coffee. I figured Rennie would be stepping out onto the porch for sunrise, as she sometimes did, but instead she said she wanted to talk about her son, about Kit. I told her what I knew was true—that his character faults included overconfidence and impulsiveness. I said that he had taken all his lessons and received his license. But whatever the license signified, he hadn't been ready, not competent, to solo pilot a plane.

※

A lot of Old Hadham showed up at Chicwategue Park for Memorial Day. Some people brought picnic dinners and thermoses or coolers of drinks. The high school's brass-and-drum corps was there. There were two burros roped to a post for the little kids to ride around a guided circle.

Chicwategue Park had ducks on a pond, and a pair of swans—the town favorites—who'd made it through the winter, and bronze statues of Revolutionary War generals, and, in the center, a white-painted, lacy-looking gazebo. On the soccer fields beyond the woods, there would be footraces and other competitions throughout the day. Rennie had given Ben a two-year-old boxer she'd purchased through a newspaper ad, and Ben had entered himself and Reebok in the Frisbee contest.

I set up camp with the baby on a faded quilt. Rennie took Bibi to gamble away some of her waitress tips from the Nutmeg at the bingo tables. Watching them go, I noticed Andrea Dennis over by the penny-toss place—sporty and pretty in spotless sky-blue sweats, with a balloon on a ribbon looped at her wrist. She and Bibi greeted each other like classmates, with a hug.

Bibi's appearance looked to me like a screaming-out-loud reaction to Andrea Dennis. Bibi had whacked her fake-blonde hair into bristles and points, and her face was dusted with chalky makeup. Her lips looked almost black, and the tank top and jeans she wore were black. Still, Andrea was giving Bibi approving looks and nods.

But if Bibi's getups scared people, at least her manner had improved. That morning at breakfast, I'd overheard her saying to Ben, "Relax and sit still. I'll fix you a fresh glass of orange juice."

Now Ben's name was called over the PA system. I carried the baby and trailed Ben and Reebok to the starting stripe on the Frisbee competition field. Ben had the dog's collar in one hand and his yellow Frisbee in the other. Ben was down on one knee and the dog was trembling with excitement as they waited for the judge's signal to begin their routine.

At the whistle, the dog bolted away down the field. Ben stood up and let fly. His first couple of tries were long, too-fast throws, and the Frisbee sailed yards over Reebok's head. The dog wasn't paying attention anyhow. On their third and last turn, Reebok watched as he ran, then leaped, fishtailed, and chomped the disk, but only after it had ricocheted twice off the dirt. At the gazebo, the Frisbee judge held up a card, giving Ben and Reebok a "4" rating.

Andrea Dennis strolled over to us. She introduced herself to the baby and sort of shook hands with him. Ben and the dog came over. Ben's young face was bright, but I couldn't tell if it was from excitement or embarrassment.

Andrea said, "Man, you got robbed! Your dog flew six feet straight up. What do they *want*? They should've given you guys a special award."

Ben absorbed this. I knew that on the car ride home he would relive Reebok's last effort for Bibi and Rennie. He'd say he got robbed.

I asked him to watch the baby a minute—to make sure the kid didn't crawl away, go swimming after the swans, or filch anyone's barbecued spareribs.

I clapped a hand on the smooth blue sweatshirt material on Andrea's shoulder.

"What did I do?" Andrea said, and I said, "A lot."

We walked along together by the rows of blankets and the outdoor furniture that bordered the competition fields. We said hello to people—fellow teachers of Andrea's, the families of some of her students, old friends of mine.

I was thinking how to tell her that she had been an important distraction for me. She'd been someone safe to focus on while the reality of having no Kit was so fierce. I realized I couldn't make my interest in her into anything polite. I said, "Generally, thanks, Andrea," and I told her how great she looked in her blue.

7

Daughters

"Now we can talk," Dell said to her daughter, Charlotte. "If you've still got your bus fare. You didn't lose it, did you?"

They had just run out of the rain and into a concrete bus shelter, which had a long wooden bench. Dell sat down on the bench and pulled Charlotte down beside her. Charlotte was eight—too old to be held on a lap. The rain was falling and blowing in overlapping sheets, and Dell and Charlotte were both soaked.

"Be still," Dell said. She jerked her head back to avoid the spokes of a toy umbrella that Charlotte was twirling. They were in downtown Erie, in Perry Square, and the sky over the office buildings across the park from them was low and bruise-colored. Charlotte got down from the bench and went to the street curb, with the umbrella trailing behind her.

"Come back here and talk to me," Dell said. "I won't ask you again. Get out of the rain."

"I've still got it," Charlotte said. She stepped back under the roof of the shelter and uncurled her fingers to show a wet quarter. Her damp hair fell onto her shoulders, and her ears were exposed.

"I found a snake," she said, pointing at the gutter.

Dell got up and went to the curb with Charlotte and held her umbrella above them. They were bending over, watching an earthworm coiled next to the river of water in the gutter, when a new Mercury station wagon pulled into the near lane. Dell straightened up and squinted at the car's headlights. A Buick swerved to get around the station wagon, and its horn blew.

A man in a black raincoat got out of the passenger side of the station wagon. "We know," he said to the Buick. He opened a newspaper over his head, and ran over to where Dell and Charlotte were standing. "We *thought* it was you," he said, and tried to catch both of them under the spread of his newspaper. He was about forty, with dark hair.

"You remember Pierce, don't you?" Dell said to her daughter. Charlotte nodded at the man in the raincoat.

"We're in a bit of a hurry," the man said.

Dell said, "You two should just go on, Pierce. Nicholas is going to get rammed from behind, the way he's blocking traffic."

Nicholas was behind the wheel of the station wagon. His hand came up, and he pressed his palm on the wind-shield in greeting. He was wearing an old wide-brimmed felt hat.

"Pierce, you really should go on," Dell said. "The bus will be along any second."

"I meant for you to hurry up and get in the car," Pierce said. "Come on. We'll take you wherever you're going."

"We're going to my father's house. We couldn't think of riding in your car. We're wet to the skin." Dell turned to Charlotte, who had the earthworm draped over her index finger. "Put that worm back," she said.

More horns blew.

"Come on, Charlotta," Pierce said. He threw his newspaper into the street and grabbed the back of the little girl's neck. Nicholas leaned over and opened the back door for her. Dell collapsed the toy umbrella and followed her daughter inside. The doors slammed, diminishing the sounds of the rain.

"Hello, Nicholas, and how are you?" Dell said.

"I'm fine," Nicholas said, looking at Dell in the rearview mirror. He was white-haired, and about ten years older than Pierce. The two men were owners of a greenhouse and garden center, and they lived together in a town house on the south side of the city. Dell and Charlotte had rented their third floor for a few months after Dell divorced her husband. Charlotte was small then, and just learning to stand.

"We're *both* fine," Pierce said, shouting a little over the whack of the windshield wipers. "We're moving books. Hey, look at you."

"I'm sorry," Dell said. She tried to fluff up the scalloped wet curls around her face. "This is a new car, isn't it? I can smell the upholstery, and we're wringing wet."

"And now you've ruined it," Pierce said. "We'll have to get an even newer one. Won't we, Charlotte?"

"So much room!" Dell said.

"It's a barge and a headache," Nicholas said, steering the station wagon into the heavy afternoon traffic that ran around the square. A truck horn sounded behind them.

"Pay no attention," Pierce said.

Dell wiped beads of rain from her handbag. She said, "Could I possibly get a dry cigarette from someone?"

"Lean up, Nicholas," Pierce said. Nicholas turned sideways behind the wheel, and Pierce fished a pack of cigarettes from his raincoat pocket. "There," he said. He flipped the cigarettes over the seat to Dell. "That thing by your arm is an ashtray if you pull it out."

"Thank you," Dell said. She snapped a paper match and looked at it cross-eyed as she lit her cigarette. "We've been swimming all afternoon at the Y.W., is why we're downtown. I'm taking a lifesaving course, and Charlotte's in Polliwogs."

"You're lucky to have your days free," Pierce said. "We're moving these books from the office at the plant store to the house, and we had more than we knew. Mostly gardening stuff. This is our third trip, and we're about out of boxes."

Dell said, "Would it be all right if Charlotte sits in one of the boxes? Because she already is."

"Be our guest," Pierce said.

Charlotte had found an empty carton in the well behind the back seat. She was sitting in the box, with only her head showing. "Pierce," she said, "do you still have Django?"

"In fact, Charlotte, we don't," Pierce said. "Django ran away."

"Did he really?" Dell said.

Pierce shook his head. "Hit by a car," he mouthed.

"I'm so sorry," Dell said in a low voice.

"Where'd he go?" Charlotte said. She was using her finger to draw in the steam on the back window.

"College," Pierce said. "He went to get his bachelor's."

Charlotte ducked her head and shoulders into the box.

"Your daughter's turning shy," Pierce said to Dell.

"She's turning into a petty thief," Dell said.

Nicholas took a quick look at Dell in the mirror. "Really?" he said. "Is she any good?"

"I guess so. I hadn't thought of it in those terms," Dell said. She unbuttoned the side pouch of her handbag and brought out a packet of dollar bills.

"It's grand larceny, not petty theft, if she took that," Pierce said.

"This is just *one* thing she took," Dell said, riffling the bills like playing cards. "Seventy-four dollars. It was in the pocket of her jumper. She says she found it on the golf course. You know the golf course next to my father's place? Did I tell you we're living with my father right now?"

"She probably did find it, then," Pierce said. "Golfers are wealthy."

Dell said, "The trouble with this much money is I can't spend it and I don't know who to give it back to."

Nicholas stopped the car for a red light. Pierce reached over and twisted a knob, halting the windshield wipers. "I think we're out of the rain," he said.

The car started with a jolt, and Dell said, "Nicholas, I don't believe I've ever ridden with you. Pierce was always the driver."

"He only just got his license," Pierce said. "It's tricky, driving in the wet."

"Do I turn here?" Nicholas said. A diesel truck blew its air horn behind them. "I guess I don't."

"He's a little embarrassed," Pierce said, "just starting to drive at his age. He's never liked being told how to do anything."

"Yes, you do want to turn here, to get to my father's place," Dell said.

"I had my signal on," Nicholas said.

Pierce said, "We'll let you alone, Nicholas. We know we're in safe hands. But you do have to merge if you want to get onto the parkway."

"We *are* merging," Nicholas said.

❧

Dell directed Nicholas down several suburban streets, then past a new shopping mall and onto a road that went uphill parallel to a golf course. "There we are," she said. "The fourth house. The drive starts behind those hedges."

The rainstorm hadn't reached South Shore Drive, but some of its clouds still streaked the late-afternoon sun that was streaming over the broad lawns and slate roofs of the houses. In a neighbor's yard, a man in yellow coveralls rolled a silent mower toward a three-door garage. Nicholas drove the Mercury up the driveway.

"This is very, very nice," Pierce said. "Is this where you live, Charlotta?" He pointed to a thicket of plum trees and then to a trim line of dogwood saplings. "Good planting there," he said.

Nicholas stopped the car on the concrete turnaround in front of the low red-brick house.

"There's my father," Dell said. She ticked a fingernail on the car window. "He must have just got home from the office."

Dell's father, Gene, was smiling at them from under one of the linen shades at a window in the living room. One of his hands came up by his ear and he wiggled his fingers.

"Let me kiss you," Dell said to Pierce and Nicholas. "I might not see you again for a while."

"Hold off on that," Pierce said.

Gene came out of the front door of the house. He was wearing gray flannels and a red cardigan sweater and a pair of slippers, which slapped against the driveway. He opened the tailgate for Charlotte, who jumped out and landed on the concrete drive on all fours. Gene picked her up and twirled her over his head, turning her small trunk in his hands. "You're a bad Charlotte," Gene said. "Say it."

"I am bad!" Charlotte said, gasping and laughing.

Gene brought her down and released her. "What's up, Nicholas?" he said. "Come on inside. I've got gin gimlets."

"We hadn't seen your gardening," Pierce said. "We are impressed."

"That's thanks to the soil," Gene said. "Use a little lime and you could even grow tobacco here. Nicholas, now I know you want a drink, don't you?"

"You have no idea," Pierce said, getting out of the station wagon. "He's just been through a trial."

"Oh, yeah?" Gene said.

"People were driving like crazy idiots," Dell said.

"Let's do have a drink," Pierce said to Nicholas.

Nicholas stayed behind the wheel. "First of all, Pierce, I'm in no mood for a drink," he said. "You shouldn't be either, at five o'clock. We were going to the racetrack tonight, remember? Plus I'd like to get the books finished, if nobody minds." He looked straight ahead as he spoke.

"Will you calm down?" Pierce said. "We have time for one drink." He came around to help Dell out of the car.

"Well, I'm going to take the boxes home," Nicholas said. "I'll unpack them myself and then I'm going to the track. Do you have the money, Pierce?"

"You have money," Pierce said. "Drive carefully."

Dell said, "Stay in touch, Nicholas. Give us a call in the very near future."

Nicholas nodded and backed the car out of the drive.

Charlotte had run into the open garage at the end of the driveway, and was throwing old toys out of a box there. The three adults walked up the lawn to a flagstone patio, which was set about with wrought-iron furniture.

"I refuse to babysit for Charlotte tonight," Gene said to Dell, "so you can't go anywhere. For once, I want to be in my bed and sleeping by ten o'clock."

"You will be," Dell said. "I'll get Charlotte to bed on time myself, if I have to force her."

"I mean it," Gene said. He led Pierce and Dell into the foyer, and hung Pierce's raincoat behind a louvered door. They entered the wide, deep living room. The table lamps were already lit, and their silk and parchment shades were glowing orange. A brass light with an emerald shade stood on top of the piano. There was a full ice bucket on a side table behind the couch, and Gene mixed gimlets and shook them up in a tall silver shaker.

"I'm interested in you and Nicholas," he said to Pierce. "I want some trees for inside here. For this room. I was thinking of little laurels." He filled a glass and handed it to Pierce. "You two have a nursery someplace, don't you?"

"We can get you a tree at cost," Pierce said. "But we're generally wary about putting hearty trees indoors. They get restless."

"I've seen them thriving," Gene said. He swallowed half of his drink and refilled the glass from the shaker. "Dell," he said, "get your daughter in here. Everybody come over here and sit down around the coffee table. This is a meeting. Charlotte!"

Dell went out and reappeared with Charlotte, who was holding a plastic doll with blonde hair. They found seats around the low mahogany table. Gene had the cocktail shaker in front of him.

"This is about you," Gene said to Charlotte. He took an old-fashioned jeweler's watch case out of his sweater pocket and tipped back the hinged lid with his thumb.

"Oh," Charlotte said. She got down from her seat beside her mother and sat on the floor.

"You know what's in this box, don't you, Charlotte?" Gene said.

"I broke his watch," Charlotte said.

"First she stole it, then she broke it," Gene said. He held up a gold wristwatch with a shattered crystal. The hands of the watch were smashed against the watch face. "This was my anniversary present," Gene said. "Your mother gave it to me, Dell, on our twenty-fifth."

"Charlotte, this is terrible," Dell said. "Look at that watch. I feel so sorry for Grandpa."

"I feel sorry for him," Charlotte said. She tugged with her fingers at the carpet.

Dell said, "It was an important, special thing of his."

"It was irreplaceable," Gene said.

"All right, we're sorry, Father," Dell said. "But I don't think this is the time for a reprimand."

"Reprimand?" Gene said. "Hell, I just want to know why she did it."

"You're on the hot seat," Pierce said to Charlotte.

Charlotte looked at him out of the corner of her eye. She rocked forward and planted her spread hands on the carpet. She tried to do a headstand.

"Getting upside down won't help," Pierce said.

Dell picked a cigarette from a lacquered box on the table. She said, "Charlotte, go get Mommy's lighter from the bedroom."

"You send a kid for a cigarette lighter?" Gene said. He gestured to Charlotte to stay where she was.

"Probably unwise," Pierce said.

"I do it all the time," Dell said. "It never occurred to me."

"Well, when you come home and your home is a charred black hole it will occur to you," Gene said.

"I just wanted to shoo her off, Father," Dell said, putting down the cigarette. "I've wanted to discuss this stealing thing with her, but not now. She's embarrassed and on the spot. Aren't you, Charlotte?" She leaned over and looked at her daughter. "Are you crying? Do I see tears?"

"No," Charlotte said. She was lying on her hip.

"Neither do I," Gene said. "Frankly, Charlotte, I could wring your neck."

Dell said, "Thank you very much, Father. Now I think it's time for Charlotte and me to take a bath."

"I wouldn't know what time it is," Gene said. "I don't have a watch."

Dell refilled her glass and tasted her drink. "My, these are strong," she said. "Excuse me, Pierce." She took the cocktail and Charlotte and left the room.

≈

Dell balanced her drink on the side of the tub in Charlotte's bathroom and turned on the tub faucets. Charlotte came into the room on tiptoes.

"A bath, and then I'm tucking you in," Dell said.

"Now?" Charlotte said. "It's so early. I don't even see the moon."

"What I see is you," Dell said. "And, unless I'm mistaken, you have completely disrobed. Hop in."

"I'm so hungry," Charlotte said.

"Didn't I offer you dinner downtown? Would you eat it? No, you wouldn't."

Dell left Charlotte in the bathroom. A few minutes later, she came back carrying a tray with a dish of sliced fruit and cheese and a glass of pink soda on it. She put the tray down on the closed toilet seat. Charlotte was in the tub, surrounded by a flotilla of bath toys. Dell undressed, dropping her clothes on the bathroom floor. She retrieved her gimlet and stepped into the tub behind her daughter.

Charlotte twisted around and sniffed. "God," she said, "why are you drinking that?"

"Don't say 'God' to me, Charlotte," Dell said. "You are in enough trouble. Your grandfather's had it with you, in case you don't know. You walked off with Dr. Hanley's paperweight. Then you brought home Trish Bydecker's doll buggy. You stole seventy-four dollars from somebody. Now you've crushed Grandpa's poor watch. Think about it."

"I'm sorry," Charlotte said.

Dell finished her drink and submerged her glass in the bath-water. "You've got one last chance, Charlotte," she said. "I think you'll agree it's better for us if you stay out of sight and under the blankets tonight. Do I hear a 'yes'?"

Charlotte heaved a sigh and nodded.

Dell's face was flushed. She said, "So you see, if you go to sleep in a while, or even pretend to go to sleep, I'll buy you a car tomorrow."

"What kind of car?" Charlotte said.

"Like Pierce and Nicholas's. You can drive around town and get some new friends."

"What will you really buy me?" Charlotte said.

"It depends," Dell said. "Stretch Armstrong?"

Charlotte made a little shiver of pleasure. "Would you really?"

"Really," Dell said. "Sleep tonight, and Stretch Armstrong when you wake up." She soaped Charlotte's back and drew nu-merals on it with her fingernail.

❧

When Dell came back to the living room, she was wearing a silk blouse, pleated trousers, and patent-leather slip-ons. She found her father pacing up and down with a library book open in his hand. He had his reading glasses on. Pierce was sitting on the couch, holding a golf putter. He looked a little stunned. Some of his dark hair had come forward on his forehead.

Gene said, "Sit down, Dell. I want you to hear this. 'It seemed as though I had left my body and was about ten yards above myself, floating in the air,'" he read. "'I could see myself down below, crushed beneath the car's tires, but I felt no pain. I was strangely detached. I wasn't even interested.'"

"Don't let Father read to you," Dell said to Pierce. "You poor thing."

"I'm all right," Pierce said. "I'm about ten yards above myself, feeling no pain or even interest."

"This proves life after death, I think," Gene said.

"What about dinner?" Dell said. "Have you offered Pierce dinner, or were you going to put him in a coma first?"

"I'm hungry, too," Gene said, "but let me finish. I was reading about this guy who was hit by a car." He closed the book. "I'll just tell you, all right? The guy is legally dead. Heart stopped. No brain waves. You know what he hears?"

"How can he hear anything?" Pierce said.

"Angels," Gene said. "A choir thing starts up for him."

Pierce had poked the golf club into his shirtsleeve and worked it up to his shoulder, so that his left arm stuck straight out. "I wouldn't hear choirs," he said. "I hate choirs."

"It's different at my age," Gene said.

"I think I have to leave now," Pierce said. "Gene's liquor has punched me between the antlers."

"Gets you, doesn't it?" Gene said.

"Come on in the kitchen with me, Pierce," Dell said. "I'll phone for a cab, and you can watch me fix dinner."

"There are some strip steaks thawing in the icebox," Gene said.

Pierce shook his arm, and the golf putter fell down his sleeve and onto the carpet.

"Everyone must have a clear conception of his or her relationship with God," Gene said. He spoke with great precision, pronouncing each syllable.

"I don't," Pierce said. He followed Dell into the kitchen.

She called a cab on a wall phone in the breakfast nook, and then she walked back and forth under the cabinets, gathering plates and shaking out napkins. She took a head of lettuce from the refrigerator and began washing the leaves under cold water at the sink.

Pierce had found a bone-handled carving knife and sharpener, and he drew the blade back and forth against the rod. "We haven't taken in another boarder since you," he said. "You left quite a hole in our lives, Delilah, which I could manage to live with if you'd phone once in a while."

"I haven't called because of guilt," Dell said. "I know I still owe you that rent money. You've been very nice not to mention it."

"Oh, for heaven's sake," Pierce said.

"No, I do owe it, and I'm working on paying you. You'll get a pleasant surprise in the mail someday."

"Don't embarrass me," Pierce said. He put the knife down and picked up his gimlet glass from the top of the dishwasher. "Don't put a strain on our friendship."

"I know how angry I made Nicholas," Dell said.

"Nicholas is an old lady," Pierce said. "Anyway, he and I are thinking of getting a divorce. We've been at each other's throat twenty-four hours a day lately. You hang on to your money. You got a rough break from your husband, and you need all the money you have. Nicholas and I don't need it, and you know I'm telling the truth, because I'm generally such a bitch about finances."

Dell twisted a knob on the stove and then looked out the bay window in the breakfast nook. A pair of headlights was moving down the drive. "I see your cab, Pierce," she said.

Pierce went out of the kitchen, and when he came back he was stuffing his arms into his raincoat sleeves. "Gene's conked out," he said. "He's using his afterlife book for a pillow." He stooped a little and squinted out the bay window. "Why, that's Nicholas. What do you know? He came back for me."

"Will he come in?" Dell said.

"He's too ashamed," Pierce said. "He'll sit out there in the car until I go to him." He leaned forward and kissed Dell on the mouth.

Charlotte came into the kitchen wearing a clean nightgown. She had a sheet of red construction paper with a crayon drawing of a dog on it.

"Is that Django?" Pierce said. "For me?"

"Yes, I drew it for you," Charlotte said. She looked at her mother.

"Instead of being asleep," Dell said.

There was a quick, loud horn blast from the driveway. Pierce shrugged and worked the collar of his raincoat into place. "I'm being called," he said.

8

Seizing Control

Wᴇ ᴡᴇʀᴇɴ'ᴛ sᴜᴘᴘᴏsᴇᴅ ᴛᴏ stay up all night, but Mother was in the hospital having Jules, and Father was at the hospital waiting.

We spent a long time out in this blizzard. We had the flood-lights on out behind the house, and our backyard shadows were mammoth. We kicked a maze—each of us making a path that led to a fort like an igloo we piled up at the center of the maze. We built the fort last, but then nobody wanted to get inside. Hazel patted the fort and said, "Victory!"—from a movie she knew or something. We didn't quit and come in until Sarah, the youngest, was whimpering.

Our cuffs and gloves were stiff and had ice balls crusted on them. Our socks were soaked. All of us had snow in our boots—even Terrence, who had boots with buckles. Zippers were stuck with cold. Our ears burned for a long while after, and our hair was dripping wet from melted snow. We put everything we could fit into the clothes dryer and turned it to roll for an hour.

Our neighbors on both sides had been asked to guard us and watch the house (there were five of us kids, not counting Jules), so when it got late and the TV had signed off we put out the lights and had a fire in the fireplace instead. We didn't sub-scribe to cable, and Providence, where we lived, has no all-night channel on weekends (this was a Friday). Sometimes we could get Channel 5 from Boston, but not that night, not with the blizzard.

Hazel, who was the oldest of us, was happy about the fire but baffled about the television. Hazel was retarded. She'd get the show listings from the *Providence Journal* and underline what she wanted to see. To do this, she must have had some kind of coding system she'd memorized, because of course she couldn't read. This was the first time Hazel had ever been awake when the TV wasn't.

She watched the fireplace, and once when she saw an up-shoot of flame she said, "The blue star!" which was what she called a beautiful blue ring that our mother wore. Hazel watched the fire some more and kept quiet enough. She had her texture board with her on her lap. "Smooth . . . grainy . . . soft," she recited, but just to herself, as she felt the different squares.

Terrence got on the telephone and called up a friend of his—Vic, who'd claimed he always stayed up all night. Terrence couldn't get anyone but Vic's very alarmed parents. He didn't give them his name. Terrence was also drinking a bottle of wine cooler—Father's—which wasn't allowed, but the rest of us had shared a can of beer earlier and now we were having coffee that we'd made in the drip machine, neither of which we were al-lowed to do, either. We figured we were all about even and no one would tell.

Hazel started to get annoying with her texture board. She had torn off the square of wide-wale corduroy, and she kept wanting the rest of us to feel the beads of rubber cement left on the backing. "Touch this," she said over and over to Willy, our other brother.

We took her to bed, to our parents' king-sized bed—which we thought would be all right this once. And Sarah, the baby, was there in bed already. At first Sarah pretended to be asleep while Hazel was undressing. She could undress herself if she stood before a mirror, and she knew to arch her back and work her hands behind to get her bra unhooked. She never wore clothing that looked retarded. In fact, whenever Father said to her, "How come you always look so pretty?" Hazel really would look pretty. She swung her arms when she walked, the same as the rest of us.

Sarah pretended to wake up suddenly. She wanted her cherry Chap Stick—her lips were so dry, she complained. Terrence must have heard Sarah—we were downstairs—because she was being so insistent. He called, "You left it out in the yard! You had it outside with you. You left it." Sarah believed Terrence, because his voice had authority. He was very attuned to voices, and he knew how to use his though he was only seventeen. He'd say to Hazel, "Don't sound like you're six years old. You're not six." Or if someone said just what was expected and predictable Terrence would ask, "Why should I listen when you're only making noise?"

Sarah wanted us to retrieve her Chap Stick. But the blizzard was still on, and nobody was going back out there, however sorry for her we felt. Most of the time when Sarah was outside, she'd kept her wool muffler over her mouth to protect it. Willy had to wrap it around her, under the hood of her parka, so it was just right. She had baby skin and the cold got to her.

Late in the night, Hazel punched Sarah in the face when they were supposed to be sleeping. Probably they were asleep, and Hazel was probably having a dream. Terrence was interested in dreams and wrote about his in a dream journal he kept. Sometimes he'd ask us questions about ours, or he'd talk to Mother and Father about the meaning of dreams. But he didn't ask Hazel if she was dreaming when she swung and socked Sarah.

We all talked at once: "I can't find a coat. . . . Wear mine. . . . Un-unh, I *hate* that coat. . . . This is wet! . . . Go look in the dryer. . . . Get a blanket—get two! . . . No one will see you except maybe the doctor. . . . It makes virtually no *difference* what you're wearing or how you look. . . . Another towel for her nose! . . . Let's just get out of here."

Terrence warmed up the old Granada out on the street, where Father had parked it because the driveway was snowed over. We left Hazel alone in our parents' bed, and we carried Sarah. We put her in the back, and then two of us got on either side of her. Sarah was covered up with a blanket and also Father's old topcoat.

The snow blew around in the headlights. No one else was out, and we urged Terrence to run the red lights. He said he couldn't afford to—his license was only a learner's permit. He also had a fake license from one of his friends, but the fake said Terrence was twenty-six, which wasn't believable. We begged him to put on some speed. We said that with a hurt person aboard, the police might even give us an escort through the storm. Terrence said, "Well, I checked her out and she's not that hurt, unfortunately."

A man walking his brown poodle loomed up beside us for a moment. The poodle was jumping around in the deep snow, loving it.

"Dog," Sarah said through her towel bandage. She was wide awake.

❧

After the emergency room, we left Sarah on the car seat. She was out cold from the shot, even though the doctor said it was just to relax her. Her nose was nowhere near broken.

We'd driven a while and then we hustled into an all-night pancake place, there off Thayer Street. Inside it was steamy and yellow-lit, although it felt a little underheated. We took over one side of an extra-long booth, each of us assuming giant seating space and sprawling convivially. Our arms were spread and they connected us to one another like paper dolls.

We spent time with the menu, reading aloud what side stuff came with the "Wedding Pancake," or with the "Great American French Toast." Willy wanted a Sliced Turkey Dinner Platter, but Terrence said, "Don't get that. It's frozen. I mean frozen when served, as you're eating and trying to chew." The waitress approached, order pad in hand. She wore a carnation-pink dress for a uniform. We fidgeted in irrelevant ways, as if finding more comfortable spots on the booth seat. But we didn't whisper our orders. We acted important about our need for food. We'd been through an emergency.

After the waitress, we discussed what we'd tell Mother and Father, exactly. They'd be so busy anyway, we said, with baby Jules. They'd been busy already. Father had painted the nursery again, same as he'd done for each of us.

We wondered if washing-machine cold-water soap might remove the bloodstains Sarah had left on the pillowcase.

"We'll tell them . . ." Terrence said, but he couldn't finish. We pressed him. We wanted to know.

"O.K.," he said at last. "We just give them the truth. Describe how we seized control."

We said, "They're going to ask Sarah, and she'll say, 'Ask Hazel.'"

✎

Our parents asked Hazel. She told them everything—all that she knew. She said, "Share. . . . Admit who won. . . . People look different at different ages. . . . Providence is the capital of Rhode

Island. . . . Stand still in line. . . . Mother and Father have been alive a long time. . . . Don't pet strange animals. . . . Get someone to go with you. . . . Hold tight to the bus railing. . . . It is never all right to hit. . . . We have Eastern Standard Time. . . . Put baking soda on your bee stings. . . . Whatever Mother and Father tell you, believe them."

9

Kite and Paint

OCEAN CITY. IT WAS the last day of August, and everybody was waiting for Hurricane Carla. Don was outside the house he shared with Charlie Nunn, poking at the roses with an umbrella. The cuffs of Don's pants were soaked with dew. His morning coughs were deep, and with each round of coughs he straightened up and clutched his cardigan at his throat.

Charlie Nunn was watching Don from an old glider on the porch. He had taken apart the morning paper, and had the sports section open on his khakis. Both men were in their sixties.

"You don't sound good," Charlie said.

"I know it," Don said. He paused in the roses and whacked at a spoke of weed with his umbrella.

A green car pulled up at the curb in front of the house. Charlie nodded at a face in the window of the car. The car door opened, and Don's former wife, Holly, got out. She was all dressed up—a pale-green crocheted dress, nylons, and alligator shoes. She came up the path of flat stones that led to the house, with one hand on her red straw hat.

"Come in, come in, Holly," Charlie said. He folded his newspaper and tucked it under his thigh. "Do sit down," he said.

"Thank you, no," Holly said. "I'm just here to check on my piano." She stepped onto the porch, and her hand dropped from her hat to one hip. She smiled at Charlie.

"I could kick myself for not moving it out of here long ago," she said. "Don can't play it. Unless he learned to play."

"No, he didn't," Charlie said. "But the piano's safe. I got it on top of the meat freezer, believe it or not. I built a frame for it so it won't warp if we get flooded, and it's shrouded in polyethylene."

"On a meat freezer?" Holly said. "My goodness. It's really nice of you, Charlie. Or did you even know the piano belonged to me?"

"I guess I did," Charlie said. "I used to keep track of what was whose. Last evening, I just decided everything had to be protected."

"Well, what are you going to do?" Holly said. "Are you two going anywhere for the hurricane?"

"Not that I know of," Charlie said. "I guess almost everyone else already left."

"Yes, a lot of them are staying over at the grade school," Holly said. "It's high ground." She turned and looked toward Don. "I wonder if he should be out there," she said. "What's he doing?"

"Picking mint, it looks like," Charlie Nunn said. "What can I do?"

"Nothing at all," Holly said. She tapped one of her shoes against the other.

"Let's go look at the piano," Charlie said. He got off the glider and led Holly by the wrist through the front door.

They went through the parlor and the kitchen to a small storage room at the back of the house. Charlie gestured at the piano, an upright, which was lying on one side on top of a low freezer. Inside its slatted frame, it was swathed in plastic wrappings.

"It looks like a coffin," Holly said. "It should be fine. It looks great. How in the world—"

"I got in some beach kids, and they gave me a hand with it," Charlie said.

"What are those?" Holly said, pointing to some flat shapes stacked in one corner.

"Sized canvases," he said. "I don't know why I'm keeping them safe. Don won't use them. He hasn't worked since he had the flu."

"He hasn't?" Holly said.

"No."

"Well," she said, "you know the only time he painted with me was when we were first married—oh, twenty years ago. Back when he was friends with some of the big names."

Charlie followed her back into the parlor.

"Oh, God, look at that," Holly said. "He left the caps off his oils. They're all clotted." She went over to Don's drawing table, in one corner of the room, and stared at the metal trays that held his paint tubes.

"I would at least like to see the canvases stay dry," Charlie said, half sitting on an arm of the couch. "They were work."

"They predict fourteen-foot waves," Holly said.

"I heard that," he said. "If we flood out, I swear I'm taking the canvases first. I had to cut the stretchers with a mitre box. They're black oak. The sizing's made with white lead from Germany and glue from Japan."

He got off the couch and went over to a closet. "Let me show you something. This makes me furious," he said over his shoulder. He knelt and eased a square of illustration board from between some storage envelopes on the closet floor.

Charlie showed Holly the illustration board. It had childish doodles of a warplane dropping a row of finned bombs, and beneath the bombs there was a pencil sketch of a pelican.

"Do you see this part?" Charlie said, circling the pelican with the tip of his index finger. "Feather-perfect," he said. "It could buy us food."

"How bad is the financial situation with you two?" Holly said.

Charlie said, "I have a pension from teaching."

"You taught? I never knew that," Holly said.

"Sure. I taught shop at the junior high for twenty-three years."

"This junior high? Then you're from here."

"Oh, yeah," Charlie said. "My dad was with the shore patrol. My mother's still alive. She lives on Decker Street. I'm told somebody already drove her to Philadelphia for the blow. One of my nieces, I think."

Don came into the parlor, carrying a handful of mint. "Aren't you scared?" he said to Holly.

"No, I'm not scared," she said. "Just exhausted is all."

"I think I'll take some of my kites down to the beach," Don said. "It's getting sort of windy already." He dropped the mint on the seat of an armchair.

"In fourteen-foot waves?" Holly said. "How smart would that be?"

Don pointed the end of his umbrella at Holly's hat. "What a thing on your head," he said.

Holly's face reddened. She said, "I'm on my way to Philadelphia, Don. I'll be at Mary Paul's." She turned to Charlie. "Maybe I'll see your mother," she said.

"Maybe you will," Charlie said, rocking forward on the soles of his shoes.

"Good-bye, Charlie," Holly said, heading for the door.

"Good-bye, Don," said Don.

"Yes, good-bye, Don," Holly said.

"I don't feel good," Charlie said, in the next hour. He and Don were in the parlor.

"Go outside and take some breaths," Don said.

Charlie frowned at the couch, which was heaped with cardboard boxes he had just brought up from the basement. He got down and lay on his back on the parlor rug. He put his left fingers on his right wrist, and cocked his arm to read his pulse against his watch.

Don had switched his pants and sweater for a bathrobe and sandals. He was sitting in an armchair and drinking from a bottle of gin. On his lap was a small wheel of cheese.

"The air is so bad in here it's making me cry," he said.

Charlie had a lighted cigarette in his mouth and was smoking it while he took his pulse. Some ashes had fallen on his unshaven chin.

Don snapped the switch on an electric fan that stood on a table beside his chair. The fan wagged slowly to and fro, cutting the smoke haze over Charlie's body.

"Chess?" Don said. "A quick game while we wait?"

Charlie stubbed out the cigarette in an ashtray he had balanced on his stomach. He glared at his watch. "No, I don't want to play chess," he said. "I just want to feel better."

"You would if you ate. Only you'd better get to it, because what you see here is about all there is, and it's nearly gone," Don said. He snapped off the fan.

"You're eating that cheese with the rind still on," Charlie said.

There was a gust of wind outside, and the parlor curtains billowed against the windowsills. "You should see it out there," Don said. "From here, it looks like the sky is beige."

Charlie rubbed his stomach.

"I'll let you see what I did last night," Don said. He got up and stepped over Charlie on the way to the closet. He brought out a shopping bag and put it on the rug by Charlie's head.

"Looky here," Don said. He pulled a half-dozen kites from the bag. The kites were made of rice paper, balsa-wood strips, and twine, and were decorated with poster paints in bright primary colors.

"They look like flags," Charlie said.

"I made drawings of each one in a notebook, beforehand," Don said. "I gave them titles. These are called 'Comet' and 'Whale.'" He showed Charlie a blue kite and a yellow one with an orange diagonal stripe.

"Yeah. What else?" Charlie said.

"This is 'Boastful,'" Don said, handing Charlie a kite. "Stay still a minute." He crossed the room, with a kite in each hand.

"I'm not going anywhere," Charlie said.

Don propped the kites against the boxes on the sofa, where the light from one of the parlor windows fell on them. "These are the next to the best," he said, standing back. "'My Beauty' and 'Moon.'"

"Right, right," Charlie said. "Let's see the best."

"This one—'Reddish Egret,'" Don said. "It's my favorite." He held the last kite flat above Charlie's face. "See?" he said, touching a stenciled figure in the center of the kite. "It's a bird."

"Why don't you send them to Zack, in the city?" Charlie said as Don took the last kite away. "He could get you some gallery space or something, I bet."

"I fired Zack," Don said. "It'd be fun to waste them in the blow."

"Not a chance," Charlie said.

"Why can't we?"

"I'm not getting off this floor," Charlie said, "unless it's to get in hot bathwater, and I mean up to my chin."

Don collected his kites and dropped them one by one into the shopping bag. He threw himself into the armchair and turned on the fan again.

"Holly was shocked at the mess your oils are in," Charlie said after a while.

"Oh, don't even tell me," Don said. "Holly! Her very presence is dispiriting to me."

"I don't know why you say that," Charlie said. "All she hopes for is to see you do an occasional day's work."

"I never liked to paint," Don said.

Charlie turned on his side on the floor and braced his head on his palm. "Would you turn off that fan? I can't hear myself," he said. "You liked painting when you had a model. Especially that one model."

The fan quit by itself, in midglance, and the noise from the refrigerator stopped.

"Uh-oh," Charlie said. "That means the hot water, too." He got off the rug and went to the window, and stood holding back the curtain. "It looks like a good one," he said. "How about flying your kites from the porch roof, if I rip up an old bedsheet? For the tails, I mean. You want to climb out there and try it?"

"I do," said Don.

10

Father, Grandfather

M Y DAUGHTERS WERE BIG, beautiful blondes who shared a loft in the East Village, but lately they'd been staying at my placc, helping me resettle. I could hear them now in the living room, the younger one, Cammie, asking as she came to, "Where is it I have to get up this second and go?"

"Supermarket," said Cake. "We need napkins, disposable cups. We have no ice tongs."

She sighed and said, "Cammie, my God. It's a good thing your clothes are all-occasion."

Cammie had slept fully dressed on my couch.

"Well, but I wake up ready to go," Cammie said.

"I think you drink," said Cake.

"What if I do?" Cammie asked as she pulled up and shook off. Now both of them arrived in the kitchen.

"Not water from a tap, though, which is something I've seen *you* do," Cammie said. "What's this we're cooking?"

They stood at the stove. On one of the front burners sat a huge gurgling kettle.

"Clothes," Cake said. "They were ugly, so I'm dying them. That sundress what's-her-name gave me, and this other stuff, if it doesn't get pitch black I'm throwing it out."

She used a long wooden wand to stir the clothing and the kettle's dark water.

"Did you make that? It's an *oar*," Cammie said.

Cake nodded. Both my girls had, like me, degrees in anthropology, but Cake had gone into the design and production of wooden spoons. Cammie served drinks at a cowboy bar.

"Hi," I said now, from my seat behind the breakfast nook. I had been sitting there, unnoticed, the whole long time.

꒰

They returned from the market with sacks of food and the idea of using my bigger kitchen to make hors d'oeuvres.

They had invited me to a cocktail party that night at their loft. I was looking forward to the party and to meeting their many friends. The past eighteen months, I'd been away traveling on a grant. I'd gone to Ciudad Juarez to live with the Okut.

"Before we do anything," Cake said. "This *kitchen*."

꒰

They cleared shelves and cabinets and flipped cans and jars into recycling bags. They used what they called the "six-sack solution"—separate sacks for paper, glass, metal, plastics, food garbage, and one for nonperishables.

I left the kitchen and hid; close, but in another room.

I heard Cammie say, "Here're all the supplements we bought for her—iodine, zinc, chromium, selenium. . . . Seals unbroken, soon to expire."

Cake called out to me in a tone that made my cat leap: "Mom! You cannot rely on food for nutrition! The soil your produce is grown in is worthless!"

"Come here, Moo," I told the cat. "You didn't do anything,"

Now they were defrosting my freezer.

"Get back! Get that blowdryer outta here!" Cake yelled. "That is so dangerous! Mom, will you tell her this is dangerous? And that she can't slam at it with a ballpeen hammer. The thing's got Freon!"

My door buzzer sounded. As I got up to answer, I saw the doorknob turn, saw the door open. My father slipped in. I exhaled relief and sat back down.

Dad was dressed for cold in a topcoat and a furry black muffler. His face and bald head were deeply tanned.

"Un*locked?*" he asked me. He glanced left, glanced right. He leaned over my chair. "Who's here?"

"The girls," I said. "You're so tan!"

He straightened. He said, "Thanks," as he unbuttoned his topcoat. He said, "I use that cream. It's not bad. Not streaky orange like in the old days. I'll bring you some."

Cammie's voice said, "Grandpa? Don't take this the wrong way, but no."

She stood in the kitchen entryway. She was holding a platelet of ice.

"It costs three or four dollars," he said.

"I know," Cammie said, "but the greater cost. There're laws now about smear-on tans. That anyone who has one can't vote."

"I'm not registered anyway," Dad said when Cammie was gone.

"Oh lordy," I said. "Don't tell them that."

"Who's in authority here?" he asked.

❧

"I've got crocuses, a few tulips," he said. He lived in Brooklyn. "Saw kids doing an egg hunt the other morning. Oh, and, Gloria, I read in *Cosmopolitan* that you're supposed to—"

"Wait," I said. "You read *Cosmopolitan?*"

He looked right, he looked left. "Only sometimes, if it's lying out and I happen to pick it up."

I hadn't moved in hours and my chair's upholstered buttons had numbed circles into my back.

"This article cautioned you to cook eggs all the way. You want to be certain of that when you're getting ready for Easter."

I didn't comment, but Cake called from the kitchen, "We're a little old for baskets, Grandpa. Though we still need Mom's help tying our Easter bonnets on."

Dad was lounging on the carpet now before the television. The cat came from the shadows and climbed onto him.

"Your husband still with that woman?" he asked me.

I said, "Why would you believe me, but I don't know or care."

"You may be fooling yourself," my dad said.

"Then I successfully have. Just shoe her away. The cat," I said.

"Oh no, don't worry about it. I'm flattered she wants to sit here."

"Except I do like these pants," he said after a moment. He lifted the cat off his lap and brushed at his trousers.

I got out of my chair and stood by a bookcase. I had heard Cake say, "You want to bet that if we go in there she still won't have moved."

"Badgering your own witness!" Dad told the TV.

Perry Mason was on, and Dad had been ahead of the prosecutor character with objections. "Not best evidence. Wasn't introduced in cross." He said, "I think this must have been a joke episode, the way Raymond Burr keeps announcing he's waiting for Mr. Right."

"Have you seen this one?" I asked.

"I don't know, I might've. I've got them all on tape. It's to the point that whatever I'm doing I move to the theme song, you know? Tahd-ah, duhd-ee, tahd-ah, duhd-*ee.*"

The smoke alarm in my kitchen sounded.

The girls, through the entryway, high-jumped. Cake swatted at the alarm. Cammie was fanning at it with a towel.

My dad scooted over to me and asked if he should intervene. "Although I'm not sure how," he said.

I pantomimed palming the lid, turning it, plucking out the alarm's batteries.

Above its shriek, Cammie screamed, "A potato! That's all I was trying to do! This is about a fucking potato!"

The spud flew past us and thumped against the wall, hard, and awfully close to the cat.

❦

We were on the way to the girls' cocktail party. Cammie had her car in a tight alley, competing with a cab. Usually I enjoyed riding with Cammie. Her driving included many tricks she'd learned in her days of pizza delivery.

Now we were caught with the cab side by side at the alley's end. The cabby hauled himself out and came around to argue.

I said, "How about if we just —"

"In fairness, I think he started it," said my dad.

"It doesn't matter who started it!" I said.

The cabby was yelling. Cammie geared into reverse.

We arrived for the party at the same time as a lot of guests. Some were carrying drinks, coolers, and bags of ice that they dumped into the sinks in the kitchen.

My dad wove through the room, chatting and introducing himself and shaking hands.

I knew no one. While I was traveling, the girls had picked up a whole new crowd.

And they had redone their loft—lacquered the floor tiles, painted murals, stenciled the woodworking.

"The guy behind you," said Cake. "Not straight behind. Five o'clock."

I turned, turned back. "He looks like Aldo Ray," I said.

"Yeah," Cake said. "But Mom, he is the sweetest person."

"He certainly does have a lovely tan. Golden! Your grandfather must've got to him. He's *older* than your grandfather."

She said, "The sweetest. You know, the last time he stayed over—because he lives out in who-knows and some nights it's too cold. The next day he kept apologizing, 'cause I guess he'd been snoring. Saying, 'God, I'm a warthog! Honk, honk!' Saying that over and over."

"*All* your guests are old," I said.

Cake looked at me as if I'd burped.

I could hear my dad behind me. He was talking to somebody, asking, "How could you tell? You remember these? Nineteen forty-three, in fact. They're my war shoes. Old, but they are perfect shoes to this day."

I thought I saw someone. I went stiff and wheeled slowly around like a rotating store-window mannequin.

"Tell me that isn't," I said and grabbed Cake by the wrist.

"Well, yes," she said, "I'm afraid it is. We have a party, they come if they want. Mom, pretend you don't notice."

"How?" I asked.

"Easy," she said. "Just pretend."

⁓

Now the crowd had me cornered. My husband and his friend were dancing close by. Their moves had flourishes, and the lacy tops of the woman's thigh-highs showed with her every turn.

I tried to look engaged. I leaned to the ear of a woman who was reading her watch. I whispered, "I, too, need to know the time."

"This won't tell it," she said, and finger-snapped the watch face. She was bare-legged. She wore a cocktail dress, a bowler hat, ugly black shoes.

"Would you just talk to me for a second?" I asked.

The woman pulled back. She said, "Glow-ria. You don't remember me. We used to be best friends."

"Oh," I said, "Bonnie. I'm sorry. I didn't see it was you."

"Catch your breath," the man with her said kindly. Rhinehart, I believe, was his name. He stared off at the speaker system and nodded at its song. As it ended, he looked back to us, still nodding. He said, "Love *is* a lie. One big lie."

"It's like you're holding an egg yolk in your hand," I said in a low voice.

Bonnie said, "You mean the *other* person's holding the yolk."

"You two are psychotic," said Rhinehart.

"Gloria," someone whispered, and took me by the shoulders and turned me around. It was Aldo Ray. "I'm Sasha. I just wanted to introduce myself."

I said, "It's nice to meet you. I already know who you are. Cake was telling me. About the night you stayed over? The honking and snoring. Not that *she* thought you were, by any means."

⁓

Dad found me in the dining room, on one of the spindle-backed chairs at the banquet table. Before me were ice buckets, and the girls' new pairs of tongs, many kinds of liquor, glasses, and drinks paraphernalia.

"I did a terrible thing," I said.

My dad said, "I heard."

"Oh my God, no. He's *tell*ing people?"

"No, I *over*heard," said my dad.

He sat across the table from me. He said, "I finally found a remedy for that jumpy stomach of yours. It's a tumbler of gin. You get into bed, you're half lying down, you gulp the whole glass, you're cured."

"No, Dad, that's being unconscious. It's not a remedy for anything."

"It works, little lady. I ought to know."

"Of course it works! You're passed out!" I said. "You're in a coma!"

After a bit, he said, "One evening, I remember coming home from work. You must have been in your room upstairs. A banana peel shot straight out your window and landed on the roof."

"Those were the days," I said.

"Well, it took me all next morning to get it down. Assembling the ladder, crawling out on those old shingles. Some of them loose."

I said, "Dad, you choose *now* to reprimand me?"

"No. I'm saying, Gloria! There's a point at which your kids aren't who they were anymore. They aren't even kids. They're over there, a couple of people."

It was Cammie who joined us and warned that we were abandoning too many traditions. She said, "This is why tribes die."

"Which traditions?" asked my dad. "Cultural? Religious ones? Our family?"

"Those're they," Cammie said.

Cake was there also. She said, "You're going to have to be more specific."

"Okay, Easter dinner. It used to be a ham covered with pineapple rings and cloves," said Cammie.

"Even if I didn't think this idea dangerous," Cake said, "I wouldn't eat ham."

She said, "And you're not going to get me out caroling. Nor do I see myself wearing a hat in church."

"Not rules, you're thinking rules. More like customs. Like holly. Or breaking the wishbone on Thanksgiving," Cammie said.

"Spankings on my birthday," said Dad.

Cammie said, "Or how about quarters under my pillow? I just had this wisdom tooth yanked."

"You floated through that on Percodan. You weren't even there," said Cake.

"Cards," Cammie said. "I will buy you all gift boxes of greeting cards to send to me."

"I like jelly beans and Easter candy," my dad said. "Not marshmallow chicks. Nobody likes those, they're always stale. Though they *look* good."

"Hershey's a decent company," said Cake.

I said, "Maybe you're right about traditions. What I missed in Mexico was anything *familiar.*"

"*Live at Five,*" Cake said. "Denny's."

My husband and his woman friend entered the room. My dad sought to distract me by starting a loud complaint about the wine in my glass. He said, "Gloria, honey, stop! I tasted that wine you're drinking. It's gone bad. And besides that, the girls say it's all full of sulphitates. You better excuse yourself immediately. Take a word of advice and go heave."

"I'm fine," I said. "Let me finish."

I said, "You know, when you're a kid, how you want everything to move really fast. So you can grow up, or get to change classrooms, or you want to have more gears on your bike. Plus, the bad things. You chip a tooth, or the way the UPS man ran over Pumpkin."

Cammie looked deep into me. She said, "You were a piece of *wood* when that guy killed Pumpkin."

"No, no, that's just what you *saw*. I was devastated," I said.

Now Cake was crying and writing our dead dog's name on a table napkin.

"Aw, little baby," my dad said to her, or to any of us, or to all.

He removed his war shoes and moved them along the carpeting and presented them to me. "Gloria," he said, "put these on."

He said, "I'm serious. Just try them."

"All right, I have to admit they're pretty good," I said.

He said, "I want each and every one of you to wear them."

The girls were nodding. Cammie said, "Me, next."

11

Trying

Friday night, Bridie's rock group were into their second set at the K. of C. dance. They were an all-girl band that went by the name Irish Coffee. They did popular songs and a handful of simple electrified versions of Celtic songs they'd been able to learn.

Some boys in St. Augustine's School jackets crashed the makeshift ticket gate, which was two girls at a card table with a spool of purple tickets and a glass jar of dollar bills. A couple of the boys had beer—bottles of Killian's Red. "You don't want to drink that," Bridie O'Donnell said into the microphone during a break between numbers. "It's made by Coors."

Three of the St. Augustine's School boys moved up front and stood there, facing the stage. They did a prepared jig during the group's next song—a three-chord, just-the-chorus rendition of "The Lads of Bofftae Bay." On the last note—a dominant chord from Karen Jorry's bass guitar—the boys whirled and let their trousers drop.

Some pushing and pulling ensued. Karen Jorry and the group's drummer, Ellen Gautier, left their equipment and stomped off the stage.

At the microphone, Bridie said, "Come on, please. No kicking. You don't need to kill them—just get them to leave. Guys? Take your teensy imaginations out of here." But the shoving went on some more.

"Save my amp from getting knocked over—*that* one, not this one!" Bridie shouted now to Proudbird.

He jumped onto the stage, spun, and crouched. The big amplifier was still attached to its wires, but Proudbird got it up and onto his back.

"What *was* all that stuff—mirth?" Bridie said.

"Yah, I guess mirth, man," Proudbird said. He shrugged under the amplifier.

The two watched as the annoyed dance crowd began to flow out of the K. of C. hall, observed by a brown-uniformed security guard.

Bridie was sitting tilted back on a folding chair, reading a basement-press newspaper she'd smuggled into the convent in a leg of her jeans. It was the day after the K. of C. thing, and she was serving detention for class truancy or some other infraction—she wasn't even sure.

The convent, an ordinary two-story wooden house on the St. Benedict's grounds, was home for a dozen Benedictine nuns. Also on the grounds, in a kind of cluster around the Romanesque cathedral, were the two school buildings, a rectory, and a gymnasium. St. Benedict's was in northern Virginia, not far from D.C.

Today Bridie was supposed to tidy the convent's kitchen and straighten the contents of cabinets and drawers. She'd been told to box up some canned goods that were in grocery sacks dumped in a corner—donations from parishioners for the Afghanistan Alliance.

Proudbird appeared at the kitchen's screen door. He was carrying a thin branch with a couple of apple blossoms on it. "Hallo," he said to Bridie.

Proudbird was a St. Benedict's senior, an exchange student from Lagos. He lived with the fathers on another part of the grounds. Bridie—she was a day student who commuted to St. Benedict's on the Metro from Washington—had got to know him gradually, from serving detentions here on Saturdays and after school.

"You driving me home? Will Father Tournier lend you a car?" she asked him. She ground open a can of apricots as she talked. The other cans she'd unbagged were arranged on the long table so they spelled out "X NUKE."

"Oh, sure, I guess," Proudbird said. He brought another young man into view behind the screen. "A surprise for you, man. My brother."

"What do you say?" Bridie said.

"Johnson," said the brother. The three of them beamed.

Bridie was seventeen and still freckle-faced. Her reddish curls were brushed into no specific shape or style. She had a wholesome look she often tried to sabotage. Above her jeans today she wore a T-shirt with a tiny stenciled reproduction of the Bill of Rights on it.

"I'll be damned," Sister Elspeth had said that morning, seeing the shirt. Bridie always reported to her to begin her detentions. Sometimes she automatically turned up at Sister Elspeth's room on Saturday even if she had managed to stay out of trouble for a whole week.

"Killer, huh?" Bridie said. "I can't take full credit, though. My mom ordered this from someplace."

Sister Elspeth had Bridie's homeroom and also her American history class. The nun suffered from giantism. She was six feet eight inches tall. Her hands and feet were absurdly large, and her face was oversized as well. Her expression—from carrying around such a large mouth and nose and brow, it seemed—was amused as well as tired.

"You want temperance or fortitude? We're still on the cardinal virtues, right?" the nun asked. She always gave Bridie something to contemplate while serving detention.

"Either," Bridie said.

"We'll hold off on fortitude," Sister Elspeth said. "That leaves temperance. That's finding the middle ground—the trick against going to extremes, you know?"

"Not sure I do," said Bridie.

The nun thought a minute. She said, "You've maybe seen a man being very rash, and he seems brave. A general, let's say. A boss. Maybe somebody's father. Instead, with temperance, he goes along steadily but doesn't omit anything that needs to be done."

"Cool. I can get that," Bridie said.

"Can you? It's sort of Aristotelian. But morals have to come before faith or the other theologicals. You could be moral but still not believe in anything, see?"

Bridie said, "Yeah, I learned all that with justice. Remember, I said in class a guy might be cheating his workers, then suddenly give them a Christmas bonus? Before he's charitable, he's got to be just."

"Right," Sister Elspeth said. "Not bad at all." And with a gesture she sent Bridie off to her detention.

Now, a couple of hours later, Sister Elspeth was in the dining room. "Who've you got in there?" she called to Bridie in the kitchen.

Bridie swallowed an apricot half. She said, "There's nobody else, Sister." This was true. Proudbird and his brother had just wandered off over the back lawns. The whole area behind St. Benedict's steep-roofed church—the rectory, the elementary school, Bridie's high school building—looked snowy, it was so littered with apple blossoms.

"Then to whom were you giving that speech a second ago?" the nun asked.

"To me," Bridie said. "I mean, no one. That's how I always talk to myself."

"Yipes," said Sister Elspeth.

≺∿

In front of the line of mirrors in the third-floor green-tiled girls' room, two sophomores were exchanging space-shuttle jokes. Bridie shoved between them. She said, "Did you read how they're saying that explosion put plutonium into the atmosphere? And it could give cancer to like five billion people?"

"Don't tell them that, O'Donnell. They might believe you," said Tasha.

Bridie said, "That could actually happen sometime—the plutonium?"

"You're always trying to scare us," said one of the sophomores.

"Yeah, who *are* you?" the other girl said. "We'd have heard of something giving people cancer if it was true."

"You go right on believing that," Bridie said. "Sure, they'd have heard," she murmured to herself.

"You slave to style," Bridie said, and touched the single tiger-tooth earring Tasha wore.

Tasha picked up Bridie's handbag and plopped it down again. "Thought you never wore leather," she said.

"I don't. That's from a rubber tree."

"And what's *this*? Where do you get such stuff?" Tasha said. With a fingernail, she ticked the button stuck to the lapel of Bridie's cardigan. The button read WORK BETTER—GO UNION!

"My parents," Bridie said.

"Who are?" asked Tasha.

"Saints. I'm being raised by saints. Honestly. I screw up totally on my own, and they punish themselves."

~

Bridie's hand had been raised a full sixty seconds. Her Latin teacher, Mr. Lefan, shook his head at her: no.

He had his chair turned around and he was straddling it, facing the class. He leaned his arms on the back of the chair and addressed the students in confidential tones. "You've seen art renderings of the Seven Hills—the architecture and the rest. The Roman baths. But what went on behind that spectacular surface, you ask. *Don't* you ask?"

Bridie's hand again went into the air.

"I'm not calling on you, O'Donnell, 'cause you'd filibuster until the bell," Mr. Lefan said.

"*Please* don't," moaned a boy in the front row.

Mr. Lefan said, "Romans were like present-day bulimics, in that they'd overindulge unbelievably. They'd get drunk, stuff themselves. Then they'd deliberately throw up and go right on back to eating."

Bridie stopped hearing him. She laid her head on her oak desktop. She was in the last seat, next to the rear door. She listened instead as the rough-voiced boy in front of her and the girl to his left quietly traded insults.

"Looks excellent," the boy murmured. "Nice to know you can walk into a pharmacy and buy yourself a tan."

"Shut up, troll. Lizard. You tick," the girl said.

Mr. Lefan was printing declensions on the green chalkboard.

Bridie scooted her desk, by inches, toward the open door. She did this most days, and most days she got caught. One time, she'd made it into the hallway unobserved. She had walked around out there in the empty corridor and taken a drink at the water fountain, waiting the time away.

✎

During lunch recess, Bridie skipped the cafeteria and walked over to the rectory, looking for Proudbird. Sister Hilma opened the door. She wouldn't let Bridie past the foyer without knowing why she was there. Instead of a habit, Sister Hilma wore a blue-flowered homemade dress and a homemade apron. Her glasses had such thick lenses that Bridie couldn't find the woman's eyes to make eye contact.

"I do have a genuine reason," Bridie said. "He promised to tune my guitar."

"Which is where?" asked Sister Hilma.

"Well, I forgot to bring it today. I meant, some other time he'd tune it for me. But I am doing this paper right now, and I have to get information about agricultural practices in Lagos," Bridie said, lying.

Sister Hilma rolled her eyes but gestured Bridie to the kitchen.

Proudbird was broiling hamburgers. Bridie watched while he stacked a platter with the cooked burgers on buns and doused them with sweet-pickle relish and ketchup.

Carrying the platter, he led Bridie up many stairs to a white-walled suite. Johnson was inside, lounging on the overpolished floor before a color Zenith. He was watching *Victory Garden.* "Hallo," he said to Bridie.

There were only a few pieces of furniture. There was a bed with boards instead of springs and a mattress. "You cannot be serious," Bridie said as she sat down beside Proudbird on the boards.

"Oh, all serious," he said, handing out the burgers.

He and Johnson talked back and forth in their complicated language.

Proudbird said, "My brother tells you it's what we like. The beds like this."

"So I guess I believe you," Bridie said. She put her spine against the powdery wall, trying to get her bottom comfortable on the board seat. "No, I don't. You'd have to be cracked to prefer this. It's cement. It's the same as choosing to sleep on the road."

Johnson looked back from the TV and smiled with Proudbird.

Bridie took a little bite of her hamburger. "Food's at least normal," she said. "What other stuff do you like?"

"Good arms. I like a girl with good arms," Proudbird said. He held back a smile. The action made a parenthesis of dimples around his mouth.

Bridie massaged her right elbow. She had removed her cardigan and tied it at her waist, and now she bunched it up behind her to form a pillow against the wall.

"We've been joking you about," Proudbird said.

"This isn't your bed, then? You sleep in a regular bed?"

"That's right."

Bridie asked, "Johnson, is it O.K. being in this country so far? What do you think?"

"Oh, yah, truly," Proudbird said, answering for his brother. "There's noplace else."

"Pleased to hear it, I guess," Bridie said. "Since it's my country."

🙶

Back at the high school building, Bridie went to the ground-floor washroom. There were a dozen or more girls lined up at the mirror, with more girls waiting in a second row. Bridie used a sink and punched up at the pink-soap dispenser. A couple of girls next to her were sharing the hot-air hand dryer. Another girl peered around at the back of her legs, looking to see if her patterned panty hose had a runner. While looking, she noticed her friend's shoes. "Tell me, Jan, why do you wear clogs so much?" she said. "They're heavy, they're noisy, they're nerdy."

"For the heels," Jan said. "I'm all of five foot one, and we can't wear—you know—heels."

"I want a sheegarette!" said a girl with hairpins clasped between her lips.

Bridie finally got to use the hand dryer. Over the roar of its blower, she heard someone behind a stall door shouting, "Holland—and then London. No Paris. Only we'll probably end up not going now. Say, you know what's written in here? 'Today is tops.' Now, that person thinks small."

Reminded, several girls produced felt pens and began to write on the stall doors and the green wall tiles. At the mirror, girls took turns writing with a wand of mauve-colored lipstick.

Bridie got out her own black marker from her purse. On the face of the hand dryer she wrote "608/256-4146," the telephone number of Nukewatch, copying it from a page in her trig notebook. "Get this down, or memorize it," she announced. "Especially if you're going on a car trip, anyone. Call it if you catch any trucks carrying bombs. Three things to look for are the truck'll be led by courier cars, and they'll be unmarked, and all have lots of antennae. The giveaway is the truck's license plate. If it begins with *E*, that's Department of Energy, and you've got one. It's carrying warheads. Call Nukewatch and say which direction the truck's going, but don't follow these guys. They don't want to make friends."

"Litzinger!" said a voice. "You're dead if you stole my chem homework."

"I *borrowed* it to copy. I *told* you. I'm giving it right back," answered another voice.

There was a huddle forming around a girl who was holding a small gold-plated drinking flask. "You each get one little sip and that's all," the girl said. "Pure Chivas Regal. I took it off my gramps. It was in a drawer in this little table, right next to his bed?"

"O'Donnell, where're you from?" a girl with seven or eight hair braids said to Bridie.

"D.C., but I can take the subway, which really isn't bad," Bridie said. "My mom went here, so it's—you know. It's like I had to come."

The braided girl said, "If mine sent me this far, just to go to St. Ben's, I'd be like 'Get out of my face.' Are you going with anybody?"

"Uh, not really. No time. I sort of date this black guy who's around."

"Your parents know? They let you?" asked the braided girl.

"My parents wish *I* were black, actually," Bridie said.

✒︎

"Here, take these. They're making me mean," Bridie said. She gave her box of Junior Mints to Tasha, who sat just to her right. It was last period—American history, with Sister Elspeth.

Bridie felt in her purse for her pack of sugarless gum and found instead a toy whirligig she saved for times when she baby-sat the kids of some of her parents' clients. Her mother and father worked for a storefront firm that practiced poverty law. She found her chewing gum, sneaked a stick to Tasha, and popped a couple into her own mouth. She reached again into her purse and clenched the spring shaft of the toy. The wheel went around, harmless colored sparks flew there inside her purse, and there was a sharp whirring noise.

"A siren? Say a Hail Mary," Sister Elspeth said, glancing up from her lecture page. She went back to reading.

Bridie chomped her gum to softness. She blew a spearmint bubble, breathed it in, and snapped it with her teeth. Immediately she said, "Pardon, Sister."

"You're pardoned. Forgiveness is a duty, not an option, for Christians, by the way."

"Rules for everything," Bridie said.

"What say?" asked the nun.

"Agreeing with you, Sister."

The nun returned to President Kennedy and Premier Khrushchev.

Bridie waved her hand, and Tasha gave a low groan.

"What?" Sister Elspeth said.

Bridie said, "The 'We will bury you' line. If you'd read Khrushchev's memoirs, you'll find out that was a faulty translation, not what he meant at all."

A boy named Chadwick raised his hand, and when Sister Elspeth nodded at him he said, "It's in a Sting song, Sister. Sting has lyrics about it."

"I don't *care*. It was a misinterpretation," Bridie said. "Anyone who can read would know that." She snapped her gum again, for emphasis. Some of her classmates tittered.

Sister Elspeth said, "Bridie, I warned you. And the rest of you can stay after school and laugh along with Bridie for ten or fifteen minutes while she does stunts with her gum."

"Aw, don't make them do that," Bridie said.

"Then stand in the corner, O'Donnell. I'm sick of dealing with you. While you're over there, you can count the holes on the cinder block at eye level. The fifth down. Block E-five. I know how many holes it has, so don't try to pull anything."

"Got it," Bridie said. In the corner, she sneaked a look at her wristwatch. The class would go on for another eighteen minutes. There was no hurry yet about counting.

"I'm opening a civics club," Sister Elspeth was saying when Bridie next paid attention. "You're my charter members."

"You're kidding—a *civics* club?" Bridie said to the wall.

"I didn't see your paw in the air to be called on," Sister El-speth said.

"I'm not being in a civics club," Bridie said, turning around. "That's for the little kids in *Ding Dong School.* You can erase my name—I resign."

"I don't believe it—you're still chewing gum! Take that out of your mouth and stick it to your chin," Sister Elspeth said, getting out of her chair.

There was some laughter, and Bridie grinned.

Sister Elspeth came for the corner, and Bridie gulped and swallowed her gum. She started laughing.

"Stop!" the nun said. "What's the matter?"

"Can't," Bridie said, from behind her open-mouthed smile. She stared up into the enormous face of Sister Elspeth.

"You *have* to," whispered the nun.

"I can't!" Bridie said, and her voice squeaked a little. Her laughter was high and unnatural. Her chest and shoulders shook.

"Please," the nun said. "None of this matters—don't you see? You're acting weird, Bridie. You're scaring me. What's the matter with you?"

Bridie shrugged, still laughing.

Sister Elspeth opened her arms and held them out for Bridie.

Later, when Proudbird was driving her home, Bridie told him that if she could take back some things in her life, she thought that moment would probably be one—when she had suddenly stopped laughing and the look of horror she must have shown as the nun, in huge concern, reached forward to embrace her.

12

Pretty Ice

I WAS UP THE WHOLE night before my fiancé was due to arrive from the East—drinking coffee, restless and pacing, my ears ringing. When the television signed off, I sat down with a packet of the month's bills and figured amounts on a lined tally sheet in my checkbook. Under the spray of a high-intensity lamp, my left hand moved rapidly over the touch tablets of my calculator.

Will, my fiancé, was coming from Boston on the six-fifty train—the dawn train, the only train that still stopped in the small Ohio city where I lived. At six-fifteen I was still at my accounts; I was getting some pleasure from transcribing the squarish green figures that appeared in the window of my calculator. "Schwab Dental Clinic," I printed in a raveled backhand. "Thirty-eight and 50/100."

A car horn interrupted me. I looked over my desktop and out the living-room window of my rented house. The saplings in my little yard were encased in ice. There had been snow all week, and then an ice storm. In the glimmering driveway in front of my garage, my mother was peering out of her car I got up and turned off my lamp and capped my ivory Mont Blanc pen. I found a coat in the semidark in the hall, and wound a knitted muffler at my throat. Crossing the living room, I looked away from the big pine mirror; I didn't want to see how my face and hair looked after a night of accounting.

My yard was a frozen pond, and I was careful on the walkway. My mother hit her horn again. Frozen slush came through the toe of one of my chukka boots, and I stopped on the path and frowned at her. I could see her breath rolling away in clouds from the cranked-down window of her Mazda. I have never owned a car or learned to drive, but I had a low opinion of my mother's compact. My father and I used to enjoy big cars, with tops that came down. We were both tall and we wanted what he called "stretch room." My father had been dead for fourteen years, but I resented my mother's buying a car in which he would not have fitted.

"Now what's wrong? Are you coming?" my mother said.

"Nothing's wrong except that my shoes are opening around the soles," I said. "I just paid a lot of money for them."

I got in on the passenger side. The car smelled of wet wool and Mother's hair spray. Someone had done her hair with a minty-white rinse, and the hair was held in place by a zebra-striped headband.

"I think you're getting a flat," I said. "That retread you bought for the left front is going."

She backed the car out of the drive, using the rearview mirror. "I finally got a boy I can trust, at the Exxon station," she said. "He says that tire will last until hot weather."

Out on the street, she accelerated too quickly and the rear of the car swung left. The tires whined for an instant on the old snow and then caught. We were knocked back in our seats a little, and an empty Kleenex box slipped off the dash and onto the floor carpet.

"This is going to be something," my mother said. "Will sure picked an awful day to come."

My mother had never met him. My courtship with Will had all happened in Boston. I was getting my doctorate there, in musicology. Will was involved with his research at Boston U., and with teaching botany to undergraduates.

"You're sure he'll be at the station?" my mother said. "Can the trains go in this weather? I don't see how they do."

"I talked to him on the phone yesterday. He's coming."

"How did he sound?" my mother said.

To my annoyance, she began to hum to herself.

I said, "He's had rotten news about his work. Terrible, in fact."

"Explain his work to me again," she said.

"He's a plant taxonomist."

"Yes?" my mother said. "What does that mean?"

"It means he doesn't have a lot of money," I said. "He studies grasses. He said on the phone he's been turned down for a research grant that would have meant a great deal to us. Apparently the work he's been doing for the past seven or so years is irrelevant or outmoded. I guess 'superficial' is what he told me."

"I won't mention it to him, then," my mother said.

We came to the expressway. Mother steered the car through some small windblown snow dunes and down the entrance ramp. She followed two yellow salt trucks with winking blue beacons that were moving side by side down the center and right-hand lanes.

"I think losing the grant means we should postpone the wedding," I said. "I want Will to have his bearings before I step into his life for good."

"Don't wait too much longer, though," my mother said.

After a couple of miles, she swung off the expressway. We went past some tall high-tension towers with connecting cables that looked like staff lines on a sheet of music. We were in the decaying neighborhood near the tracks. "Now I know this is right," Mother said. "There's our old sign."

The sign was a tall billboard, black and white, that advertised my father's dance studio. The studio had been closed for years and the building it had been in was gone. The sign showed a man in a tuxedo waltzing with a woman in an evening gown. I was always sure it was a waltz. The dancers were nearly two stories high, and the weather had bleached them into phantoms. The lettering—the name of the studio, my father's name—had disappeared.

"They've changed everything," my mother said, peering about. "Can this be the station?"

We went up a little drive that wound past a cindery lot full of flatbed trucks and that ended up at the smudgy brownstone depot.

"Is that your Will?" Mother said.

Will was on the station platform, leaning against a baggage truck. He had a duffel bag between his shoes and a plastic cup of coffee in his mittened hand. He seemed to have put on weight, girlishly, through the hips, and his face looked thicker to me, from temple to temple. His gold-rimmed spectacles looked too small.

My mother stopped in an empty cab lane, and I got out and called to Will. It wasn't far from the platform to the car, and Will's pack wasn't a large one, but he seemed to be winded when he got to me. I let him kiss me, and then he stepped back and blew a cold breath and drank from the coffee cup, with his eyes on my face.

Mother was pretending to be busy with something in her handbag, not paying attention to me and Will.

"I look awful," I said.

"No, no, but I probably do," Will said. "No sleep, and I'm fat. So this is your town?"

He tossed the coffee cup at an oil drum and glanced around at the cold train yards and low buildings. A brass foundry was throwing a yellowish column of smoke over a line of Canadian Pacific boxcars.

I said, "The problem is you're looking at the wrong side of the tracks."

A wind whipped Will's lank hair across his face. "Does your mom smoke?" he said. "I ran out in the middle of the night on the train, and the club car was closed. Eight hours across Pennsylvania without a cigarette."

The car horn sounded as my mother climbed from behind the wheel. "That was an accident," she said, because I was frowning at her. "Hello. Are you Will?" She came around the car and stood on tiptoes and kissed him. "You picked a miserable day to come visit us."

She was using her young-girl voice, and I was embarrassed for her. "He needs a cigarette," I said.

Will got into the back of the car and I sat beside my mother again. After we started up, Mother said, "Why doesn't Will stay at my place, in your old room, Belle? I'm all alone there, with plenty of space to kick around in."

"We'll be able to get him a good motel," I said quickly, before Will could answer. "Let's try that Ramada, over near the new elementary school." It was odd, after he had come all the way from Cambridge, but I didn't want him in my old room, in the house where I had been a child. "I'd put you at my place," I said, "but there's mountains of tax stuff all over."

"You've been busy," he said.

"Yes," I said. I sat sidewise, looking at each of them in turn. Will had some blackish spots around his mouth—ballpoint ink,

maybe. I wished he had freshened up and put on a better shirt
before leaving the train.

"It's up to you two, then," my mother said.

I could tell she was disappointed in Will. I don't know what
she expected. I was thirty-one when I met him. I had probably
dated fewer men in my life than she had gone out with in a
single year at her sorority. She had always been successful with
men.

"William was my late husband's name," my mother said.
"Did Belle ever tell you?"

"No," Will said. He was smoking one of Mother's cigarettes.

"I always liked the name," she said. "Did you know we ran
a dance studio?"

I groaned.

"Oh, let me brag if I want to," my mother said. "He was
such a handsome man."

It was true. They were both handsome—mannequins, a pair
of dolls who had spent half their lives in evening clothes. But my
father had looked old in the end, in a business in which you had
to stay young. He had trouble with his eyes, which were
bruised-looking and watery, and he had to wear glasses with
thick lenses.

I said, "It was in the dance studio that my father ended his
life, you know. In the ballroom."

"You told me," Will said, at the same instant my mother
said, "Don't talk about it."

My father killed himself with a service revolver. We never
found out where he had bought it, or when. He was found in his
warm-up clothes—a pullover sweater and pleated pants. He was
wearing his tap shoes, and he had a short towel folded around
his neck. He had aimed the gun barrel down his mouth, so the

bullet would not shatter the wall of mirrors behind him. I was twenty then—old enough to find out how he did it.

⤶

My mother had made a wrong turn and we were on Buttles Avenue. "Go there," I said, pointing down a street beside Garfield Park. We passed a group of paper boys who were riding bikes with saddlebags. They were going slow, because of the ice.

"Are you very discouraged, Will?" my mother said. "Belle tells me you're having a run of bad luck."

"You could say so," Will said. "A little rough water."

"I'm sorry," Mother said. "What seems to be the trouble?"

Will said, "Well, this will be oversimplifying, but essentially what I do is take a weed and evaluate its structure and growth and habitat, and so forth."

"What's wrong with that?" my mother said.

"Nothing. But it isn't enough."

"I get it," my mother said uncertainly.

I had taken a mirror and a comb from my handbag and I was trying for a clean center-part in my hair. I was thinking about finishing my bill paying.

Will said, "What do you want to do after I check in, Belle? What about breakfast?"

"I've got to go home for a while and clean up that tax jazz, or I'll never rest," I said. "I'll just show up at your motel later. If we ever find it."

"That'll be fine," Will said.

Mother said, "I'd offer to serve you two dinner tonight, but I think you'll want to leave me out of it. I know how your father and I felt after he went away sometimes. Which way do I turn here?"

We had stopped at an intersection near the iron gates of the park. Behind the gates there was a frozen pond, where a single early-morning skater was skating backward, expertly crossing his blades.

I couldn't drive a car but, like my father, I have always enjoyed maps and atlases. During automobile trips, I liked comparing distances on maps. I liked the words *latitude, cartography, meridian.* It was extremely annoying to me that Mother had gotten us turned around and lost in our own city, and I was angry with Will all of a sudden, for wasting seven years on something superficial.

"What about up that way?" Will said to my mother, pointing to the left. "There's some traffic up by that light, at least."

I leaned forward in my seat and started combing my hair all over again.

"There's no hurry," my mother said.

"How do you mean?" I asked her.

"To get William to the motel," she said. "I know everybody complains, but I think an ice storm is a beautiful thing. Let's enjoy it."

She waved her cigarette at the windshield. The sun had burned through and was gleaming in the branches of all the maples and buckeye trees in the park. "It's twinkling like a stage set," Mother said.

"It is pretty," I said.

Will said, "It'll make a bad-looking spring. A lot of shrubs get damaged and turn brown, and the trees don't blossom right."

For once I agreed with my mother. Everything was quiet and holding still. Everything was in place, the way it was supposed to be. I put my comb away and smiled back at Will— knowing it was for the last time.

13

While Home

THE DEFOREST KIDS WERE in the Lakebreeze Laundro
mat. "Whose treat is lunch?" asked Jonathan. He and little
Lana looked over at their older brother, Shane. Severely handsome, he was taking his ease in a kelly-green scoop chair. Lana,
who was seven, had been lifted up and set on top of a broken
clothes washer.

"I guess I'm the only one with money," Shane said morosely.

A machine, beginning its spin cycle, let off a shivery whir.

"Tie my shoe for me," Lana said.

Jonathan, who was eighteen, had already flicked through all
five of the laundromat's magazines. He gave up pacing now and
drew what string remained of Lana's shoelace back and forth between the lowest eyelets of her sneaker, evening the shredded ends.

"Tight," Lana said.

From his chair, Shane said, "I know who *had* money. The
dog. This morning, I found the corner of a ten in its bed, Lana.
The rest of the bill obviously chewed up and swallowed."

"No, sir," Lana said. Rosalie was her dog.

"Probably my ten," said Jonathan, as he secured a bowless
double knot on Lana's shoe.

"You ate the money, if Rosalie didn't," Shane said to Lana. He sighed. "O.K., I'll cover lunch," he said. "But one of you has to bring it here to me. I'm not sitting in any restaurant in a swimsuit. You've got to go get the food—is that agreed?"

Shane was conscious of his nice good looks and his light voice, which made these orders seem less than demands. He was a sometime model and actor who had come back for a while to recover from a year and a half of spectacular unsuccess in Los Angeles. If he found a decent job here at home, he might just change his plans. His present role, of returned prodigal and older brother, was the best of his career so far.

"Sure, sure, agreed," Jonathan said.

Their town was Ophelia, Ohio, on the lake. The three of them had been swimming in Erie's friendly little surf. Jonathan's blond hair formed into stiff bunches now as it dried.

"Let's get pizza from Sub Hut," Lana said dreamily.

"Too much salt," Shane said. "I like a subtler pizza." He took a sandwich Baggie, folded many times for waterproofing, from the buttoned pocket just below the waistband of his swim trunks and extracted a twenty-dollar bill.

"Hey!" said Lana, in admiration.

"I'll have a BLT, rings, and a Strawberry Blizzard," Shane said.

"That a regular or a Blizzard Supreme?" Jonathan asked.

"Second one," Shane said. He almost had to shout, because water was firing into a nearby machine.

They had been waiting for their beach things—towels, Levis, a pullover, and Lana's terry cover-up—to finish in the tumble dryer. They had a clothes washer and dryer at home, on the other side of town, but they were temperamental machines, tricky to operate, and their mother had forbidden their use while she was away. She was in Milwaukee, taking care of their grandmother after an operation. "That means especially Lana," she had said. "No, especially *you*, Jonathan."

Jonathan was on his way out of the laundromat now, but he circled back. "Look outside," he said, and directed Lana to the front bank of windows. "At this man. He's coming by any second. You've got to see this, Shane. It's like his hair was sculpted on. Like it's carved out of wood putty."

"Here he is," Lana said.

"Here, Shane, quick!" Jonathan said. "Is that not carved hair?"

But Shane did not get up. He sat lower in his chair, with his neck bent. He was hugging himself.

"Uh-oh. Shane's thinking again," Jonathan said.

"I believe I might be going to have a damned seizure," Shane told them after a moment. "I only said 'might,' so try not to get hysterical."

"Nah, you're not. Are you?" Jonathan said. "Please say no, because I don't remember what to do. Maybe you just have water in your eardrums. I get it every time I swim."

"It's more than that," Shane said.

Lately he had been using a new anticonvulsant for his epilepsy. He had developed an allergy to his regular medication.

Lana kicked the machine beneath her with the heel of one sneaker. "But this is the first time I was allowed out!" she said.

Lana had been confined to the Deforests' front yard for the past couple of weeks. This was for her own good, her mother had reminded Mr. Deforest and the boys before she left, because Lana had recently come home, after an afternoon at the little Kristerson boys' house, with her dress on backward and the buttoning sequence missed by two.

"Please wait until after we eat, and then you can," Lana said to Shane. "You shouldn't lie down here or anything."

"Lana, he can't control *when*," Jonathan said.

Without taking his eyes from the floor tiling, Shane said, "No, and I really think I'm going to."

✌

Back home, Shane rested in a rope hammock that was strung between two sweet-apple trees. He had not had a seizure. "Quit waiting!" he ordered Lana.

She kept watching him. She was lying on her belly on a green upholstered chaise outside the trees' shade. She had stripped down again to her red-checked gingham swimsuit, which she had worn at the lake. "I'm not bothering you," she said.

"You're waiting for me to have a convulsion. If you weren't, you'd be helping Jonathan dig or you'd chase Rosalie. You'd be doing anything but lying still, Lana. I know you."

"I don't care," Lana said.

"Not responsive," said Shane.

"Tomorrow I want to help Jonathan. Today I'm getting more suntan," she said.

Jonathan was on the other side of the modest yard, working a patch of worn lawn with a shovel. Whistling rhythmically to himself, he jimmied loose a stone and then kicked the point of the shovel into the ground again for a new bite of dirt. He was digging a shallow trench around a mound of earth he would eventually dress with rocks—making a strawberry patch, he had announced. His real idea was to strengthen his back and shoulder muscles. He wanted to be able to manage a more serious, faster motocross bike than his aging Suzuki. He had talked this over a few days before with a mechanic at the Cycle Corral—a fellow who had once raced professionally.

"I'd forget about a KTM or a Husky, if I were you," the mechanic had said. "A real thunderbutt bike'd just intimidate you.

Way too much power in the midrange, with your little arms. You'd get blasted out of the saddle. See, I could give you this 495 and take your old bike and in the woods I'd still beat you, because you have to stay lower in the power band or lose it. While you're fighting, I'm gone. And you won't want to take a monster bike off to college with you anyway. Not freshman year, you don't."

Jonathan twisted his shovel on a carrotlike section of root he had struck. He chopped at it, rested, and chopped. He looked up as two young women approached the split-rail fence that bordered the yard. The Deforests' neighborhood was old enough to be very shady, but the women were in a stretch of sun at the moment, walking jauntily and seeming carefree and entertained by each other.

"Shane," Jonathan said in a low voice. "Two girls coming."

"Describe them," Shane said without raising his head.

"They look nice. One has sort of beaming red hair. I mean bright-bright."

"It's Kay," Shane said. "A chatterbox and sort of a rival. I don't want to see her. Are you positive they're coming here?"

"They're *here*," Lana said. "Open up your eyes and find out, Shane, instead of always asking Jonathan."

"Can it, Lana. I have a good reason. I can't just gape around at them. I mustn't show interest. Kay works at the store where I've been desperately trying to get a job."

"Well, I'm not here," Jonathan said. "They're your problem, Shane. I'm not talking to them."

Sitting forward in the hammock, Shane said, "Kay—hey, hello."

The girls had stopped, still in the sun. They had roller skates slung around their necks.

"Shane? I remembered your name," the redhead said. She folded her pretty freckled arms on the fence's upper railing and planted a green espadrille on the lower. "And you remembered mine."

"His name is *what?*" the other girl asked. She was more delicate than Kay, and darker.

"It's Shane. Isn't that cool?" Kay said. "Hey, there, Harpo!" she called to Jonathan.

"He'll never forgive you," Shane said. "He hates his curls."

Jonathan had turned abruptly and was facing in the opposite direction now, digging away at the already trenched earth.

"That, whose whole life you've just ruined, is my brother Jonathan," Shane said. "This is Lana, my illegitimate child."

Lana made a show of covering herself up to her nose with her beach towel.

"He's joking," the redhead explained. "That's not his kid."

"So let me take a guess where you two are going," Shane said. "I have the gift of sometimes seeing right into the future. You're on your way to . . . to Skateland."

"Astonishing," the red-haired Kay said.

"One of my gifts," Shane said.

"You didn't get the job at Carlton's," Kay said to Shane. "Have they told you yet? They're hiring this other guy."

Shane had met Kay before his interview at Carlton's two days ago. She worked in the ladies' half of the apparel store, which specialized in expensive tailored wear. He had applied for a position as a clerk and salesman. With his modeling history and his looks, he figured he'd be good at fitting and convincing menswear customers, although he had no experience at the work.

"They haven't said anything *official*," Shane said.

"Well, they're not hiring you," Kay said. "Say, I forgot. This is Maria. Remember, I told you about Maria? My friend that lives in the other half of my double? Only she owns, I rent. She's my landlady! Aren't you?" Kay said to Maria.

"It's true, I swear," Maria said. "I'm sorry about it." She patted Kay's arm.

Shane closed his eyes again for a moment, and both girls were instantly quiet, watching his beautiful profile.

～

Later on in that week, Mr. Deforest sat in his carpeted kitchen, watching TV. He was home on his lunch hour. The air in the kitchen was cool and full of the aroma of the oniony egg salad Mr. Deforest had just prepared.

"Looks good. Thank you and greetings," Shane said, as he entered through the archway. "Now, please, Dad, say only the best things you can think of about my appearance." He was dressed in a poplin suit, a blue shirt, a navy-and-yellow silk tie. He was going to another interview in the afternoon.

"You're good enough for a royal wedding, but you'll have to model somewhere else, honey," Mr. Deforest said. "You're blocking Beirut."

"Dad, this suit failed me once before at a job interview. Does it look cheap or something?" Shane said.

"Affordable, I always say, not cheap. But no. Hell, no, Shane. It's a better summer suit than anything I own. You look like a store-window dummy."

"Maybe that's the trouble." Shane scraped some egg salad from its bowl with the wire whisk and ate very carefully, his head far out over the table.

Lana darted into the room and immediately took her father's lap for a seat. Jonathan came in from the yard, shirtless and newly sunburned. "Surprise, surprise, everybody. Egg salad for lunch," he said, sitting down.

"If you know how to make anything different, I pass the apron to you," said Mr. Deforest. "I'm a genius with thermocouples, but this and potpies are just about it for me and cooking."

Lana was eating handfuls of the salad, straight from the bowl. "Sure hope you washed your hands," her father said.

"A *month* of eggs," Jonathan went on. "Our family cholesterol level must be right off the charts."

"We've had lots of other foods," Lana said. Her face was smeared with mayonnaise.

"I'm seeing this guy today, over in Lorain—a sporting-goods store," Shane said. "My last shot. If he doesn't hire me, I'm closing out my savings and heading back to L.A."

There were groans of protest from the table. "Your mother wanted you around at least until she got back," Mr. Deforest said. "Grandma's getting better every day. Why don't you hang in here a little while?"

"Because it's devouring my pathetic bank account, Dad, and I'm also sponging off you. When I was out on the Coast, I made fun of this place, and now I don't feel good enough for it, since nobody around here will hire me to shine shoes. So to hell with it."

"Will you be in movies?" Lana asked.

"Yes," Shane said absently.

"He really could be. That was next," Jonathan said, more to Shane than anyone else.

The television news ended with an admonition from the anchorwoman: "It's twelve twenty-eight and ninety-four degrees, so have yourselves a record-buster, but take it slow out there. Stay cool."

"Talking directly to you, Jonathan," Mr. Deforest said. "You ought to take some salt pills if you're still going to work on those strawberries."

"Salt pills after this egg salad? I'll be the only teen-ager to die of sodium poisoning," Jonathan said.

An old episode of *Hawaii Five-O* started up, and Mr. Deforest ticked his spoon on the table in rhythm to the show's opening theme. "I wish I could stay for this," he said.

"What's the big deal about ninety-four degrees?" Shane said. "In L.A., that's the norm."

"Well, for June," Jonathan said.

"You'd think it was some *crisis,*" Shane said. After a moment, he said, "You know, things were looking up out there. I had a sort of letter of inquiry from the William Morris people after my commercial. That's what hurts. To get turned down here by some pimp in a button-down collar."

"Don't be too hard on your home area," Mr. Deforest said.

"*Will* you be on television, Shane?" Lana asked.

"I already was, Lana. You know about that. And can't you eat with slightly better manners than Rosalie—which you forgot to clean the burrs off," Shane said. "You have to *groom* this sort of dog, Lana."

The chimes of an ice cream truck sounded out on the street. "I hear dessert coming," said Mr. Deforest.

"Quick, Pop, give me money," Lana said, hopping down from his lap.

"We just hoped you'd stay around for the summer, before you go chasing your stars," Mr. Deforest said to Shane, reaching into his pocket.

"It all depends on this job," Shane said.

"I'm sure glad it's not me," Jonathan said. "I might do all right during actual exposure time, during the interview, but right now, beforehand, I'd be throwing up."

❦

It was Sunday. Lana was on the screened porch, fixing round stickers onto her tissue-wrapped gift for her father. The stickers said things like "Grin and Ignore It" and "Things Are Getting Worse—Send Chocolate!"

Shane was lounging on the wicker sofa with a copy of *Variety.* He wore a black polo shirt and white trousers today. "Lana, tell me again, did you really check for ticks in your hair?" he asked. "There were three on Rosalie last night."

"Yes, Shane."

The east wall of the porch held tendrils of ivy. Through the ivy and the screen's mesh, out above the trees, the sky looked chalky with clouds. It was much cooler this Father's Day morning.

Jonathan lay in the hammock outside—a curled sleeping bundle. One hand dangled loose, still wearing a cowhide work glove.

The day before, Jonathan had ridden Lana on his Suzuki through a meadow and a shady woods where they knew they'd find butterflies feeding on the wildflowers and among the willow and wild cherry trees. It was Lana's plan to supplement her Father's Day present with a framed specimen. They captured and let go a few cabbage whites and one faded viceroy. Then, in a lucky swoop, Jonathan netted a red-spotted purple. Back home, he chloroformed the butterfly in their killing jar—a thing he had learned in biology class. "It's gone to sleep," he said to Lana.

"He stayed in the hammock last night," Lana said now to Shane. "I had another present for Dad, but Jonathan let it go."

"I know," Shane said.

Jonathan had confided to Shane about pinning the butterfly the evening before, only to find that it wasn't quite dead. Its wings rose and quivered, and now and then beat rapidly enough to make a fluttering noise. Jonathan fled his bedroom, leaving the butterfly impaled, and hadn't yet gone back there. He told Lana he had changed his mind and released their specimen.

"Everything set?" Mr. Deforest yelled to them on the porch.

"Sixty seconds!" Shane called. He collapsed his paper. "Lana, get Jonathan. Those're enough stickers."

Lana went out and returned with Jonathan, who looked sun- and sleep-dazed. He took the seat next to Shane on the wicker sofa.

Mr. Deforest entered with his face bright, his hands folded behind him. "Well, hot ziggetty, a holiday for me. What have we got going here?"

"Cards first," Lana said.

Her father obeyed. "Great card, Shane. Your mother's is nice too—I opened it after breakfast. She asks how you're doing on that new medicine. I'm wondering the same."

"If the moon's full, I grow huge hands and fangs, and hair all over my face, but those are the only side effects so far," Shane said. "I'm settling into it."

"This one, of mine," Lana said.

Mr. Deforest opened Lana's envelope and showed around the contents—a bumper sticker with the message "I Love My Mutt!"

"And if that's not Rosalie's picture on there, I'll eat it with mustard," Mr. Deforest said. "Good for you, Lana girl. This goes right on the car."

"Over my dead corpse," Jonathan whispered to Shane.

Mr. Deforest opened his gift from Lana, saving the wrapper stickers for her. "Lana, you are a shopper! Men's-formula hair spray. I do need this."

Lana took the can from her father and showed him how to work the nozzle.

"Excellent, baby, but not so much on the ivy. The ivy doesn't need it too bad today," Mr. Deforest said.

"Mine," Jonathan said. He reached under the wicker sofa.

Mr. Deforest hefted the big package, wrapped in gold foil. "Is this a joke? It's too big."

"I still had some graduation money and nothing to do with it," Jonathan said.

"Well, you made me look awful," said Shane. "Aside from my card, I didn't do anything. I've been pinching every cent for L.A." He had not been hired by the sporting-goods store.

"Holy mother! Look at this, Shane. Lana, look," Mr. Deforest said. He swept aside tissue wrap.

"Damn, it is nice. Really nice," Shane said. He got to his feet
for a closer look.

"Extraordinary. A duffel bag you would call it?" Mr. Deforest said. "Get a load of this leatherwork. A place for socks, toi-
letries. I got a hundred zippers here."

"Where'd you buy it?" Shane asked.

"Carlton's—before they didn't hire you. Sorry," Jonathan
said.

"I thought so," Shane said.

Their father said, "You could put a *suit* in here."

"You wouldn't, though," Shane said. "You'd wear the suit."

"Thank you, Jonathan, thank you," Mr. Deforest said.
"Now I have to think of someplace nice enough to go."

"I've got a nice trip all lined up for a bag like that," Shane
said. "You wouldn't want to let me break that in for you, would
you, Dad?"

"Hint," Mr. Deforest said.

"Are you really going to go?" Jonathan said.

"Yes. I wish I could wait for Mom, but . . . I'd sure feel better about myself if I were stepping off the Trailways bus with
that bag over my shoulder. I'd send it right back to Dad."

"It would have to be in virgin condition," Mr. Deforest said
to Shane.

Shane said, "Well, you know me."

Lana was in the yard now, running with Rosalie and giving
off screams.

Jonathan stretched, groaning. "Lana had a butterfly for you,
Dad, but I messed it up trying to mount it."

"From the meadow? You check her for ticks?" Mr. Deforest said.

There was a silence on the porch and Shane and Jonathan and Mr. Deforest all looked out at Lana, who had straddled the dog.

"I better rescue Rosalie," Shane said. "Lana still doesn't believe you can't tickle a dog and make it laugh." He pushed the screen door open but then paused and said to Jonathan, "You maybe ought to come to the Coast with me. We could have a wild time."

"Yeah, it'd be fierce," Jonathan said.

"Feelings aren't hurt, are they?" Mr. Deforest said to Jonathan when Shane had gone. "It was your graduation money, I know."

"I can't believe I'd ever pick out anything he'd like so much. That's truly a first," Jonathan said.

"But you wouldn't consider what he said. I mean about going with him. I don't think he meant it literally."

"No, I know he didn't," Jonathan said. "Don't worry, I know."

Mr. Deforest had picked up the bag again and now practiced walking up and down the porch with it. "This is first-class," he said. "You can hang it on your shoulder or carry it by hand." He put it down again and directed a look at Jonathan. "O.K., the truth. You're hurt," he said. "And you want him to stay here, stay home with us."

"Yes, but no—no, I'm really not. There's something else. I have to go up to the bedroom to make sure that butterfly's croaked, once and for all. And throw the damned thing away. It'll put a couple years on me, so expect an older son to come back down. I'll be about caught up with Shane."

"You might want to rethink," Mr. Deforest said. "Before catching up with Shane. I sort of remember being his age. It was terrible. Maybe just skip it when your turn comes."

14

In Jewel

*I*COULD BE GETTING MARRIED soon. The fellow is no Adonis, but what do I care about that? I'd be leaving my job at the high school. I teach art. In fact, I'd be leaving Jewel if I got married.

I have six smart students, total, but only two with any talent, both at third period. One of them might make it out of here someday. I don't know. Jewel is coal mining, and it's infuriatingly true that all the kids end up in the mine.

One of my two talented students is a girl. She's involved with the mine already—works after school driving a coal truck for them. I've had her in class since her freshman year. She's got a ready mind that would have wowed them at the design school in Rhode Island where I took a degree ten or so years ago. "Dirty Thoughts," she titles all her pieces, one after another. "Here's D.T. 189," she'll say to me, holding up some contraption. She does very clever work with plaster and torn paper bags.

Jack's the name of the man I might marry. He's a sharp lawyer. He looks kind of like a poor relation, but juries feel cozy and relaxed with him. They go his way as if he were a cousin they're trying to help along.

Jack's a miner's best friend. He has a case pending now about this mammoth rock that's hanging near the top of a mountain out on the edge of town. And the mountain's on fire inside. There's a seam of coal in it that's been burning for over a year, breaking the mountain's back, and someday the rock's going to come tumbling straight down and smush the Benjamin house, it looks like, and maybe tear out part of the neighborhood. The whole Benjamin family has seen this in their dreams. "Hit the Company now," Jack says, "before the rock arrives."

Jack first met me when a student was killed a couple of years ago and the boy's parents hired Jack to file suit against the Company. As I understood it, there were these posts every few or so feet in the mine, and the Company had saved a buck skipping every third post. Well, Rick, the boy—he was a senior at school but he worked afternoon half-shifts in the mine—was down in the shaft one day, and some ceiling where there wasn't a post caved in and he died on the spot. Rick was a kid who was *never* going to be a miner. His ceramics, done for me, weren't bad, when they didn't explode in the kiln.

Jack asked me out for coffee one of those days when court was in recess. We blew a couple hours at the Ballpark Lounge, playing a computer game called Space Invaders.

"You could win money at this," Jack said. "You ought to have your own machine." Don't I wish. That's how Jack thinks: big.

My gifted student who might get out of Jewel someday is Michael Fitch. "Maybe I'm nuts," he said to me after homeroom had cleared out one morning. I have him for art and homeroom.

"I don't mind," I said.

"There's a lot of noise because I won't say the pledge of allegiance in assemblies," Michael said. "I refuse."

"You got to stay alert from now on, Michael," I told him. "For the next little bit, you'll have to be on your toes."

He took a pink stick of chalk to the blackboard and worked in thick, porous contours. Clouds, maybe. "I think the entire town's afraid of me," he said.

"Probably," I said. Why would anyone balk at the pledge?

کہ

Jack and I would go live in Charleston if we got married. We've talked about being there by the end of August. He even has a house lined up. Actually, it's half a house. The downstairs is a crisis center where they take "hotline" calls. Jack says I could work there, if I want to work. He got me to spend an afternoon with the people, learning their procedure. They listen to these calls, I found out, and then they more or less repeat back whatever the caller's just said. Such as "You discovered your dearest friend in bed with your husband." Then they add something like "You sound angry."

Jack thinks I'd be terrific at this sort of thing. He doesn't realize my worst moments as a teacher are when somebody confides in me. Brad Foley, for example. He confessed about some stuff he was going through with his dad, and when we were all finished talking, Brad, crying, asked if he could kiss me. I said he could hug me, the poor thing, but just for a second.

I wouldn't mind waving good-bye to Jewel, but it would be tough leaving my family. Mom's all right here, and so is Russell, my big brother. Russell recently got Mom a new clothes washer. He does things like that, and they're a very contented couple.

Russell's nuts, though. I mean, here's a guy working in three feet of coal every day, contending with a couple kinds of gases that are there, also the dust from the machines, and all he wants is to be allowed to smoke cigarettes. He says it isn't because of methane that you can't smoke in the mine, it's dollars. Most of the miners roll their own cigarettes, see, which takes a minute or two.

So you figure a couple of dozen smokes would cost the Company a half-hour's time every shift.

I get sad for Russell. The biggest achievement in his life is being respectable. He'd cheat and lie before he'd do anything that's frowned upon.

But I was always respectable, I admit. Two years in a row I won the Jaycees' Good Citizenship award—Women's Branch. Really, though, that was for my dad. I couldn't like Dad, but I often pleased him. He was superstitious about women ever working in the mines, and very confident about his opinions, which weren't backed by anything but his fears. He would hate that there are five women down there now. If he were alive, he'd be yelling about it.

The women won't last long. They'll get sick or quit for some reason. You can't blame them—it's no fun making everyone nervous.

My fiancé doesn't get too excited or too blue. He won't allow himself. He's learned to take comfort in small things. Say, if he finds a word he likes he speaks it with relish. He makes you enjoy the word with him—its aptness or strength. "I like a shower head that throws an aggressive spray," he says, and leans on that word "aggressive." Or he tells you that for supper he can get by gladly with a plate of fresh yellow tomatoes and just a mug of coffee, so long as the coffee is "pitchy."

One thing that bothers me about leaving Jewel is that I just wallpapered my bedroom at Mom's. The wallpaper I put up has a poppy pattern that's like Matisse.

Charleston wouldn't thrill Jack for long, I bet. He's headed for growth: Atlanta, Seattle, Santa Fe.

You name it and it went wrong for me up in Rhode Island. I got mangled or something. I was at the School of Design there. I finally did graduate, or some version of me graduated. I really wasn't present. I'd be walking on Thayer Street and all of a sudden realize I was looking for my reflection in every shop window.

Back in Jewel again—surprise—I was fine.

Imagine teaching at the same high school where you and your whole family went—it can't be good. I figured out my dad was a freshman there in 1924.

Some days, the Rhode Island thing seems like a dream. I'll be pushing a cart around the market here, say, and it comes to me that I know all the people in the store—first and last names. I know the meat cutter. I was a Camp Fire Girl with Marsha, who works the checkout counter. I went through twelve grades with the milk guy, Lewis, who loads the dairy refrigerator. I even know what grief sends his family running to the therapist at the new guidance center. And, outside, those Leahy brothers, with their beef-red faces, on their bench on the courthouse lawn I know, and Sue Forrest, pacing around carrying a sandwich board for her son's bakery, and the guys crowding the Ballpark Lounge and the Servo Hardware. I like feeling at home, but I wish I didn't feel it here.

Little Brad Foley sent me a note of congratulations when he found out from the newspaper that Jack and I are engaged. "I hope for your sake you'll be moving," he wrote. The note's still on the shelf of my secretary. I don't throw anything away. No, worse—I don't put anything away. All that I've ever owned or had is right out here for you to examine.

15

Happy Boy, Allen

ALLEN WAS DRIVING HIS father's Dodge up Light Street, in Baltimore, looking for an empty parking space near Cheshire Towers—the old hotel turned apartment building. As he drove close, Allen noticed an odd-faced teenager who was on the steps of the Cheshire. The boy had an involuntary giggle. He wore shorts and a cowboy hat. He was seated in the white sun, up from the shadows of the mighty shrubs that flanked the Cheshire's entrance doors.

Allen began breathing through his teeth. People such as the teenager made him anxious. People who were happy for no clear, visible reason.

The teenager bounced from his seat, and threw open the Cheshire's doors for a nurse in pale hose and crisp uniform. Allen pointed his father's car into the far-left lane of the street and kept on driving.

Allen's paternal aunt, Mindy, had a rental suite on the eleventh floor of Cheshire Towers—a creamy stone building, distinguishable for its many windows and the various drape styles and colors in each. Allen had left his home in Towson that morning on an impulse. He had felt the urge to chat his problems out with someone more mature.

"Aagh," he said, and stamped the brakes for his fourth stoplight. "I hate this damn town. I really do! Row houses, shmow houses. Couldn't they think of something else?" His generator light blinked on. With a little jump and intake of breath, Allen saw the light and snapped off the air conditioner. When the blowers quit, Allen heard the car radio, which was sputtering, forgotten, between stations.

He found a parking slot, at last, on an alley in front of a necktie shop. The shop was open for Saturday business, but empty except for a stout saleswoman, who was planted, angrily, in the doorway.

"Bless you," Allen told the parking meter as he read its orders. He drew a shade with his hand over his eyebrows, and squinted at the facades for his aunt's apartment building. "Please, please be home," he said to the upper-floor windows when he found them. "You must." He adjusted his right foot in its penny loafer, and walked.

The teenager in the cowboy hat had come out onto the broad sidewalk, and was watching as Allen approached.

Allen stalled, and got his bearings under a lilac bush. He busied himself with his wristwatch, shaking it, and scowling at its face. It was eleven-forty.

"Guess how much I used to weigh," the teenager said. He held open the vest he wore instead of a shirt, and showed Allen his tiny waist and rib cage.

"You're crazy," Allen said.

"Yeah, but just guess," the teenager said.

"Four hundred and fifty pounds," Allen said. He headed up the sidewalk, past the teenager, toward the entrance doors to the Cheshire.

The cowboy followed, close on Allen's heels. "You belong back in your room at the mental asylum," Allen said. "You're late now, so you better hurry if you want lunch. Let me by, this instant."

"There you go," the teenager said. He took his hat, waved it with his hand, and did a low bow. "Monsieur."

Allen looked at the bent-over teenager, who had a zodiac pendant dangling from his throat. The boy wore archless sandals of stitched plastic.

"You look about the right weight," Allen said, and swallowed.

"That's what I think," the teenager said. He straightened up, and took a soldierly stance. "It took willpower."

✎

Mindy was propped on her couch, on foam pillows the colors of Easter candy. She had a crocheted afghan spun twice around the calves of her legs.

The old suite she rented had been restyled with lowered ceilings and a pink-beige carpet. There was a new folding door on the bathroom, and a line of little appliances in the kitchen.

The central room was hushed after the street racket below, and the floor and furniture were striped with light that came through the window blind. Low on a wall, an air cooler was chugging.

"Ooh, thank heavens, you're here," Allen said. "Do you have any idea what would have happened to me if you'd gone out to lunch or something?" He flopped down on the floor in front of Mindy, gripped the back of his neck, and let his head roll back on his hand. "Whew, I'll tell you. I'd be at the police station, right now, filling out reports. That's a tricky downtown, on a good day. But on a day like today—a Saturday, when everything's thronged, the people get irritable enough to kill one another, and they don't even know why. It's because they're hot."

Mindy was watching Allen without interest.

"Aunt Min, I hope you can help me," he said. "I need desperately for somebody to talk me out of doing something stupid."

Mindy creased the pages of the newspaper she had been reading, the *Sun,* and tossed them over her shoulder onto the floor behind the couch. She reached for a glass on the lamp table—a brown drink with a bobbing cherry.

"Give me a minute to get my equilibrium," Allen said. "Then I'll unload the whole problem. Your place sure is coming along. It looks better and better, every time I come. Is that a new painting?"

Mindy lifted herself, and craned her neck to see the wall behind her. "No," she said. She relaxed back into place, and tapped the cherry that floated on the surface of her drink. "I got that at an estate sale, almost a year ago."

"What does it remind me of?" Allen said, thinking. "My head is full of names. I've been taking a course on the history of art—which I love. I was smart, for once, and got the jump on my graduating class. They don't start college 'til fall quarter. Rousseau is the name that keeps sticking in my mind for some reason—in relation to that piece." He nodded at the wall. "Someone, either the textbook or my T.A., says the whole pageant of art history stops right with Henri Rousseau. I think I already knew that, but, anyway, his work sort of reminds you of looking through a magnifying glass. He can take you out into a field or a jungle, say, and leave you standing there. Painting, I found out, is all done with the eyes." Allen straightened his posture, and pulled his feet into a lotus position. "To prove what I mean, we saw these amazing films of Auguste Renoir, in his last and final days, where he was painting with brushes strapped onto the backs of his wrists—which were crippled up with something, but even that didn't stop Renoir."

"No, it wouldn't," Mindy said.

"O.K., you're not interested," Allen said. "But what brought all this up is I really do like your picture, if nothing else, just for the winter theme. I love winter, and I hate summer. You wouldn't believe how lazy I am because of the humidity, recently. I just drop when it gets too bad, and Dad leaves our air conditioner off overnight, so you wake up, already sick. One morning, I was fixing cinnamon toast, or something, and I had to practically lie on the counter to keep from going into a complete faint."

"How is Paul?" Mindy said.

"Fine," Allen said. "So, what I do is I throw a whole tray full of ice cubes into the bathtub with me, first thing, and then I just stay in there until the air conditioner's working enough to make some difference. I know it's not good for you, to go from red hot to freezing cold—it's probably why I'm so hoarse. Dad says I go around coughing twenty hours a day."

"Is Paul still thinking of remarrying?" Mindy said. She untangled her legs from the afghan, stood, and circled where Allen was positioned on the rug.

"That's the whole thing I came to talk to you about, Aunt Min." Allen looked up, and turned slowly on his seat, following Mindy. "The woman, it turns out—I've never met her. I just heard about her from Dad, and, of course, he left out all the bad stuff. She's older than he is. She's been married before, at least once. She's got four kids, which're grown, thank God. He wants to move her—Laura Glinnis is, I guess, her name—into the house with us. You can imagine what that'd do to me. I've never had to live with a woman. Not since we lost Mom."

"You never lived with your mother, Allen. She died in childbirth."

"I know," Allen said, looking sad for a moment. "Everyone always tells me not to blame myself for it."

Mindy said, "Your father never forgave me for missing Marguerite's funeral. Though I was in Germany then, with Carl. We waited a day too long before flying home. I had no idea they'd bury her so quickly. And then Carl was dead within the year, and I found out how they do things."

"I'm sure Dad forgives you," Allen said. "See, he's forgot all about Mom. That's what gets me." Allen pulled a burr from his sock and threw it onto the carpet. "I had the Dodge out one night, driving around, and thinking over this whole thing. I got off the beltway at some exit, and went to a bar, and had a couple of mixed drinks. No one even asked for an ID. They just served me the drinks, one on top of another. I was completely exhausted by then. I didn't care if Dad moved Mrs. Glinnis and her brood right smack into the dining room and fed them T-bone steaks. I started smashing my fist on the table top of the booth they had there. I didn't hurt anything, really. Just my own hand. But I realized I have a capacity to be very destructive. It's like there's some monster inside me, that wants to kill everything in my way."

"Why don't *you* get married, Allen?" Mindy said. She was between him and the couch, snapping at her manicured fingernails with her thumb. "Why don't you get a wife somewhere, and marry her, and move away? Let your dad find a way out of his loneliness, if he can. Because you'd still have the *idea* of you and your father. I'm sure that'd be better than the real relationship."

"Hmm. Maybe I could," Allen said. He took Mindy's drink, which she had refreshed, and sipped from it. "But you forget I'm underage."

"No, I remembered that, Allen. You could lie. Or you could get permission from your father."

"This is crazy, though, because I don't have anyone to marry," Allen said.

"I know dozens of people."

"That'd marry me?"

"In a minute," Mindy said.

"Yeah, O.K. Only, so many people make me nervous. There was a guy out front, today, for example . . . "

"Tex? Tex is usually out front. You'd delight in him, Allen. He's got just the right touch of . . . "

"You must be thinking of someone else," Allen said.

Mindy was in a beanbag chair, in the corner, loading color film into her camera. "You know, I bought this camera with money I won in the football pools," she said. "I always win. That's why I love to gamble. I especially like circulating the floors of the office where I work, to see who else won, and what teams the poor losers bet on. Oops!"

"What?" Allen said.

"Nothing," Mindy said. "Don't worry." Her chignon had come undone, and the left side of her hair—blonde, though she was fifty-one—had fallen onto the shoulder of her kimono. "I clicked off a couple that I didn't mean to. It'll be all right."

"It will," Allen said, in a low voice, to the cowboy-hatted teenager who sat on the couch with him. "She's really more or less a professional. Her work's appeared in a couple of the D.C. galleries—places you'd recognize, if I could remember the names."

"One gallery, and they just showed two of my self-portraits," Mindy said. "A picture of me, at the stove. One of me, petting Abra. . . ."

"Cat that ran away," Allen told the teenager.

Both young men had been drinking, earnestly. Allen tugged off his cotton shirt and laid it out on the floor. He removed his loafers, and his wristwatch. The teenager took off his vest.

"What may I call you?" Allen asked.

The teenager puffed his right cheek full of air, then noisily let the air out. "Baker," he said.

"First, or last?" Allen said. The teenager shrugged.

"Baker, alone, is fine," Allen said. "Easier to remember."

"One more minute," Mindy said, from the corner. "I'm truly sorry this is taking so long. It isn't my fault. The spool's in backwards or something. I wouldn't have had Allen get you up here," she said to the teenager, "if I'd known this was going to happen."

"These'll be great photographs," Allen said.

"Yeah, if I can. . . . Oops," Mindy said. "Damn."

"Now what's the matter?" Allen said.

Mindy said, "Oh, I did something, and now I can't—do you know anything about cameras?"

"I had a basic film theory and technique course," Allen said.

"Loading," Mindy said. "L-o-a-d-i-n-g."

"Not for *any* camera," Allen said.

Mindy struggled out of the beanbag chair. She came toward them, stepping over the coffee table, and showing one of her legs from the thigh down. She dropped the camera. Its self-timer ticked off fifteen seconds against the floor carpet.

Allen squeezed his forehead and sighed.

"The joke is, I do make good photographs," she said. "Maybe—who's to say?—great ones. But you've got to do daily work to be great, and for that you need a darkroom in your house, and not way across the g.d. town." She sat on the coffee table, with her skirt hitched up.

"That's true," Allen said.

"I had a camera," Baker said.

"Good for you, Tex," Mindy said. "Seriously, I got two rolls of thirty-six people each. . . . What did I just say? Did I say, 'thirty-six people each'? Isn't that a scream? Thirty-six *exposures* each, on each of two rolls. They came up brilliant, brilliant. And the reason was those faces."

"Faces?" Allen said.

"Yes, honey, that's what the world is. There's no world without faces to reflect it. Look at that face."

Allen and Mindy looked at Baker. He was whistling through a cavity in a front tooth. He wiggled his eyebrows at them, hard enough to move the brim of his cowboy hat up and down.

"What's in that face, Allen?" Mindy said.

Allen narrowed his eyes at Baker, and asked him to turn his head left, then right.

"Well?" Mindy said.

"Well, because of the hat, he looks . . . I'd say Western."

"You're a sharp boy," Mindy said.

"I wasn't done," Allen said. "It also looks like a face that's recently lost weight."

"Yeah, I did," Baker said.

"You don't see any pain in those eyes?" Mindy asked Allen.

"Yes. Well, really, no. I don't, frankly, Aunt Min."

"Good, because I don't either. There isn't any. How about fear? Do you see fear in his eyes? Never mind." Mindy got up and headed for the bathroom.

"Do you like it hot, like this?" Allen asked Baker. Baker looked around his feet, and then around the apartment.

"I mean, do you like hot weather?"

"Sure," Baker said.

Mindy came back and Allen stood. Baker gathered his vest and stood up as well.

"Here's a face. Sit down, both of you," she said. She showed them a photograph of a young male whose head was shaved, and whose eyes were wild-looking. There were markings, or scratches, on the photo, above the dark eyes. "This one is disturbed. People call him 'disturbed,' but he made perfect sense to me the day I took shots of him. If you look deep enough, you see the calm behind the chaos. It's one reason I wanted to photograph you two," Mindy said.

"Not that you're retarded," Allen said to Baker. "Or me—that I am."

"Oh, you're retarded, all right," Mindy said. "I don't know how, Allen, but you stopped your emotional growth at the age of six."

"Hey, that's the bottle talking," Allen said.

"This was nice," the teenager said to Mindy. "I'd like to visit you again, sometime, in the future."

❦

Mindy had felt sick, grabbed up Allen's shirt, and gone swiftly into the bathroom, with the shirt held against her mouth. For a long while, Allen heard faucet water running. Eventually, he tried pushing open the folding door. "Aunt Min?" The door moved a few inches, and caught on Mindy, who lay over the floor tiles, with Allen's shirt balled under her cheek for a pillow.

Allen pulled the door shut. He paced around the apartment, in just his slacks, hissing and swearing to himself. He perched on the back of Mindy's couch, and brought the telephone to his lap. He dialed "one," and then his home phone number.

"Hello," said a woman's voice, startling Allen.

"Is this my house?" he said. "Who is this?"

"I'm Laura Glinnis," the woman said.

"Well, put Dad on, if he's there. I need to talk with him, immediately."

"Just a second, Allen," Mrs. Glinnis said. "Paul?"

"What do you want, now?" Allen's father said into the phone.

"Just to let you know what I'm up to," Allen said.

"Is it serious?"

"I feel that, this time, I'm in deep water, Dad. Things are completely out of my control. I'm sauced, for one thing. There might even be an ambulance case in the bathroom. I'm so messed up," Allen said.

There was a long silence at the other end of the line. Allen heard the whispery scrape of a cupped palm over the phone's speaker. His father's voice came back, slowly, saying, "Relax, boy. Run this thing down for me, step by step."

"O.K., the first thing you should know is I came here to tell Aunt Mindy about what's been happening—my side of the story."

"Who's in the bathroom, hurt?" Allen's father said. "Is it Mindy? Tell me straight. Take it slow now, son."

"Aunt Mindy'll be fine. I'm not worried about her," Allen said. "She's used to being drunk." He laughed once.

"Allen?" the voice said. "Do you know how you make me feel?"

"Yeah, yeah," Allen said, and smacked down the phone's receiver.

He straightened the apartment a little, tidied the kitchen, and perked coffee. He opened the bathroom door the few inches it would go. He hoped the coffee aroma would revive Mindy.

"You know Charles," Mindy said in her sleep.

Allen got the camera off the floor, and sat down, and tried until he was sweating to get the roll of film untangled.

"I feel so . . . regretful," Mindy called.

Allen looked in on her. She was awake, but in the same prone position. Water still splashed from the opened faucet. "This is disgusting, I know," she said. "It must be disgusting for you to see, Allen. A young boy. I'm really so, so sorry."

"You're forgiven," Allen said.

"Do you mean it? You're not really angry?"

"Hell, no. Not at all," Allen said.

Whistling to himself, he borrowed a tailored blouse from a hanger in Mindy's closet. He rolled the cuffs, where there were

pearl, flower-shaped buttons. He turned the collar under, un-
comfortably.

In the kitchen, Allen poured coffee into one of his aunt's
pretty tea cups. He sat in the tiny dining annex, with his legs
crossed, and sipped coffee, and considered his day. He
thought he'd drive out around the Baltimore zoo—maybe buy
himself dinner.

16

I Am Twenty-One

I HEARD RINGING, AND I realized that what I had done was continued my answer to Essay Question I—"What effect did the discovery of the barrel vault have on the architecture of thirteenth-century cathedrals?"—writing clockwise in the left, top, and right-hand margins of page one in my exam book. I had forgotten to move along to page two or to Essay Question II. The ringing was coming from in me—probably from overdoing it with diet pills or from the green tea all last night and from reading so much all the time.

I was doing C work in all courses but this one—"The Transition from Romanesque to Gothic." I needed to blast this course on its butt, and that was possible because for this course I knew it all. I needed only time and space to tell it. My study notes were 253 pencil sketches from slides we had seen and from plates in books at the Fine Arts Library and some were from our text. I had sixty-seven pages of lecture notes that I had copied over once for clarity. Everything Professor Williamson had said in class was recorded in my notes—practically even his throat clearings and asides about the weather. It got to the point where if he rambled, I thought, yeah, yeah, cut the commercial and get back to the program.

Some guy whose hair I could've ripped out was finished with his exam. He was actually handing it to the teaching assistant. How could he be *finished,* have given even a cursory treatment to the three questions? He was a quitter, a skimmer, I decided; a person who knew shit about detail.

I was having to stop now and then, really too often, to skin the tip of my pencil with the razor blade I had brought along. I preferred a pencil because it couldn't dry up or leak. But this was a Number 2 graphite and gushy-gummy and I was writing the thing away. The eraser was just a blackened nub. Why hadn't I brought a damn *box* of pencils?

The teaching assistant was Clark—Clark Something or Something Clark, I didn't know. He was baggy and sloppy, but happy-looking. He had asked me out once for Cokes, but I had brushed him off. That was maybe stupid because he might've been in charge of grading exams.

I decided to ignore Essay Question II, pretend I hadn't even seen it. I leaned hard into Question III, on church decoration, windows, friezes, flora, fauna, bestiaries, the iconography in general. I was quoting Honorius of Autun when the class bell fired off.

I looked up. Most people were gone.

"Come on, everyone!" Clark called. "Please. Come on now. Miss Bittle? Mr. Kenner, please. Miss Powers?"

"Go blow, Clark," I said right out loud. But I slapped him my exam booklet and hurried out of Meverett, feeling let down and apathetic all of a sudden, and my skin going rubbery cold.

I biked home with a lot of trouble. I went on the sidewalks. I was scared that in the streets I'd get my ringing confused with car warnings.

I was still ringing.

Last semester I had had a decorating idea for my apartment, this monastic idea of strict and sparse. I had stripped the room down to a cot, a book table, one picture. The plaster walls were a nothing oatmeal color, which was okay. But not okay was that some earlier renter had gooped orange—unbelievably—paint on the moldings and window frames. So where I lived looked not like a scholar's den, finally, but more like a bum's sleepover, like poverty.

My one picture up wasn't of a Blessed Virgin or a detail from Amiens of the King of Judah holding a rod of the Tree of Jesse. Instead, it was an eight-by-ten glossy of Rudy and Leslie, my folks. Under the backing was written *Gold Coast, the first cool day.* The photo had been shot out on North Lake Shore Drive around 1964, I'd say, when I was three. Leslie, my mom, was huddled into Rudy, sharing his lined leather jacket. They appeared, for all the eye sparkle, like people in an engagement-ring ad. I kept the picture around because, oddly, putting away the *idea* of my folks would've been worse than losing the real them. In the photo, they at least *looked* familiar.

They had been secret artists. Rudy was a contractor for a living, Leslie a physical therapist. So they worked all their art urges out on me on my school projects, for instance, which they hurled themselves into. One project "I did" for seventh grade that they helped me with was, I swear, good enough for a world's fair. It was a kind of three-dimensional diorama triptych of San Francisco Bay with both bridges—Oakland and Golden Gate—that may have even lit up or glowed in the dark. We had to borrow a neighbor's station wagon just to get the thing safely over to Dreiser Junior High—it lined up as long as an ironing board.

I got my bike tugged inside, left it leaning against the wall under the photograph. I clapped a kettle onto the midget stove

in the kitchen part of my apartment, and paced, waiting for the
water to heat. The pitch of the steam when it got going was only
a quarter-tone below the ringing in my head.

My folks were two and a half years gone.

I used to drive out to the site of their accident all the time—
a willow tree on Route 987. The last time I went, the tree was
still healing. The farmlands were a grim powdery blond in the
white sun, and the earth was still ragged from winter. I sat there
in my tiny Vega on the broken crumbly shoulder. The great tree
and the land around—flat as a griddle for miles and miles—
didn't seem as fitting as I had once thought, not such a poetic
place for two good lives to have stopped.

I had my tea now and grieved about the exam. Leaving a
whole essay question unanswered! How could I expect to get
better than a C?

Just before my first sip of tea, my ringing shut off as though
somebody had punched a button, said, "Enough of that for her."

I decided it was time to try for sleep, but first I used a pen
with a nylon point to tattoo a P on the back of my hand. This
meant when I woke up I was to eat some protein—shrimp or
eggs or a green something.

On the cot I tried, as a sleep trick, to remember my answer
to Essay Question I—word for fucking word.

17

Independence Day

HELEN HAD NOT DONE anything all June. She did not have to. Nothing was required of her. Her estranged husband was in Detroit somewhere. Her retired father was housing her in a grand stone house in Port Brent, a lakeside resort town in northern Ohio. The house was on a cove and the backyard led to a private pier where Helen's father moored his boats, an old wooden Chris-Craft with an Evinrude engine, and a Lido sailboat.

It was not good for Helen, having nothing to do. If you didn't do things to your life, she decided, it would begin doing things to you. She decided this while lying in bed at four-thirty in the morning. She was looking at her knees, and, as if to confirm her thought, she heard a clunk sound that she recognized as the air conditioner breaking down.

She turned onto her side.

❧

She woke up sweating at one o'clock the next afternoon, and stepped into some beach thongs and a sundress. It was almost a hundred degrees in her third-story room.

Down in the kitchen, her sister, Darla, who was twenty-five, had her elbows splayed on the open morning newspaper; she was reading Maggie and Jiggs.

Helen peeled an orange over the kitchen counter and considered her sister, who was sweating, too, in an immodest calico bikini. Darla snorted a laugh through her nose at the paper, then raised her eyes to stare at a hose that connected the dishwashing machine.

Darla had a cottage somewhere on the lake, but she was an in-and-out visitor at the Kenning house. Since May, she had been mostly an "in" visitor, as she was low on money and boyfriends.

"Where's Father?" Helen said.

Darla nodded toward a backfiring engine noise out the window.

Helen lifted herself on her toes and looked through the double windows over the sink. She saw her father on his riding mower, in the west stretch of the lawn. He and the mower were bounding over the crest of a little slope.

Helen said, "Why isn't he fixing the air conditioner? Why is he mowing the lawn?"

Darla shrugged, studying the washing instructions on the inside of her swimsuit's bra cup.

"I'm getting sick," Helen said. "I'm going to get Father."

"Terry called," Darla said. She moved a butter plate and some juice glasses around on the table so she could roll the paper over.

Terry, Helen's husband, had been calling from Detroit five times a day. Helen refused to talk to him because he usually had only one point to make, and that was that she should clear out of her father's place and get her own apartment.

She walked around the counter to the windowed aluminum door that led onto the patio and yard. Art Kenning had U-turned his mower and was charging for the house.

He eased the machine onto the patio's gravel apron. A pebble flew from the grass blower and stabbed the side of a wooden toolbox that was on the ground. "I thought that was a bullet," Mr. Kenning said, staring at the chip of stone. He said, "Your husband called this morning."

"What's wrong with the air conditioner?" Helen said, over the idling of the engine. "Can't you fix it?"

"No," Mr. Kenning said, and sighed. "You'll have to live without it."

"I can't live without it," Helen said.

"I'll look at it," Mr. Kenning said. "But I'm leaving in fifteen minutes. Where's your sister?"

"Inside," Helen said.

Her father stopped the engine and leaned back on the mower's saddle. He brought his feet up one by one and removed his shoes and socks. He stuffed the socks into the shoes and climbed down and picked his way, barefooted, over the gravel.

Helen followed him back into the kitchen, and they stood looking at Darla and the pattern on the tablecloth for a minute.

"This is Communism," Darla said, rapping a column in her newspaper. "I think we whipped the wrong damn army."

Mr. Kenning said, "You know, girls, this is a workday for most people."

"Tomorrow's Fourth of July," Darla said. "Not a workday. So you'd better get a repairman out here." She wet the tip of her finger and turned a newspaper page. "Helen, get me a Coke while you're over there."

"Watch the handle on the refrigerator," Mr. Kenning said. "It's falling off."

⁓

Helen swam in the cove.

She and Darla rode the house bike, an old Schwinn, along the beach road. Helen pedaled, standing, while Darla sat on the bike's narrow seat with her pelvis thrust forward, her legs dangling, a cigarette in her hand.

After they swam, they lay side by side in the sun on the dock, their hair wrapped in colored towels.

"What are you writing?" Darla said, with her eyes closed. "I hear you writing."

"A book of days," Helen said. She had a sheaf of papers in a folder that she had brought along in the bike basket. She was flipping through the papers. She paused and scribbled with a red Flair pen.

"About Terry?" Darla said.

"Why would I write about Terry?"

"I don't know," Darla said. "What else have you got to write about? You don't date. You don't work. A book of days is supposed to be autobiography—about things happening. What's been happening to you?"

"I've got plenty in my life besides Terry," Helen said, but after a while she closed the folder, which contained mostly notes on movies and TV shows she had seen.

Helen swam again in the early evening. She brushed her wet blonde hair into a spike and put on the same sundress. She walked a quarter-mile of shady road through the resort town of Port Brent. On the edge of the town was a lounge Helen liked that was called—from what Helen could gather from the pink neon sign that marked the place—Seafood Liquor.

The lights in the lounge flickered on as she entered, although it was only six o'clock. She passed a line of men at the bar who were watching a trunk-sized color television that showed a horse race. She passed the little placard on a stand that read: "Please wait to be seated," and went to her usual booth, in the rear, under a stuffed, board-mounted, varnished lobster.

"Double White Horse, neat," Helen said when the waitress came.

The waitress, a big-boned pretty girl in the gingham house uniform, brought the drink right away, on a round tray with a cork mat and a book of paper matches.

Helen's Detroit husband, Terry, came into the bar. He went to Helen's booth. He lay on the bench seat across from her, with his legs up and crossed at the knee.

"It's Crayola at the clubhouse turn," said the TV announcer. "Crayola by a length."

The men along the bar cheered and punched each other, pulled each other's clothing, rearranged their standing and seating positions.

"I suppose it means something that you can always find me," Helen said to her husband.

Terry put a hand under his dark glasses and rubbed his eyes. "No. It just means you always go to the same places."

The pretty waitress brought Terry a menu, and he said, "No. I don't need it. The Bosun's platter and two of those." He pointed at Helen's drink.

"When did you drive down from Detroit?" Helen said. "It's a horrible drive, I know. I've done it."

"Have you?"

"Once," Helen said.

Terry said, "I had to come down because you never answer the phone. You know how many times I've called?"

"I know. I'm sorry," Helen said. "It's just that so many times I pick up the phone and the caller hangs up, or asks, 'Who is this?' To *me!*"

"That's nuts," Terry said. "That isn't the real reason. You don't come to the phone because you don't want to talk about what I want to talk about."

"You do kind of play the same violin, Terry."

"Well, I've got a different violin," he said. "I need to talk to you." He settled his dark glasses back on his face. "Something good's happened."

"Yes?" Helen said.

"Silly Brat. Silly Brat. Blinko and Silly Brat at the rail," said the TV.

"It's my birthday," Terry said. "I'm thirty-three."

"Oh, God. It is. I forgot all about it," Helen said. "July third, of course. I'm so sorry. Is that what you've been calling about?"

He looked sourly at Helen, and took her drink and finished it.

"Something very nice has happened," he said.

"You got a job," Helen said.

"Never mind," Terry said. "Thank you," he told the waitress, who put two wide, full glasses and some napkins on the table.

"I won the state lottery," he said. "Legally. I won twelve thousand dollars on a ticket I bought in Euclid."

Helen said, "You really did?" and Terry began to nod with his lower lip fastened by his upper teeth. "That's incredible. That's wonderful. That is good news. Congratulations. I should say so."

"Yep," he said. "But there's an angle. There's a strong possibility I'll win a lot more, Helen. I'm likely to come out of this a millionaire."

"How?" she said. "This is remarkable. You!"

"Friday," he said. "There's another drawing, between me and some other people—five of them—and one of us gets the million dollars."

"Jesus," Helen said.

"Yeah, really," Terry said. "But don't worry. I'll win."

"You probably will," Helen said. "Whew!"

"Anyway," Terry said, "I'm going to give you some money. Whether I win more or not. I want you to move out of your dad's house."

"Oh, no," Helen said. "Same old violin."

"I want you to move," Terry said.

"I'm fine there," Helen said.

"I want you to get your own apartment," Terry said. "You've never spent a single night alone in your whole life. You don't know the first thing about just day-to-day getting by— earning money."

"Why would I want to spend a night alone? My father has plenty of money."

"I want you to move," Terry said.

"I'm fine where I am," Helen said.

"Yes, but, Helen," he said. "Okay," he said. "When I win the million dollars, I'll just buy the place."

"You can't buy the place," Helen said. "It's our home. My father has boats there. It's where I was raised. My mother *died* there, in the laundry room."

"She had a stroke in the laundry room. She died in a hospital," Terry said. "I'll buy it, and kick you out. I'll evict you."

The waitress brought him a small porcelain plate with a powdered dinner roll and a tablet of butter between waxed-paper squares. On a larger plate was a bowl of salad.

"I'll need cutlery," Terry said to her.

"Sorry?" the waitress said.

"Oh," Terry said, "skip it. I'll eat this junk with my fingers."

He picked up some chunks of lettuce and wedged them into his mouth.

There was a motorist's inn, a circle of shingle-roofed, paint-blistered buildings around a blacktop court, where Terry had taken a cabin. Helen woke up there, on the morning of the Fourth of July, to a local explosion. The room was queerly lit.

One tall ceramic lamp, smoothly sculpted into a seahorse shape, threw the illumination from a low-wattage light bulb onto a wall of cheap paneling, and there was a tiny window with white drapes. The room smelled faintly of gunpowder and of the refrigerated air that blew from the air conditioner.

Terry had left the TV on and from her pillow Helen watched about ten minutes of an Abbott and Costello movie.

She stretched and got out of bed. She put on her sundress and stepped out the door. The sky was white. There was a yard with some playground equipment behind the circle of cabins. It was hot, and Helen spotted Terry, shirtless, with some young boys. Terry was supervising the firing off of cherry bombs, Chinese twisters, sparklers, paper tubes that foamed and smoked and boomed.

The neighborhood dogs were barking. Terry shaded his eyes. "You're up," he said to Helen. "Good morning."

"How could I help being up?" she said. She went back inside and tried to fix her hair with a tin comb from her handbag. The only mirror in the cabin was over the bathroom sink and it was missing big chips of silvered surface. Helen bent at the knees to fit her face between two flaked-off, black sections.

Terry came up behind her. There was a boom from outside the cabin. It shook the single window in its mounting.

"Did you leave your fireworks with those kids?" Helen said. "They'll blast off their thumbs and you'll spend your twelve thousand on some lawsuit."

"They aren't my thumbs," Terry said.

❧

Terry took Helen to the Port Brent parade. They sat on the courthouse lawn, near the curb, and watched the floats and the high-school band pass by. A man on ten-foot stilts in an Uncle Sam outfit stalked over them. Helen waved up at him.

"How are you today, darling?" the man said. His face, under the tall striped hat, was tiny.

Darla, Helen's sister, was in the parade, in a beige Ford that was part of the automobile show. She looked sad and pale, perched on the hood of the car.

"She was dreading this," Terry said.

"Who was?" Helen said.

"Darla. She was dreading this. Your father made her do it, I guess," Terry said.

"How would you know?" Helen said.

"I talk to Darla," Terry said. "Whenever you don't answer. I've talked to her a lot about her life."

"Have you? And what else?" Helen said. She had trouble holding a match still to light a cigarette.

"I came down to see her once. Maybe I shouldn't be telling you this."

"No, it's all right, I guess," Helen said. "So you want to buy my father's house?"

"If he wants me to," Terry said. "I get the impression he does. He doesn't want the responsibility for the place anymore. But I don't mind the responsibility. I'll buy it up and kick you out."

"That'll be all right," Helen said.

18

Apostasy

Donna was late. She left the Camaro running alongside a dumpster and jogged to the all-night drugstore.

Sister Mary Divine Heart stood waiting before a backlit wall of creams and ointments. Her eyes were bruised from lack of sleep. She wore a trenchcoat, and her hair was bound with a yellow rubber band.

Donna ticked a coin on the display window, and her sister, Sister Mary, covered her grinning mouth with a tissue and came out into the harsh light of the predawn. It was Sunday morning—a watery October. A lake breeze blew, tangling a *Plain Dealer* between Sister Mary's legs.

The women drove along the lakefront, listening to a rebroadcast of the Texaco opera on Donna's car radio. Sister Mary said wasn't it a peculiar sound track for the bait shops and sagging cottages that rolled by the windshield.

"Were you waiting very long?" Donna said, pushing in the cigarette lighter. "The reason I'm late is Mel and I had to work all night. You remember him? He's my boss. The congressman? He's done an article on prosecutorial immunity, and it's really something. It's really getting to him. It's getting to both of us."

Sister crossed her feet. She said, "I don't mind waiting. I watched *Les Girls* on the pharmacist's portable TV. Anyway, I slept plenty. I slept the whole way back on the Greyhound."

"What did they tell you in Rochester?" Donna said. She slowed the car and stared at her sister. "They said you're dying."

"Probably," the nun said. "Your last pal."

"Well, Jesus Christ," Donna said.

"Well, I'm dying," Sister said.

The road bent sharply and hugged a little industrial canal that ran by a mile of warehouses before rejoining the sliding surface of the lake.

Donna parked on the yellow grounds behind the cloister's tamed woodbine and herbarium. Sister Mary got out of the car and stood in the blotchy shade of a partly stripped plum tree, and Donna slid over to the passenger's seat.

"In a way, I envy you," Donna called through the window frame.

Sister shrugged. She scooped a bee off a spear of fern and held it under her eyes. She said, "I'm willing you my Saint Augustine."

"Goody," Donna said, and exhaled on the wings of the bee Sister was holding. The bee stung Sister, who brandished her palm with a white welt blooming for Donna to see.

Clouds hurried over the convent's grounds. On the drive adjacent to the refectory, kids were unloading pieces of a public-address system from the back of a Ford Pinto.

❧

John Manditch was on the front porch of Donna's rental house, his hands pressed on his hips, doing deep knee bends. "Hold it a second," he said. "I might be sick." He looked down at his stomach and then he paced around in a small circle.

Donna opened the screen door and went into the house. A fat boy in a poplin blazer was sitting in the living room on top of her Utah loudspeaker. The couch had been moved. On the TV, a cheer-crazed commentator announced the morning news.

Manditch caught up with her when she stopped at a sideboard in the hallway. He filled a tumbler with Tanqueray and used the tail of Donna's jacket to mop a puddle of gin he splashed on the tabletop.

Amy, Donna's housemate, appeared at a mirror in the hall and waxed on some lipstick. "It was my idea to have a party," Amy shouted, "but nobody will go home."

Donna went over and cupped a hand on Amy's ear. "Is there any food left?" she said.

"Who knows?" Amy said, and shook loose.

Donna stomped into the kitchen. She opened cabinets and flapped the breadbox. Proudhead was stretched out on the floor in evening clothes and fancy new shoes. He was eating fried chicken and drinking brandy.

"I have twin brothers," he said to a crouching girl. "Thirteen and eleven, with hair down to here." He pointed to his nipple with a shredded drumstick.

"Who ate the roast beef?" Donna said. She threw the refrigerator door shut.

"Some of this left," Proudhead said, pushing his paper chicken bucket toward her with a glossy dress shoe.

A young man in white slumped into the kitchen. He said, "I think I just backed over a Great Dane."

"That's our neighbor's Great Dane," Donna said. "You ran over Lola."

"I'm sorry," said the young man.

"I'm sorry," said Proudhead.

Donna squatted and sipped from Proudhead's Hennessy bottle. John Manditch walked by, holding his belly, and headed for the sink.

"John, get these people out of here," Donna said.

Manditch said, "The neighbors on all three sides have phoned the police. Thanks to you," he said to the young man in white.

"Lordy, Lordy," the young man moaned. "Why do these things happen to me?"

"Don't ever come back here," Proudhead said to him.

❧

Donna woke up wearing a rope of cotton underpants and a madras jacket she had left over from high school. "What's that noise?" she said.

Manditch was beside her in bed, with a bottle of carbonated wine and a paperback novel. He pointed to Proudhead, who knocked a croquet ball across the hardwood floor with a hearth shovel.

"He has a nosebleed," Donna said.

"I know it," Manditch said, flattening his thumb on the bottle spout. "I told him. I forgot to shake this."

"Lift up," Donna said, trying to free her arm from under Manditch. "And who opened the windows in here? I can see my breath."

"I did," Manditch said. "We had a pipe-smoking visitor."

"We did? Who?" Donna said. "This morning?"

"About a half-hour ago," Manditch said. "Want some of this?"

Donna took a drink from the wine bottle and coughed.

She said, "My sister has cancer."

Proudhead sat down on a ladder-back chair and wadded a piece of white underwear against his nose.

The bedroom door came open and Amy put her head in.

"I'm moving out," she said.

"Fine," Donna said. "Proudhead? Toss me my pants."

Proudhead threw the trousers. Donna pulled them on and climbed over Manditch, who had taken off his horn-rims and was massaging the bridge of his nose.

Donna stood at the window. She found and lit a half-smoked Kool. She could see Congressman Mel Physell down there in the yard. He wore a clear, floor-length raincoat, and he was knocking pipe ash into a puddle of mud.

"That was going to be my zinnia garden," Donna yelled at him. Congressman Mel Physell jumped backward. He looked up and down the street. He threw his pipe into a clot of shrubs and moved away to the sidewalk, where Amy was busy loading a floor lamp into her Peugeot truck.

❦

Proudhead and Donna were in the kitchen, leaning against the stove eating scrambled eggs from a skillet.

Congressman Mel Physell came through the side door. "Your lock's broken," he said.

"I know," Donna said. "For about two months."

She took him into the living room. John Manditch was lying on the floor carpet with his hair wrapped in a soap-smelling towel. "Aaah," John Manditch said. He unbuttoned his corduroys and revealed a full stomach.

"Who are these guys?" Mel Physell asked.

"I know them," Donna said. "Don't ask me how. I just do."

Amy walked by carrying a blow dryer and a CB radio.

"I've written some poems on prosecutorial immunity I'd like to read to you," Mel Physell said, opening a spiral-bound notebook.

"That's wonderful," Donna said. "Please do."

"I worked the whole morning on these," Mel Physell said, "though they're rough, you understand. These are just the roughs."

"That's okay," Donna said. "We'd be honored."

"Keep in mind, these are not the finished products. In fact, they're just an outline, really, a pastiche. Don't pay any attention to the first five or so. They're just scribbles and doodles, rough drafts, not worth thinking about. I just scratched them down without a nod to rhyme or meter. They're utterly worthless," Mel Physell said, and threw his notebook into the fireplace. He sat with his face in his hands.

Proudhead came from the kitchen, carrying the skillet and scraping out bits of egg with a spatula.

"Now stop being foolish," Donna told Mel Physell.

"I kag hab id," he said. He had a pen between his teeth and was searching for something in his raincoat pockets.

John Manditch got to his feet. He picked up the morning paper and sank into the sofa beside Proudhead.

Donna said, "I really want to hear the poems."

"Okay," Mel Physell said, lifting the notebook and brushing off a page. "Here we go. Don't listen to this first one. It's just a preliminary draft." He smoothed the page with his palm. "It's so wrinkled," he said, "I don't think I can read the handwriting. I can't seem to make it out. Just forget I mentioned it." He threw the notebook into the fireplace again.

John Manditch had the newspaper spread out on the coffee table. "Carborundum's striking," he told Proudhead. "Doesn't your father work there?"

"Cathcote," Proudhead said. "He works at Cathcote."

"I know Dick Burk at Cathcote," Mel Physell said.

Donna locked her teeth. "Mel," she said, "look at us."

"Three people," the congressman said, grinning. "Constituents."

Donna sighed and looked at the ceiling.

"Things are not so good," Mel said.

"Well, you've got that right," Donna said.

"They used to be good," Mel said. "Things were proper, and that's a cherished goal. Now—who knows? Now it's here come the firemen, here come the chilly-willies. You know?"

"You don't have to tell me," Donna said.

Mel Physell broke into full-throated laughter, which John Manditch and Proudhead parroted.

"You know?" the congressman said, wiping at his eyes. "Really."

19

For Real

I WAS IN THE DRESSING rooms, comfortable in my star's chair, a late evening in October. We had taped three shows. My lounge chair was upholstered in citrus-green fabric. My section of the studio dressing rooms was all lollipop colors, in case a Cub Scout troop or something came through.

I was alone, confronting a window. I could see lights around the Dutch Pantry restaurant, and a single truck enduring the horrific eastbound uphill grade on the Pennsylvania Turnpike. Beyond that, the mountains—which were florid in the autumn daylight—had darkened to a hostile black-green, as if they were closed for the night to visitors. Their pointy peaks were brushed with beautiful cloud smoke, though, and on the piece of Lake Doe that I could see, there lay a startling reflection of the night's quarter moon.

I was Boffo, the girl clown, who hosted Channel 22's *Midday Matinee.* We ran old bad movies on the *MM*—or worse: old TV pilot shows we passed off as movies. My job was to ridicule the films and gibe at our sponsors, so the viewers at least would have something to smile about. The job was complicated. I felt tested, whenever the cameras were aimed at me, to improve the little monologues and jokes I had written—to act funny, as if I really was Boffo.

Three years of playing her had told on my face. I used an expensive, hypoallergenic clown white that I special-ordered from Chicago, but my complexion was coarsening. My wigs were coral-pink acrylic, with tubes for hair; I wore a skullcap, under which I had to keep my real hair cropped short—an inch or so at most. The fact was, I never wanted to be a clown. I hadn't gone to clown school in Florida or anything, but I'd studied broadcast journalism here at our own Penn State. I didn't even particularly like circuses. I was pushed into the job by management.

Gradually, two things happened. I stopped feeling so reduced by the clown suit. The first months, putting on the nose and wig and the purple gloves with gigantic gauntlet-style cuffs, I had always winced and apologized repeatedly to myself. I got around that by deciding one day that the suit was only a disguise—something to do with my act, not me. I hadn't invented Boffo or her costume. What else happened was that I became convincing, actually pretty good at playing her. Also, I grabbed a crazy amount of pay.

I came back from the window and tried to call Dieter, using the special oversize clown telephone near my chair. I had to thump the out-call tablet four times, because Channel 22's phone system was no better than its movie library. Arranging the receiver so it didn't touch my greased cheek (I had another show to tape, so I was still in full Boffo gear), I tapped off Dieter's number. In the mirror, my cheek was porous and as white as a sheet of rag paper. While Dieter's telephone rang, I found myself trying to loosen some of the coils in my phone's exaggerated wire cording. I permitted ten rings. No Dieter. *"Wo ist Dieter?"* I asked myself.

Dieter was the only guy I bedded with just then. He was a few years my junior—a recent college grad, in fact—which was part one of the problem. He was employed by the Channel 22 news department. He was all set as long as his student visa remained valid, which it wouldn't for long. Dieter was a West German citizen, and he was going to get shipped nicely back there soon if he didn't come up with a legal reason to stay.

"So what the goddamn hell is this not-there jazz?" I asked in my shrill Boffo voice. I often reverted to character when I was in clown rig. I pretended to abuse the enormous receiver, throttling it before I dropped it back onto its rest. "Dieter is always home *in die Nacht. Nacht* is ven the news happens!"

Dieter wanted to marry me, and plenty of times I had agreed, so he could stay on in the States. But I didn't want to marry Dieter, really, and that was part two of the problem: he knew.

I made fun of him a lot, for being such a tidy person and so formal-acting. He wore starchy white shirts always, with cuff links. The line in his side-parted hair was ever straight. *"Was ist das?"* I would say to him. "Did you use a slide rule and a T-square to get that straight a part? It's centered perfectly over your left eye!" An outsider might think I treated him condescendingly, but I wasn't asking any outsiders.

I plucked up four rubber balls and juggled them. I flapped my Stars and Stripes shoe, as long as a diver's fin, on the tile. I got a rhythm going with the soft pops of the rubber balls and the splat of my shoe. That's what I was doing—that and worrying about Dieter—when Terrence, the floor director, opened the dressing room door and said, "We need you for the spot."

"See the moon?" I asked Terrence.

The spot was a little promo for a coming show. Out in the studio, I stood where they told me to, before Cary Williams's camera. I juggled the balls and kept slapping my shoe.

Terrence said, "Three, two, one," and pointed to me before he was distracted by something happening over his headset. We waited.

I liked Cary Williams, the cameraman. He was in his fifties, dimpled and shy, with an impossible laugh. I said, "Hey, *hi!*— it's Boffo. For tomorrow—whoa, brother. We've got a movie that'll bring up your breakfast, brunch, lunch, *and* dinner. And next you'll get to hear me read a medical review on toxic shock syndrome. Lastly, we'll have a visit from Sam and Janet. Sam and Janet who?"

Pete, who was holding up the cue card, said flatly, "Sam and Janet evening." That was our oldest joke.

"Yeah, yeah, could we just do it right for once?" asked Terrence.

I peeked around the trunk of Cary Williams's camera. He was not even smiling. I said, "If I had to do it right, I'd quit."

꙰

I had a pretty comfy condo, with a view of the mountains and Lake Doe. When I was home there, nobody knew I was Boffo the clown. Tonight, because of a flood watch and drenched roads, Dieter was staying over.

I got into bed with him, but also with a vinyl-bound notebook that I balanced against my knees. I tried writing some material—just dumb puns and so on—for a Gregory Peck movie we had scheduled. The film also had Virginia Mayo in it, so I was goofing around with "Ham on rye, Greg, and hold the mayo," and variations of that kind of low-grade snorter.

I couldn't get much written. I was too conscious of Dieter and how much more convenient the future would be if I loved him some, or at all. He was sharp-looking enough—cool-faced, with a romantic broken nose, from being a wrestler for a while in college. He had a slippery grin that was a trick to summon.

"Laugh, Dieter! This is honestly funny, and I'll think more of you," I'd tell him sometimes as he helped me get dressed.

He'd hold up the big stiff costume while I boxed my way into it. Then he'd steady me, so I could fold myself way over to strap on the floppy, dazzling shoes.

"Right, *ja,*" he'd say, his face entirely sober.

He tried especially hard whenever we watched a taped *Midday Matinee* rerun together. But he always failed because he didn't have the same references. At first, I figured I'd just catch Dieter up—give him the lowdown on somebody like Charlton Heston and why it was a pleasure to crack on such a jerk. But that wouldn't have done much good.

Other times, too, Dieter kept missing the jokes. In the supermarket, when I was helping him shop, he'd look down and see that I had slipped nine or ten packages of pigs' feet into the basket. If Dieter knew this was odd, he didn't know it was funny.

And then, *Dieter* would do things, himself, that to me were a laugh, but they weren't to him. I mean, I've never been to West Germany, but there must be less space there. Because Dieter would go into a coffee shop or someplace like that and walk right up to a booth where a couple of people were already sitting, and he'd *join* them. He'd just sit there and read his newspaper, or he'd start a conversation. I'd hear him calling them *"meine Herren"* or *"gnädige Fräulein"*—"Your Lordships" and "Gracious Lady"—and then I'd discover they'd never met before!

A scary thing about marrying Dieter was that it could also mean three years of being spied upon. We'd have to be completely true to each other and very intimate, because I had heard awful stories of immigration inspectors doing spot checks, or calling in one member of a couple like us and asking all manner of personal questions. What's her perfume? What color towels were in your bathroom this morning? What was she wearing when she left the house this morning?

I squinted now at Dieter and asked him, "What's my favorite perfume, that you see me putting on all the time?"

He shrugged. He said yellow-colored—*"Gelb."*

"Dieter, that's any or all perfume," I said, and rocked my head on my pillow. "We are doomed!" I threw my Boffo jokes notebook into the corner. *"Ich bin müde,"* I said. "I am ge-sleepy."

❧

I watched through a separation in the draperies while Dieter parallel-parked his car in the condo driveport. The wipers quit when he killed the engine. He didn't get out of his car right away, so I waited some more in my foyer. I ended up taking a place on the little settee there, waiting for Dieter to ring my doorbell—after which he would bow and usually shake my hand before he kissed me hello and finally came inside.

Today I rushed him through all that. I pulled his angora scarf away and kissed his throat. I held his rain-chilly face between my hands and kissed him some more, although he hadn't even taken off his perfect topcoat. Today I wasn't going to put up with fussiness. We were going right into action, and this time that would change my heart.

But this was Halloween. Dieter had a gift for me, and, he said, hopeful news. His gift was a gold locket. The locket was pricey, I sensed, but there was no photo. "Hey, it's Claude Rains," I said.

Dieter gave me a tilted head, a curious look. At last he said, *"The Invisible Man?* Because in my locket there is no *Lichtbild*—photograph?"

"Way to go, Dieter! That's exactly correct. How'd you get that?" I clapped him on the back in congratulation.

He also had a box of candy for me. He had signed the card, "On Halloween, to my clown."

I slowed up and made coffee for us. We sat by the fire I had laid earlier. Our view through the bow window at the end of the living room was of mountains and the lake, more brilliant than ever, against an ashy sky.

The fire rustled busily and we sampled some of my chocolates. "So far, I've had bad draws," I said. "A cream thing and an orange center, and now this one is jelly."

Dieter's eyebrows went up. It occurred to me to tell him about Halloween candy: chicken corn and those tiny orange pumpkins. I decided the info wouldn't have much utility. I also wanted to hear Dieter's hopeful news.

It turned out he had been to the lawyers'. There was a chance that Dieter could get a job as a translator for an international news service. He was smart. He could read six or seven languages. The catch would be convincing an immigration inquiry board that he wasn't taking the job away from a qualified American. Dieter said he'd have to prove he was the only person qualified. But I was still bent on seducing Dieter and falling in love with him. I stood him up and kissed him hard, no doubt tasting of raspberry jelly.

ᴦ⌣

I watched the red light on Cary Williams's camera and held for the noise of the five-second buzzer. I had been on the set only an hour and the wig was toasting my scalp. I didn't usually admit this even to myself, since it wasn't a solvable problem. What I did mind was that my cheeks were pasty and stiff because my whiteface had dried to chalk. Like an idiot, I had left my makeup kit in my car trunk overnight. Instead of floods recently, we'd had a snap of fearsome cold—excessive for November. At night, in the car trunk, some of my Boffo cosmetics had actually turned to ice.

The Halloween visit was our last serious get-together, Dieter had announced. He hoped he'd be around town, maybe still
be my friend, but he said he couldn't go through with a marriage—because, he said, I *shouldn't,* not out of simple goodwill.

He had asked me a question I couldn't exactly answer:
"What if you fall in love with somevun for real?" He said I
couldn't be with the hypothetical someone for three long years.

I spoke the movie's lead-in now. The card on Dieter's candy
box had said, "To my clown," hadn't it? The few times I had
got to Dieter, he had a barking, punctuating laugh that would
have been an incentive to me, I guessed, had I heard it more often. It would have helped me be funnier. I probably hadn't been
funny lately, I realized, even on Boffo's level, because I'd been
shoring up all my energies while I aimed at being a better person than I was.

I interrupted the movie's intro. I said to Cary Williams's
camera, "Excuse me, viewers? Ladies and germs? You've been
being cheated, in all truth. You've been seeing a lazy job of
Boffo. But stay watching. We're about to press the pedal to the
floor. We're about to do it right."

On the set there, that got a laugh.

20

May Queen

"I SEE HER SKIRT, DENISE," Mickey said to his wife. "It's blue. I can't see her face because her head's lowered, but the two attendants with her are wearing gloves, right?"

He was standing on the hood of his new tan Lincoln Continental, in a parking space behind the crowds of parents outside St. Rose of Lima Church, in Indianapolis. He had one hand over his eyebrows, explorer style, against the brilliant noonday sun. He was trying to see their daughter, Riva, who had been elected May Queen by her senior high-school class, and who was leading students from all the twelve grades in a procession around the school grounds.

"There's a guy with balloons over there," Mickey said.

Denise stood with the small of her back leaning against one of the car headlights. Around her there were a good three or four hundred people, scattered in the parking lot and on some of the school's athletic fields. They held mimeographed hymn sheets, loose bunches of garden flowers, little children's hands. Some of the women wore straw hats with wide brims and some of the men wore visored golf hats, against the sun, which was cutting and white, gleaming on car chrome and flattening the colors of clothes.

Mickey and Denise had been late getting started, and then Mickey had had trouble parking. "It's a damn good thing that the nuns picked Riva up this morning," Denise had said. "We'd have fritzed this whole thing."

Mickey moved cautiously along the hood of the Lincoln and jumped to the ground. "They're headed our way," he said. "They're past the elementary annex and rounding the backstops."

Denise said, "How does she look, Mick? Scared?"

"Sharp," Mickey said. "Right in step."

"I know," Denise said, clapping her hands. "I love that dress, if I do say so."

"I keep forgetting it was your handiwork," Mickey said.

Denise pushed her glasses up on her nose and made a mad face. Her glasses had lenses that magnified her eyes. "So is this, you forget," she said, pinching the bodice of her dress. She stood away so Mickey could admire her sleeveless green shift and the matching veil pinned in her shining gray hair.

After a while she said, "You know, three other parishes are having May processions today. I don't care. Ours is best. Ours is always the best, though I do like the all-men's choir at St. Catherine's."

"Mi-mi-mi," Mickey sang, and Denise elbowed him.

"Shhh," she said. "There they are."

"So grown up," Mickey said. "I ought to be hanged for leaving the movie camera at work Friday."

Altar boys with raised crucifixes headed the march, and behind them came a priest in a cassock and surplice, swinging a smoking bulb of incense. Riva came next, flanked by two boy attendants, who held the hem of her short cape. Beneath the cape Riva wore a blue bridesmaid's frock. She carried a tiny wreath of roses and fern on a satin pillow. Her face was lifted in the white light. Her throat moved as she sang the Ave Maria.

A family of redheads who were grouped ahead of Denise and Mickey turned around and grinned. Mickey wagged his head left and right. "Great!" he said.

Denise slipped a miniature bottle of spray perfume from her pocketbook. "One of us smells like dry-cleaning fluid," she said. She wet her wrists with the perfume. "Unless I'm reacting to the incense."

"It's me, I'm afraid," Mickey said. "This suit's been in storage nine months." He brought his coat sleeve to his face and sniffed. "Maybe not. I don't know. Who cares? Let's enjoy the damn ceremony."

The procession had moved into the church and most of the people went in, too. Mickey and Denise threaded quickly through the crowd to the church doors. Mickey took the handle of Denise's pocketbook and guided her skillfully, but when they got inside the church, all the pew seats had been taken. They stood in back, in the center aisle, directly in front of the tabernacle. Riva was way up in front, kneeling between her attendants at the altar railing. The children's choir began a hymn about the month of May and the mother of Christ.

When the hymn was over, a young boy all in white got up on a stool near the front of the church and sang alone. Riva and her attendants got off their knees and moved to the left of the altar, where a stepladder, draped in linen and hung with bouquets, had been positioned next to a statue of the Virgin Mary. The arms of the statue extended over a bay of burning candles in supplication.

Riva climbed the stepladder, still carrying the wreath on the satin pillow. She faced the church crowd and held the wreath high. Mickey and Denise grabbed hands. Riva's eyes were raised. She turned and began to place the wreath over the Virgin's head.

"Am I right?" a man standing next to Mickey said. "Her dress looks like it's caught fire."

"Dress is on fire!" someone said loudly. There was quiet, and then there was noise in the church. People half-stood in their pews. A young priest hurried to Riva. She was batting at her gown with the satin pillow. The fern wreath wheeled in the air. Her attendants pulled her down the steps of the ladder.

Mickey shouted, "Stop!" and ran for the altar. He pushed people out of the way. "I'm her dad," he said.

The priest had Riva by both shoulders, pressed against him. He folded her in the apron of his cassock, and a white flame broke under his arm.

"They *both* caught," a woman in front of Mickey said.

The priest smothered Riva's flaring skirt. He looked left and right and said, "Everybody stay back." Riva collapsed on the priest's arm and slid toward the floor.

Mickey vaulted over a velvet cord in front of the altar. He and the priest picked up Riva and between them carried her quickly across the altar and through a doorway that led into the sacristy.

❧

An usher with a lily dangling from the lapel of his suit jacket came into the room with a folded canvas cot. "Put her here," he said. "Just a minute. Just one minute." He unfolded the cot, yanking at the stiff wooden legs. "There she goes," he said.

When they got Riva lying down, an older priest, in vestments, began sending people away from the room. Denise was allowed in. She helped Mickey cover Riva's charred dress with a blanket.

"That leg is burned," the first priest said. "Don't cover it up."

"I'm sorry," Denise said.

The two priests sat facing each other in metal chairs, as if they were playing a card game.

"We called for an ambulance, Father," the usher said to both of them.

"It doesn't look too terrible," Mickey said as he folded the burned skirt back and examined his daughter's leg. He glanced around at the priests. "I think we're going to be okay here," he said.

Riva was sobbing softly.

Denise stood at the base of the cot and clutched each of Riva's white slippers.

"Listen, sweetheart," Mickey said, "your parents are right here. It's just a little burn, you know. What they call first degree, maybe."

Riva said nothing.

"When this thing is over," Mickey said, "and you're taken care of—listen to me, now—we'll go up to Lake Erie, okay? You hear me? How about that? Some good friends of mine, Tad Austin and his wife—you never met them, Riva—have an A-frame on the water there. We can lie around and bake in the sun all day. There's an amusement park, and you'll be eighteen then. You'll be able to drink, if you want to."

The priests were looking at Mickey. He blotted perspiration from his forehead with his coat sleeve.

Denise said, "I'm surprised they are not here yet." Her glasses had fallen off and she was crying with her mouth open, still holding Riva's feet.

"Give them a little longer," one of the priests said.

"You know," Mickey said to Riva, "something else I just thought of. Tad's wife will be at Erie some of the time. Remember how I told you about her? She's the one who went on television and won a convertible."

"Will you shut up?" Riva said.

21

Your Errant Mom

My High School Art Teacher

"AND THERE WENT KURT Schwitters's *Merzbau*—an incredible piece of art—devoured by the Nazis. He built another one, also destroyed," said Mr. Lee. We were outside on the grounds of my old school in my home state of North Carolina, where the soil is sandy loam and the state motto is "To Be Rather Than to Seem."

There was a warm crosswind from the sea just over a wall, down from the school grounds, below the baseball diamonds. I said, "That must be like what happened to pointillism. When Seurat died so young, I mean."

"Nope," Mr. Lee said. He wasn't a patient man, nor did he have time for expected details. For instance, he was now in need of a haircut. His black-and-white mane flopped left to right in the wind. And he wanted a diet, and a more careful shave.

Over the sea's pounding, I heard one of my twin daughters. She said, "I've been bitten by something. Now I get polio!"

"Malaria, maybe. Not polio," said the other twin.

Mr. Lee was sipping from an aluminum can of Diet Slice. He fished three neatly folded sheets of paper from his trouser pocket. He opened the pages and said to me, "You know what this is? An essay you once wrote for me. The criticism exercise? I still keep it."

I confided in Mr. Lee about my girls. I said, "The best thing about Hallie's being back from Chapel Hill for the summer is she persuaded Susan to come with her. So I get them both. But now that could go out the window. Susan has been talking to Army and Navy recruiters."

"You may have the wrong kind of kid," Mr. Lee said.

The twins closed in on us. They wore seersucker shorts, huge T-shirts. Their heads had crisp blonde hair, Peter Pan style—youngish for twenty-one-year-olds. Susan was saying, "It's just a welt, Hallie. A small—it's sort of a big welt."

"Now you've met the twins," I said to Mr. Lee.

I was suddenly overcome with the chills that accompany a serious headache. I was suddenly sick, and I told them so.

"You?" Hallie said. "I'm the one with yellow fever!"

My Birthday Present from My Boyfriend

I turned forty-three, and Devin gave me a white Alfa Romeo Spider. He took me out to Blackbeard's Galley for supper—a long trek. We rode the car ferry across Pamlico Sound to Ocracoke Island, on the Outer Banks.

I stayed in the Alfa on the ferry. I was savoring the car, and I didn't want to wreck my dinner dress and hair. Devin hung on a rail and watched the sunset playing on the crinkled water.

The light was fading as we entered Blackbeard's—named after the pirate who was captured off Ocracoke by the British and executed. We sat on a plush sofa in front and drank Campari, waiting for our name to be called. The place was in season, bustling. There were antique mahogany furnishings, high ceilings, Waterford chandeliers.

My temples stopped throbbing eventually. They'd been at it for two weeks. And eventually Devin put his chin on his palm and told me about his wife. "She dropped dead the first day of nineteen ninety-four," he said. He smiled. "I had to miss the Rose Bowl Parade."

"What did you think of my daughters, truthfully? Did you like them?" I asked him.

"No."

"Come on," I said. "Didn't you think Susan was funny, telling about—"

"No," Devin said.

"You've got to admit that for their age they are very, very attractive."

"Not to me," Devin said.

"Well, I like them. I was proud of them," I said finally. I was furious with Devin, but I couldn't help smiling about my birthday present.

The Palmetto

A porter in a linen jacket and alligator shoes took care of me on the train. He gave me a newspaper. I read the obits while I ate a raisin Danish. I had brought my own Twinings China Black tea bags. I drank the tea, plain. I had steeped it in Amtrak's pot of boiled water.

"Should've flown," said the dapper man in the seat ahead of me. He had mentioned he was from South America. He was talking to a woman in a suit of twilled silk.

"Are they crossing you up?" the woman asked. Her voice was rich, from deep in her throat.

I listened only selectively to the two of them. I heard the phrases "backup crew on the way . . . new people going to make it tough ... kick off a week from tomorrow—no later ... if we plan to get out clean, which we do."

"I must explain," the South American said. He got back all of my attention. I was interested in an explanation.

"Please don't. I don't care," his woman friend said.

"Only take a second," said the South American.

But the cars rattled over bad track and I splashed tea on my newspaper and missed whatever came next.

A Visit from Mick's Folks

Our house was a raised ranch with multiple additions, east of the East Dismal Swamp and west of the Outer Banks—Pea Island, the National Wildlife Refuge, Kill Devil Hills, Kitty Hawk. It was a nice house, a long way from people.

The twins were watching a PBS production of *Francesca da Rimini.* I heard one twin say to our bulldog, "Shut up, hound. Here comes the saddest part."

My husband, Mick, took the dog out onto our front lawn, recently mowed. I followed. He walked with dragging, heartsick steps.

Mick's parents came cruising up the road. They turned onto the snaking line of pavement that was our driveway. I had the Alfa Romeo parked where they wouldn't see it, behind some prop-rooted mangroves.

Mick smelled of Canoe and he had on a polo shirt—lemon yellow. He pushed up a shoulder of the shirt, threw an arm to wave hello. "This," he said through a gritted-teeth smile, "will be the worst day of our lives—I know, I know. But I wanted them to have a whack at seeing the twins."

His father heaved himself from their car. Nearly seventy, the man was bullish thick. He wore chinos that were flat in the rump. His face was the hue of pie dough. Mick's mother fluttered a hand at us. She was already weeping. She was just as big as her husband.

My High School Art Teacher

Mr. Lee's house was set high on pilings. On the desk in his living room was a Plexiglas box with a collection of fossil casts marked INARTICULATE BRACHIOPODS.

"Don't you hate it when there's both a knock at the door and the phone rings?" Susan said, beside Hallie on the main couch.

"It never happens. So no," Hallie said.

"Does to me," said Susan.

The living room had a lot of black lacquered wood and white leather furniture. There were photographs of faces—very intense—blown up to single-bed size. They hung on three of the walls.

"Aren't you two impressed with this place? How could you not be?" I asked them.

"Sure," Hallie said.

Mr. Lee said, "The trouble is, you bring in a bucket of Colonel Sanders, the whole effect's ruined. Next a Sunday newspaper, a bad pair of bedroom slippers. Horrible. Or your cat drops a Hartz Mountain toy."

The Palmetto

The woman in the silk suit had a good vocabulary, I decided. Her deep, dark voice made a kind of music I didn't have to listen to all the way to appreciate.

The train smelled sweetly of disinfectant. Our seats were swivel loungers, upholstered in red. There were napkins clipped over the fabric of each seat's headrest. The windows were red-curtained, and filtered the dying light so it flattered the passengers.

The sounds kept me awake—the metal door rocking and, from the adjoining club car, splits of champagne being opened and the buzzer for the microwave.

A few passengers were trying to sing the show tune "Once in a Lifetime," and they were trying to stand close together despite the slamming and lurching of the train.

A Visit from Mick's Folks

"Are the twins ready for this?" I asked Mick, too late for him to answer. He threw our bulldog a fluorescent ball. The dog came obediently back to Mick with it. The dog's coat was tawny, brindled.

Mick's dad stepped up to pump my hand. I hugged Mick's mom. "Rough trip, Elise?" I asked her.

"I just cry," she said.

"She cries at the television," said Mick's dad. "At bowling shows."

Hallie came outdoors and Mick's dad called, "There you are. Whichever the hell one you are."

"Sometimes I forget," Hallie said with a tired smile. "Mother? I'm biking into Dunphy for a split second."

"You're not!" said Mick.

"Let her go. She needs some things. She'll be right back," I said.

Hallie spun off on her ten-speed. The bike made the promising ticking noises of time speeded up, of escape.

"Mickey kid, this lawn's a sorry thing," Mick's dad said.

Mick despised the name Mickey. He said, "We're sort of French about that, Dad. We let some of it go on purpose."

"I'd love to weed it, deadhead it for about an afternoon."

"He talks big, but he would drop right over in this humidity," Elise said. Mick's folks were from Michigan, and they did not like our steamy days—my steamy days, my state.

"Sometime, could you show my parents that painting you did?" Mick asked me.

"What painting?"

"The one with the airplane and the Japanese man," Mick said.

"I had to burn it," I said, and acted sad.

My High School Art Teacher

Mr. Lee's telephone was ringing. He said, "Don't answer that, under pain of death." We were headed out back to view his yellow fringed orchids, which were over three feet tall, many of them, and all with spikes of orange flowers.

We stayed on the deck. Mr. Lee asked me to go to his kitchen. He asked me to bring him soda and a whiskey glass and his whiskey, and he told me where I could find everything.

"Children," he was saying to the twins when I returned. He was implying picture frames with his hands for Susan's and Hallie's faces. "My glory, you're good-looking girls!"

I shook my head at him, yes. I had been waiting to hear that.

"Our noses are like doorknobs," Hallie said.

"I think we're fat," Susan said.

"Fat kids with doorknob noses!" said Mr. Lee.

"Would you possibly—this is awful—would you maybe have a spare cigarette?" Susan asked him.

He said, "I don't smoke. If you do, at your age, you're an idiot."

"Well, I do," Susan said. "You think your—uh—friend in there would mind if I had one of his menthols?"

"I think I'd ask him," Mr. Lee said.

"I got the habit from studying," Susan said. "And now I've just, you know, got the habit."

"Break it," said Mr. Lee.

With My Car Parked at Devin's

I was thinking it was interesting, and ominous, that the furniture Mick and I had chosen for the raised ranch was expensive, but all of a movable, temporary kind. We had foam flip chairs, lightweight couches without frames, futons instead of beds, many wicker pieces with detachable cushioning. Our shelves and tables could collapse or fold. Things were stackable.

Mick was answering our telephone, telling Devin, "She's not here." Mick said I had gone to Charlotte to negotiate a contract—probably off the top of his head. I owned a gallery over in Raleigh. Our next exhibit of Jim Dine prints was not to be mounted for a week. Our last show was by a local hyperrealist who did gleaming oils of drag-racing cars. Those were just coming down.

"Devin's looking for you," Mick said to me, after he'd hung up the phone.

"Well, I'm not crazy to talk to him," I said.

"Lie away," Mick said, and laughed.

The heavy things in the raised ranch were the paintings crowding the walls. There were so many, and some by big names—an Oldenburg cartoon, a Katz oil, a panel by Helen Frankenthaler.

I said, "Mick, I could lend you twenty thousand, you know. Substantially more, in fact. Painlessly. You could travel. You could set yourself up somewhere pretty nice."

"Me?" Mick said. "You're the one who's leaving, baby."

"If," I said.

"If what? No ifs. My house, you're out."

"If you think you can keep it up," I said.

"Don't judge me by my parents," Mick said. "I can pull my own oars in this world."

Mick either never understood or he never believed how much I liked his parents. Elise was close to loving, whatever that meant anymore. I didn't remember my own mother. Long, long ago she had died.

The Palmetto

The couple ahead of me kept their reading lights on through the night until dawn. I wasn't disturbed, but almost grateful I was awake for the night ride.

I saw, by a linesman's shed, a lot of finely chewed sawdust on the ground. We drove over a gorge on a rickety-seeming trestle. The train was late. The South American man was talking. "Could you please speed it up?" his woman friend asked him.

"Quantico!" our porter called out.

My High School Art Teacher

Mr. Lee was the nearest thing I had to a best friend, but I wanted to shake him now with all the strength in my arms and scream, "Wake up!"

"Don't disturb him. He mustn't be awakened at this time of day. Please. The living room," whispered Mr. Lee's housemate.

We both stared at the sleeping form in the blue wash of light from the bedside clock radio.

The housemate was a thin, neat man in a gauze shirt and straw sandals. There were crow's-feet by his eyes, but he was as soft-haired as a preteen.

We moved out of the bedroom. "You don't know. I have to leave town soon!" I said.

"That may be, but why tell us?" asked the housemate.

"Because. It's necessary to say good-bye to *someone.*"

"Look," the housemate said kindly, mildly, in the tones of total understanding. "If it's come down to Lee, you should just go."

A Visit from Mick's Folks

Mick's arms were all chigger-bit. The scent of his cologne seemed so thick now, it renewed my headache.

"Tell the truth. Are the twins going somewhere?" I asked. I had heard their voices, coming animatedly from upstairs.

"You're going somewhere," Mick said.

Our bulldog crept under the dining table, where we were. The table was a collapsible kind, on casters. The dog was hiding from the beckonings of Mick's mom and dad, who were in the next room, pretending ignorance of us and interest in art magazines.

"Then they'll come with me, and enroll in schools up North," I said.

"They'll visit you up North. Eventually."

Later, before I closed the bedroom door on Mick, he asked, "Why'd you have to take them to Mr. Lee's? Let alone their meeting Devin."

"I figured you'd be hurt. It's too bad you found out," I said. "I just couldn't stop myself from showing them off." I meant *any* of them—Hallie, Susan, Mr. Lee, Devin.

Two Steps Forward, Two Steps Back

The faucets in the new place gave the coldest water I ever felt from a tap. And the rooms were appealing shapes—not all square. Bushes of bittersweet grew like mad against the edifice.

Entertainment most evenings was dancing with Devin to jump versions of old songs. He called me his heart tonight. He used the French word *coeur.*

I watched a Richard Burton movie on the tiny Quasar, had a snack of toast and well-chilled beer. There was a street map for here, wonderfully thorough, that I had scheduled to study. Instead, I chatted with my own twin, Fran, over the phone. At first, this was punishing for me. My situation revealed failure in at least two of my biggest roles. But Fran said, "Relax. Modify and revise your plan, is all. You try to be a hundred things, you're bad at all of them, no?"

"Time to learn to swim?" I said, and I could hear her smile through her answer: "Probably." Between us, learning to swim meant not asking others to buoy us up and keep us safe.

A bronzed reproduction of Degas's *The Spanish Dancer* had arrived at last—a nostalgic doll for me. Also delivered was a photo collage that the twins had made. It had pictures of a living crocodile and the bait shops at Nags Head, and some artsy snapshots of dried swamp grass.

I would sleep on my stomach now, without a pillow, and with no sustained thoughts. I wanted what I wanted. Before bed, I had read stories with I-narrators who could've been me.

22

The Wellman Twins

"You never lie to me," Bluey wrote before the nose of his cedar pencil snapped. He shrugged, reread the page. He had meant to come off as someone firm, plain-minded, blunt; someone deliberate. He thought in the past he had too often seemed moony and fragile.

He was on his hip, on the discreet floor matting. He was comfortable, with his elbow buried in a cushion he had filched from the great couch. He lay near a box speaker—one of six that was wired into the house sound system. The song that raged was "Take Her," a twenty-minute song with locomotive rhythms, done by an English band called Island of Agathas.

Bluey thought the music might warm him into his new attitude.

He kept his writings, his "Letters to Ivy," in a loose binder that was now so fat you needed two wide rubber bands to keep it square and manageable. There were seventy letters, something in the region of five hundred sheets. He wanted to finish this latest one with a lie. But his pencil was broken and, besides, the lie was so ill conceived it dissolved in Bluey's mind even as he was trying to frame it in words: "So I'll tell you. I've met a girl who is lovely, who is a model, who is much older, who is much younger, but wise, and a mermaid in the moonlit breakers. . . ."

There was noise at the front door—calling and banging. The family dog left his toy, a cherry-red plastic mouse, and went to answer. Bluey followed, shutting up the Island of Agathas as he passed the turntable.

He opened one of the double doors to Greer, his twin sister, whose arms were busy with a nylon tote, a cased viola, a bottle of champagne, and a fountain of sweet rocket—flowers that were fitted into a tissue-paper cone. She had knee-thumped the door.

"At last!" she said, and, "Guess what? Sixty-seven tax-free dollars I made! So there!"

"Yeah, but you spent it on flowers and wine, right?" Bluey said.

"Up yours," Greer said.

She was a street musician, or had been recently. She played to the lunch crowds in Newport. This was instead of having a real summer job, though neither twin had to work just yet. They were provided for by their mother, who was provided for by the life insurance, the stock portfolio, and the investment planning of her late husband, the twins' father. He was Wellman of Wellman's Valve in Kingston, Rhode Island. He had never seen his children. He had died during his wife's pregnancy.

The twins were one-month alumni of U.R.I., where they had graduated without honors, but had both been pre-med, and had both been accepted at University of Maine's medical school.

"You're not really wearing all that eyebrow makeup. Tell me I'm seeing things," Bluey said.

"Lemme by," Greer said. "Goddamn it, Deuce, stop!"

Deuce the retriever was bounding at Greer. Bluey hooked the dog's choke collar with a finger and took the champagne bottle from his sister with his free hand. He let Greer pass, though he gave her a look of impatience.

Greer went right, to the kitchen.

Bluey tapped the dog's flat head very lightly with the bottle. "You get peaceful, I'm warning," Bluey said, and then loosed the dog and went Greer's way.

ㄑ

She was whistling, already stacking together a sandwich of raw vegetables on protein bread.

"What do you do, comb your hair with a scissors?" Bluey said. "And what's with the survival wear?"

Greer was in a shirt with a camouflage pattern. The shirt had deep pockets and long sleeves that were turned back in big rolls over her delicate arms.

"Is that sandwich for you? It looks like rodent food. It looks like you're making it for a gerbil or a ground chuck."

Greer said, "You don't mean a ground chuck. Where's the clover honey, please? Ground chuck is meat. You mean a wood-chuck or a groundhog. Maybe a hedgehog."

"I mean it looks too dry for a human being to swallow— and, wow, will Mother do a back flip when she sees your *hair*."

The twins' mother was having her summer in Hawaii, in a time-share condo she had bought into.

"Are you listening at all, Greer?"

"Go be someplace else. Give me my booze," Greer said.

Bluey did, but said, "You're lucky you're still young. Soon your body won't be able to metabolize these ungodly amounts of alcohol."

"Oh, spare us. I'm allowed to celebrate."

Bluey remembered the letter he had been writing and hurried to put it away.

Deuce was in the parlor, coiled on the center seat of the mammoth couch. "You're not serious," Bluey said to him. Deuce beat his tail and ducked his head.

"Leave *him* alone, too!" Greer shouted.

Bluey took his notebook and new pages to his room—what had once been his father's study and at-home office. The walls were tacked over with blank watercolor paper, which was Bluey's idea, and the furniture was white-painted cane. Matchstick blinds screened the window light. Bluey propped a side chair under the knob of his lockless door.

꙰

Deuce was allowing his haunches to be used as a pillow for Greer's head. They were on the sofa—both drunk, Bluey decided.

"Good. Savor the fruits of your labor. I am jealous, I guess. Not about the money, but of the nerve you must have to stand up and perform in front of an audience. Real people who can react—good or bad—right there to your face. Did you give Deuce some Mumm's?"

"Oui," Greer said.

"Congratulations on the sixty-seven dollars," Bluey said.

"Who's this different person from an hour ago, Deuce? Do we know this guy?" Greer asked the dog.

"I like your clothes, too. I like the fatigue pants," Bluey said.

Greer did a leg raise. "These pants fought in the D.M.Z."

"Aha," Bluey said.

"Also, did you know Deuce has a girly friend? Yes, he does. She came calling while you were—whatever you were doing. Getting sweet. She's a demure red spaniel."

"Unh," said Bluey, sounding defeated and far away.

"Say, if you're at loose ends . . ." Greer said.

"No, I just feel weird."

"Well, I was going to suggest you build a nice hangover like me and Deuce are doing. It's all right. We're twenty-one, all of us."

The sky had pinked up nicely in the west, was going gray in the east. The twins were on the high back deck, playing canasta on a picnic bench with X-shaped legs. The view behind them, over a kind of porch of leaves, was of nice houses like theirs.

The next lawn was big like a playing field, and it tilted steeply down. A bare-chested man was fighting the grade, shoving a green mower. His shirt was tied to the mower's handlebars.

"That's Bing," Greer told Bluey. "Bing Litzinger and his grinding machine kept me from napping, and not only that but Buh-Buh-Bing will get all the insects moving from over there to over here. Yes, he will. Triste but true."

"Knock off the French," Bluey said.

"Oh, no, Deuce, Bluey the crank is back. Hey, where is Deuce?"

"I let him run," Bluey said.

Greer jumped from the table, went indoors, and was gone for a while. Bluey, wearing only swim trunks and a baseball cap, shuffled the cards as if they could warm him. He heard his sister's shrieking whistle from the side of the house. Finally, Greer was back, carrying clothes.

"Dog's gone forever. Probably eloped," she said. "Here. These'll ruin your bad mood." She traded Bluey's cap for one of her straw picture hats. Its brim was enormous. She wrapped a long scarf at Bluey's neck, telling him, "You were cold." She draped his black blazer over his shoulders.

"God, I wish you'd sober down," he said.

"Paging Dr. Wellman," Greer said. "You're wanted in Pre-Op. Stat. Code Blue."

"Dr. Wellman, you're wanted in Detox," Bluey said.

Greer sat and dealt. As she fanned her cards, she nodded agreeably, acknowledging each one.

Bluey watched her, re-aimed his gaze, fidgeted. He said, "I'm sorry, I can't stand this." He plucked the straw hat off and sailed it over the deck rail. "Why am I so jittery?"

"It's all right," Greer said. "We'll get bold. I've got some great things stored away."

Getting bold was the twins' name—a name thought up when they were younger—for a session of truth-telling.

"Let's crowd the last available boundaries of decency and privacy," Greer said.

"Yeah, trample 'em," said Bluey.

"O.K., I'll start. I read your letters to Ivy," Greer said. "Good start?" she added after a minute.

Bluey kept a long silence, and his eyes, Greer could see even in the dimming light, blinked too much.

"Well, I'll never forgive you. I can't imagine forgiving you," he said at last.

"Naturally. Way to play."

Bluey said, "I've got to get Deuce."

"I'll wait. No, change that. I'll wait inside," Greer said.

Bluey went barefooted down the deck steps, walking a little sideways to avoid splinters. He ducked through a five-tree orchard of crab apple his father had once devised.

Bluey was slapping at mosquitoes when he saw the flash of the dog's silky coat, and then he saw Deuce pile out of tall grass and galumph into Bing Litzinger's yard. The dog lifted himself onto the birdbath there and drank.

Bluey was sneaking up on him when Litzinger, who had finished mowing, came from his house.

"Get him out!" Litzinger called.

"I'm trying, damn it," Bluey said. The dog bucked at the sound of Bluey's voice and sprinted in a meaningless circle.

"There's a leash law. I can't have a dog in the yard," Litzinger said. He watched the contest as Bluey tried to capture Deuce. The dog was taunting, getting just beyond reach, his butt raised up, his front legs flat on the grass.

"I know your mother," Litzinger warned before heading back to his house.

﹏

Greer was in the kitchen, wearing the picture hat that she said she had climbed over the deck to retrieve. She was eating a bran muffin and a cup of lemon yogurt.

Bluey had dragged Deuce with him. The dog's nails scraped on the polished floor. His tail was stuffed down, his ears back.

"You're *still* purple with rage," Greer said to Bluey. "Why don't you crash a dish or two?"

Bluey freed the dog, straightened, removed a brandy bottle from a cupboard. The ship calendar on the cupboard door flapped. Bluey measured out a full glass. "They do this in movies," he said, and tried to drink it all. He couldn't manage even a full swallow.

"They probably have their stand-ins do it," Greer said.

Bluey gasped and breathed for a bit. He said, "Okay, where were we? Ivy, the girl I write to, I met at an Iggy Pop concert. You couldn't know her; she didn't go to school with us. She lives in Boston. We were both high when we met. I, you know, liked her. Really, tremendous . . . "

"Got it," Greer said.

"I thought we were high. So we agreed, after that night, we'd keep in touch. Next day, phone call from her. I was very flattered. But the thing being, she *wasn't* high the night before. She's always like that. Babbling. She's probably got maybe a brain tumor or a limbic disorder. She thinks her brother had something to do with killing Lennon. That kind of thing. I mean, I liked her for her looks, but what's the use?"

"Bluey, this all sounds like a lie. One of your lies," Greer said.

"So who I'm writing to is sort of Ivy, but sort of not, and what would be the point of mailing the letters? Most of all, they're for me."

"Well, that's a violently unpleasant story if it's true," Greer said in a summarizing tone. "Now. What've you got to crush me with?"

The dog, under the table, charged Greer's shoe—a pale moccasin. She crossed her ankles in halfhearted defense.

"Nothing," Bluey said.

"Don't be cruel," Greer said.

"I have nothing for you. Live with that one, Greer."

"Go ahead and gnaw off the whole heel. What the hell," Greer said to Deuce.

"Except this," Bluey said. "Mom told it to me, though it doesn't mean much. You were not expected. You were not prepared for. Your body was behind mine—in the womb, I mean. Shadowing mine. Our father died and never even knew you were there. Now I'm sorry I told you," Bluey said.

"No, don't be. I think it's interesting what's going on. You hoped I'd feel unwanted?"

"Somewhat. To pay you back for reading my letters," Bluey said.

"My, my," Greer said, and sighed.

Eventually she said, "I don't think you're playing this game well at all, Bluey. I mean, I don't know which lie is bigger—Ivy of Boston or the shadow in the womb."

"Hey," Bluey said, alarmed.

"Or *my* lie. I never read your letters. Relax. I never saw them but for the 'Letters to Ivy' title."

"You didn't read them? Never even looked through them?"

"Nope," Greer said.

"Well, someday you were going to get to. You were supposed to," Bluey said.

"Look at what the moonlight's doing to the grape trellis," Greer said. "Out the window."

"You hear me? The letters are to you," Bluey said.

"You didn't have anyone else to write to?" Greer said. She touched her sternum.

"No one else to write to," Bluey echoed.

Greer pressed back in her chair seat, her neck stiffening. She spoke slowly and purposefully, as though Bluey were a stranger. "Then I shall read them. Sometime. Whenever it is to your liking."

"No, forget it. I don't think so," Bluey said.

"Well, were you sort of kidding about their being written to me?" Greer asked.

"They aren't to anybody, really. Or they're to every girl. Only I don't deeply know any other girl. They're to a fantasy I have in my brain."

"Aw, Bluey, wait a while," Greer said. "Lots of things could change for you. It doesn't seem like it, but they've got to, don't they?" Greer said. "Don't they?"

23

Mirror

EHIND US WERE COUNTERS with cool basins and cabinets framed with white or amber bulbs. There was overhead, overbright lighting as well. And music—piped from somewhere above—to which Lolly kept time with her duck boot. We were side by side in swivel chairs, at a hair salon near the Watergate.

I asked Lolly what was so absorbing in her magazine—a young women's thing, with frantic announcements about dreams and skin tone on the cover.

"This asinine survey," she said indignantly. "'What Women Want Most in a Man.' Can you believe it? Intelligence is ranked fourth here, behind security and good eyes. An athletic build is number one."

"Yeah, prizefighters," I said, and sighed happily.

"You're as bad as they are," Lolly said.

In the mirrors, my eyes looked fierce beneath straight black brows, which were like charcoal strokes. My lips are dark naturally, but here they looked stained by red wine.

"Hopeless," Lolly said with sudden affection.

Our heads were prickly with perm curlers. We were draped in blue plastic ponchos with fresh cotton shoulder bibs on top. Under her poncho, Lolly wore careful layers of expensive clothes. Her ears, with their gold dot earrings, were worried pink at the lobes. We are longtime friends. We went from kindergarten all the way through Potomac Senior together, in Baltimore. We graduated at the same time, four years ago. I live in Boston, but I'd been visiting Lolly in Washington lately, camping at her place in Foggy Bottom—a third-floor two-roomer on H Street.

"My head tickles," she said. "Is yours burning? I think they're making us keep our curlers in too long."

"Oh, yikes," I said.

Lolly ejected from her swivel chair, leaving it wiggling.

"Where are you going?" I said to her back.

She stalked across the deep main space and headed through one of the enameled doors at the back—the washroom, I guessed.

Aside from a few snipping sessions, I hadn't had my hair really cut since I was fifteen. I had kept it side-parted—a straight veil about my face. I didn't think my hair needed a professional to tangle it. Today's hair job was Lolly's idea and her treat. "To thin your hair, but give it a fluffier look, with more body," she told me severely. She knew I'd always preferred to mow my own split ends.

"Things in D.C. are all right—trustworthy, the best next to New York," she said. "You wouldn't let a Baltimorean *near* your hair." Since she'd moved to Washington, she took responsibility for everything about it. She was proud of this but embarrassed too.

Now I was looking around, panicky. The salon's walls had a pink-and-black wallpaper, with many gold French poodles descending a winding staircase. All the hairdressers were up at the front of the salon, in a conference of some kind. I tried to lose myself in Lolly's magazine. I went through it once and then, caught by nothing, started again with the first article: "Envy—What It Does to *You*."

This was Christmas season, a wintry day. The salon was full of noisy customers, chattering, knitting, thumbing paperbacks. More women arrived, in furs, mufflers, and galoshes. They carried shopping bags stuffed with varnished red paper and glinting foil. One woman I could hear was saying she had just spotted Baryshnikov over at the Star Market. "He was in floor-length sable," the woman said. "I swear it."

There was a blonde child loose. She was two or three years old, dressed in a doll's version of the salon's livery—a tiny smock and nylon trousers. She came stumpily over to me and offered a round complexion sponge pad.

"My friend's missing," I told the little girl, who fitted the sponge into her mouth and left.

Lolly returned by and by. "Hi," she said cheerfully.

"Is it O.K. you didn't take out the curler rods?" I said. "That's good? It means our hair isn't getting scorched?"

"I was once here with my father," Lolly said absently. "I mean, here in D.C., of course. Father took me to dinner in Georgetown. This was over ten years ago, when we were in middle school. Anyway, Father saw John Mitchell in the restaurant where we were eating. Mitchell had been sick and he looked like the air had been let out of his face, although he was dressed in a very nice cashmere topcoat when he came in."

Lolly hoisted herself into her chair and swung sideways to face me. "Father said, 'Sweetheart, that's John Mitchell,' and I said, 'Who is John Mitchell?'"

"Was everything O.K., Lolly?" I said. "Are our heads all right?"

"Yeah," Lolly said. "On that same night, in the ladies' room in the same restaurant, written on the mirror there in crimson lipstick was 'If you're looking for the future, you're looking in the right place.'"

"Why is my scalp on fire?" I asked. I patted the spiky rollers. "What do I smell burning?"

"You won't believe this," Lolly went on, "but the same woman just wrote the same thing in *this* washroom. Whoever she is. I mean, she could be here with us today."

Lolly and I peered around.

I said, "Seriously, Lolly, could something be going wrong with my hair? Am I going to come out of this with a Mamie Eisenhower?"

"Possibly," Lolly said. "I think I should have told them I'm pregnant. It can make a difference as to what chemicals they dump on you."

"I'm worried," I said.

Lolly was slumped low on her spine now. She stretched her legs and yawned expansively. "I was just kidding. You're completely fine," she said.

The hairdressers' team conference had broken up. A man with Inca features and a brown line of beard came over to us.

"All is well? Very bored?" he asked. He checked his gold wristwatch. The watch was nestled in several gold wrist chains. "Soon now," he said.

"Good, Kenny," Lolly said. Her eyes were closed.

"I'm glad I brought up the subject of the baby," she said when Kenny had drifted on. "What's your opinion of Doug, really?" Doug was the father. He and Lolly weren't married. They weren't even dating anymore.

I studied my fingers, frowning some.

"Come on, tell me—it's O.K.," she said. Her head bent forward. She was trying to get me to look at her. "He's not husband material, is he?"

"He wouldn't be for me," I said.

"So that's out," Lolly said. "One down, out of several big decisions."

"Do you *want* a child, here and now?" I said. "On your income?"

Lolly's job was clerical, at the Library of Congress.

"Next year I'll be a G.S. three," she said. "And besides, money isn't quite at issue, thanks to my folks." She had pushed back in her seat and thrown one long leg over the other. She was in the earnest posture of a talk-show host. "My mother and father could shelter us nicely and do a lot of the work, and they'd probably love it. The routine *and* the baby."

I was considering the other people in the shop. "Maybe the lipstick writer is one of the help," I said. "Maybe a manicurist."

"I think my father would especially enjoy a grandchild. My little sister would get to be an aunt."

"The help?" I said. "Did I just say 'the help'? See how you get me talking?"

"Two different worlds," Lolly said. She was mopey-sounding and hurt.

"I'm sorry. It's just—do you know how stupid I feel right now in this stuff? I can't discuss anything, looking like this, let alone something like your entire future life!"

Lolly seemed appeased. After a moment, she said, "I've thought about that lipstick message once a week, at least, every week of my life. And now here it is again."

"Well, people are funny," I said.

Lolly had reclaimed her magazine. She dabbed her thumb, with its steep lacquered nail, on her tongue and swished through pages. She said, "Yeah, like who'd guess from your appearance that you're a life model?"

A woman three chairs down tilted forward to stare at me.

"I would think that, even for some of those college guys, you're the first woman they've seen up close completely noodle," Lolly said.

One of my jobs is to model nude for the Francis Scott Key College adult-education evening art classes.

I put my hand on the razor ad in Lolly's magazine. "This is the last time I'll explain it to you," I said. "For me, the work is like an athletic event. It's an endurance test. For the students in the class, I'm a headache, an equation to be solved. I'm their homework."

"I know," Lolly said, and I could tell she wanted me to calm my voice.

"One guy actually said he wished I'd gain weight, so there'd be less anatomy to draw and more volume," I went on. "He said he does better with volume."

"Easy—just get pregnant," Lolly said.

I began to loosen my curler rods. "I want these out," I said.

"You cannot!" Lolly said. "They have a special way of removing those. You could end up bald."

The hairdresser, Kenny, hurried over. I was undoing the curlers and uncoiling damp squiggly hair. He started dripping neutralizer onto the curls I had undone. He said, "You pay anyway. I mean that emphatically."

"Attention!" I said to the room. "Who wrote that message on the bathroom mirror? Who of you here did that?"

✍

We were going along Pennsylvania in a cab. Bits of snow, like flecks of paper ash, blurred the view. The avenue was hectic but festive with snow.

"You're not talking," I said.

"I'm so angry," Lolly said. Her lips were pursed. "You know I'm not a conformist, but still. Do you have to be so stubborn, always making a statement? I think of looking attractive as a favor to others. I do it out of respect for my fellow beings. It's considerate toward them."

I put a kind of half-nelson on Lolly, who was horrified until she realized I was being friendly—that the grip was an embrace. "When did you become a little teacup?" I asked her.

"I was paying for your new look," she said, laughing. "I wanted to see how you'd turn out."

The cab dropped me on H Street, at Lolly's apartment building. She was going off to lunch with Doug, to discuss her pregnancy and, more likely, to hear more about Doug's never-ending struggle to get graduated from G.W.

"I'm sorry," I said, leaning in through the open cab door to look at her.

"*You're* sorry," Lolly said. "Jesus, you just go back to Boston—problemless, unfettered. I'm here with nothing and no one, and I need so much help. I need you, for instance."

The cab took off abruptly, and I was left with the impression of Lolly's scared and beautiful face.

The lobby of her building had a lot of silvered glass, and marble the color of tangerines. I had forgotten to get Lolly's key, and I sat down in a waiting area on one of the cushioned pews that made a ring around a fountain. The fountain's bowl and cherub wore garlands of pine, and strands of Christmas bulbs were wound into the garlands. A tiny white nylon fir tree, hung with blue bulbs, stood in the corner between the switchboard closet and a wall of brass mailboxes. The switchboard area was watched by an attendant-doorman who had the looks of a wrestler. He had refused to take me up to Lolly's apartment and let me in.

I was glaring at him now, as I went into my second hour on the pew. "Come on, mister," I said.

He was reading a newspaper. His face had a burnt-red color, as if he had been out in the cold, which he hadn't. The ledge of his brow jutted out into a prominence that shaded his tiny eyes.

"Come *on*," I said. "You know me. You've seen me with Lolly a hundred times."

"You bother me again and I call the cops," the guy said. "It's not me locking you out, it's policy."

"You're a scary guy," I said.

I had gotten tired of my own reflection, which was coming at me from three directions. My hair clutched at my temples and neck; I couldn't get it to hang down. My substance seemed to have left me, and it was as though my body had become an armature supporting my coat and clothes. And I was hungry.

"You shouldn't be here anyway, this long in a private lobby," he said. "Go find yourself a grating. Outside."

I went through my wallet, discarding a visitor's pass to the Senate, which I'd never use, a note sheet of directions to someone's house near Rock Creek Park, and the worn end of an emery board. I let these things drop onto the rug by my shoe. With a pencil I made a few notes in the margin of a comic page in the *Post,* after I had read "Judge Parker" and "Rex Morgan, M.D." It was a little list about Lolly and me.

"Is that your mess?" the attendant said when he noticed. "I say to you, Is that your mess on the floor? Because I'm dialing the police." When he stood up he looked bloated. His belly sloped out well beyond the belt line of his uniform trousers. "For all I know, you're plotting a robbery," he said. "I don't want any company on my job here all evening. I'm working, see, no matter how it looks to you. If you belonged, you'd have a key. If you were supposed to be here, I'd know it."

With each of these pronouncements, I nodded my head yes or no, mocking him.

"I'm saying stop that. Fair warning."

I kept thinking of Lolly's apartment, just three floors above. It was a beginner's place, mostly—neat and bookless.

"I'm culturally bereft," Lolly had told me once. But there were fresh sheets, taut on her double bed. There was a glazed dish of Granny Smith apples on the Formica kitchen counter. There were draperies that Lolly had lined and sewn herself, from fabric she got at Laura Ashley. There was a clay pot containing a four-foot avocado plant. There was, on a shelf, a collection of stuffed pandas. Each bear was pristine; two were still in cellophane, and Lolly had displayed the boxes for the bears that came in a box.

I knocked off taunting the attendant and said, "So O.K., I'm sorry I bothered you. I'll pick up the papers."

"That's all I wanted, pick up," he said. "How am I supposed to know who you are?"

"That's true. And it's actually good that you're vigilant."

"Whatever that means," he said. "Are you sticking around for your friend? I have to know."

I was collecting the stuff from my wallet. I told him yes. I thought how his question and my answer had two meanings. I had decided—back in the cab, I realized—to stick around at least a little longer.

The list I made analyzing Lolly and me said that we were both waiting for something, that we had both been lucky and spoiled, and that we expected a lot. We thought alike sometimes. We remembered the same stuff. We were used to each other and could still be a help to each other. Of use.

I went over to the revolving doors. What snow there was had been chased from the street by the wind. A Federal Express truck slid up. The uniformed driver was rushing a package into the building across the street. The pink sodium-vapor light, from all the D.C. streetlamps, gave the sky a hopeful blush, as if it were not twilight.

24

Care

BARBARA LED LEAH THROUGH a coalyard to behind the elementary school. "Now look at that," Barbara said. "It's human." She pointed into the cinders at a blade of bone studded with teeth.

"That's from a cow," Leah said.

"No," Barbara said, shaking her head. The back and shoulders of her coat were soaked with dissolved snow.

"Well, I guess I ought to ask you about Jack," Leah said. She kicked a coal chip at one of the school's caged windows.

"I refuse to see him," Barbara said. "We're separated, as I'm sure you heard. We've been separated four months." She was still staring at the bone. "For a lot of good reasons. One is that I found this in his tool drawer." She opened her coat and showed a nickel-plated handgun tucked in at the waistband of her skirt.

Leah said, "Jack is the one person who shouldn't keep a revolver."

"He's so much worse since you've been gone," Barbara said. "My dad thinks it's because Jack reads so much. You know who Jack always liked, though?" Barbara leaned over and snapped one of the buckles on her galoshes. "Your sister, Bobby."

"Yes, I think he really did," Leah said. She sighed, and turned the shard of bone with the toe of her shoe. "You can tell him Bobby's wonderful. Just remarkable. She takes a lot of speed still. She's chewed a nice hole in her lip."

"Bobby's disturbed," Barbara said. "You can tell that just from the way she walks."

Leah blinked at a tiny maroon car that was circling the playground, and Barbara said, "That's Jack, and I'm leaving." She turned up her coat collar and ran away along a narrow alley that edged the back of the schoolhouse.

"Now wait just a minute!" Leah called.

"I will not see him!" Barbara called back before she disappeared around the corner of the school's library annex.

Jack drove his car onto the playground and hit the brakes when he had pulled up beside Leah. "My wife moves pretty good whenever I'm around," he said. His face was chapped red with cold under his watch cap. He used his coat sleeve to scrape at a rust scab on the car door. "I heard you were back in town."

Leah got into the car. She said, "What have you done to Barbara?"

"My wife is just afraid of me," Jack said.

"Afraid?"

"Um-hmm," Jack said. A block away, his car began to shimmy as if it might explode. A waxed cup full of cigar butts slid off the dashboard and into Leah's lap.

Jack laughed and clicked a fingernail on the windshield, where a helicopter was wading into view.

"What do they want?" Leah yelled over the terrible beating of the machine.

The copter bobbed directly overhead, then canted off toward the lake.

"Not us," Jack said.

He bought lunch for them at a grocery cafeteria. Leah put her feet up on the seat of the vinyl booth, and watched out the bank of windows. The room smelled of warm food and of the laundered cotton blotters under the casserole trays.

Jack said, "Look at the snow flying." He nodded at the window.

But Leah saw a boy go by, pushing another boy in a shopping cart on the icy parking lot. The boy in the cart sucked cigarette smoke into his nose, and adjusted a dial on the plastic radio he was holding.

"Want to hear what I've been thinking about you?" Jack said, turning to Leah.

"Sure do," she said.

"I've decided that Europe didn't change you," Jack said, "like I hoped it would. You still want for something, as if somewhere you've been robbed."

"What have I been robbed of?" Leah said.

"Something important," Jack said. He spilled soda into his mouth. "The crux, the thrust of what—as I see it—is going on with you. And I'm talking about your whole life, not just here this afternoon." He grinned. "I mean it," he said. "What you oughtn't to be afraid of is a little more rarefied stratum, Leah. One thing I learned about being young is that there's a kind of purity of insight. You know? For example, right now I could decide to be a proletarian, a laborer, an artist, an executive." He was counting the possibilities off on his spread fingers. "But I wouldn't be you."

"I'm sorry you feel that way," Leah said. She munched ice from the rim of her water glass.

"Because," Jack said, "you're just walking it through. Just saying your lines and walking it all through. My wife is the same way."

"What way?" Leah said.

"Scared," Jack said.

"What of?"

Jack fit a piece of meat loaf into his mouth. He said, "I haven't any idea."

***

Jack plowed his car into a five-foot cone of dead leaves in front of Leah's father's house. Leah's father, Sweet, grinned widely and banged on the hood of his Lawn-Boy. He was driving snow off his parking spaces with a blade, and hauling a steel utility cart in which Leah's little sister, Bobby, reclined, smoking a Russian cigarette. "Park it up the street," Sweet yelled, glowing and glad for company.

Bobby pulled herself from the utility cart and came over to Jack's car. "You slept on your hair wrong," she told Leah. She threw down her cigarette. She wet her fingers and crammed a curl behind Leah's ear.

"Don't do that," Leah said.

"Jack!" Bobby said. She leaned in the car window and almost spit her chewing gum. "I just had a birthday. Guess how old I am. I'm twenty-two."

Sweet climbed down from his tractor. He yelled, "I'm going inside now for dry socks."

Leah moved Bobby and got out of the car. She brushed a ball of ash from her lap and then she walked up the snow-sopped lawn. "Wet," she said, touching the lip of the postbox. "The same color Sweet painted his station wagon."

"The same color he's painting everything," Bobby said, chewing. "Including my bicycle. Don't mess with the mailbox, Leah. Sweet'll kill you."

✕

"But I'll tell you where the big money is," Sweet said, leading Leah into Bobby's bedroom. Sweet had been trimming baseboards and patching nail pops in the family den, and he was still dressed in working whites, his hands and face flecked with spackle. "Spraying high-rises. Just get a masking pattern cut for you, and a pump, of course, and you can go in there with a gun in each hand and your eyes closed. At fifteen hundred dollars a floor, you figure the numbers." Sweet stared at the blotter on Bobby's desk for a minute, then he picked up her wood-burning kit.

"What're you going to do with that?" Leah said.

"I don't know," Sweet said. "Make something."

They studied Bobby's closet door, where a collage of photos and cutouts was pushpinned. In one of the pictures, Bobby's boyfriend, Doug, was poking from an Army tank. There was a clipping about J. Paul Getty's grandson getting his ear sawed off. Bobby had one of Leah's sketches tacked up. It was a pen-and-ink on vellum, of a girl balanced tightrope-style on a strand of wire fencing.

Sweet squinted at the sketch and said, "A high-school friend of mine knew how to draw. He's worth a hell of a lot of money now. He's a sign painter, and he raises Afghan dogs. Which made him rich. One bitch alone gives him thirty-eight pups. At three hundred fifty dollars a dog, you figure it out."

They had moved into Leah's room. Sweet leaned on his elbow, which rested between two ceramic birds on the clothes dresser. "I'm proud of this room," he said. "I tried to keep the walls nice while you were away."

Bobby came in carrying a shopping bag. She pinched off her rubber boot and emptied water from it into a terrarium that sat in a dying spray of light at the window. "Watch," she said, as a lump of slush dropped from inside the boot and spattered dirt and moss on the terrarium walls.

She sat on the end of the bed and opened the string handles of her shopping bag. "I bought a puzzle for Doug," she said. She showed a box, which was still tight in plastic wrap. "It's Niagara Falls."

⤬

Leah sat with Sweet, warming their knees before the opened gas oven. Sweet turned a wet-looking blue porcelain jug in his hands. "I think your mother wanted you to have this," he said, "after me."

"It's nice," Leah said.

"It is nice, isn't it?" Sweet said. "It's from the war."

Bobby was bent over the kitchen counter, banging the counter surface with her fist every time the coffeepot perked. She had a transistor radio plug stuffed in one ear and she was shouting a little. She said, "So a friend of Doug's offers him a hundred dollars for his motorcycle, and Doug's license is suspended for two more years anyway. Right?" She splashed coffee into a shallow cup and used it to wash down a capsule from a tinfoil wad she kept in her pocket. "But will he take it? No."

Sweet shifted his position in the folding chair and coughed through his nose. He said, "*War of the Worlds* is on tonight."

"I've seen it," Leah said. "Anyway, I'll be gone. I'm staying at my girlfriend Barbara's. Remember her?"

"The one that married Jack," Sweet said. "And didn't poor Jack get skinny? I thought he was your cousin Caroline at first."

Leah said, "Jack tells me I'm just walking through life. He says I ought to start changing."

"Could be," Sweet said. "How are you supposed to change?"

"I don't know. He wouldn't tell me," Leah said. "Incidentally, he's going back to school, he thinks. To Yale, in Connecticut."

"I know where Yale is," Sweet said.

Doug appeared at the side door holding a white sack of hamburgers and a bottle of Rock & Rye. "Remember the guy I told you about who was called Grandma?" he said to Bobby.

"The Polish guy," Bobby said. "About three and a half feet."

"That's him," Doug said. "He got blowed up when they were dropping bottom today. He flew all the way across the foundry and landed in the aluminum furnace."

Bobby crossed the room on her toes and gave Doug a kiss. "I was telling them how that guy at the Shell station is always expressing his interest in your bike."

"Forget it, Bobby," Doug said. He dumped the hamburgers out on the kitchen table. "That bike's worth fifteen hundred dollars."

"Then don't cry to me when it rusts," Bobby said.

"Listen," Doug said, putting a pickle slice on his tongue, "I'd give it away before I'd take a hundred dollars."

Around midnight, Leah saw Jack drop over the chest-high cyclone fence. He crossed the yard, and then she could hear him letting himself into the house, where she and Barbara were in bed. Leah propped herself against the headboard and tried to wake up Barbara.

"Go away," Barbara said through her pillow.

Jack opened the bedroom door and stepped into the room. His dark hair and eyelashes and his gloves and raincoat were wet, and his glasses had fogged over in the wet wind. He said, "It smells like furniture polish in here."

Leah said, "Shh. These are rich people."

"My own rich mother-in-law is lying on the floor in the next room," Jack said, "with a stack of magazines for a pillow, and a cocktail shaker still floating with ice cubes in her hand."

"What?" Leah said. "Is she kidding?"

"I forgot to ask," Jack said. He went to the glass back wall of Barbara's room. "Whitecaps," he said, "all over the lake, and the sky's full of snow." He came back beside the bed and settled into a beer-colored chair. He took out a thin green cigar and set fire to it. "I liked you better," he said, holding the burning stick match over his head and squinting at Leah, "when you had hair."

"You worry me," she said. Sleep and the cold night were in her voice. "Look at how much you're sweating."

Jack waved out the match and picked up a pair of rough wool trousers from the end of the bed. "Who does your tailoring?"

"In Italy," Leah said. She shook Barbara, who wouldn't turn over.

"Leah, what a lovely back you've got," Jack said.

She said, "You came to talk to Barbara, I think, so I'll leave."

Jack started to cry.

"Damn it," Barbara said. She got up and walked on the bed, and went naked into the bathroom. Jack threw his cigar after her. Lighted ash showered into the carpet. A drop of sweat broke on his eyebrow and ran over his chin.

"Because I believe you two should be alone," Leah said.

"Get him out!" Barbara called over the rush of shower water.

Jack pulled his fingers over his cheekbones. He said, "I can't concentrate on anything."

There was noise in the hall. Barbara's father came in. He had a big head and he was wearing dark, expensive clothing. "What is this?" he said.

Jack said to him, "Let me know when you find out."

"I wasn't here," Barbara's father said, nervously. "I've been at a GOP reception for the governor. I was a little drunk, having a pretty good time."

He led Jack from the bedroom. Leah pulled on her wool pants and a tiny sweater of Barbara's and followed the two men to the lighted library. Barbara's mother was up, sitting in a swivel rocker. She was wearing dark glasses, holding a highball in one hand and a pink Kleenex in the other.

"Listen, Jack," Barbara's father said as he threw his body into a deep armchair. His wing tips didn't reach the parqueted floor. He drummed his fingernails on a tray that supported a thirty-cup percolator and clean china cups. "I have a lot of stuff to do. Stuff I'm going to hate like hell doing. Why don't you make some other friends? How about it? Why don't you give Barbara a little breathing space?"

"I didn't come to see Barbara," Jack said. He raised his voice to a shout: "Hey, Barbara, I didn't come to see you!"

❦

Doug was up, laboring over his motorcycle, which he had taken apart on some newspapers on the rug in Sweet's living room. Bobby lay beside him on her stomach. She was drawing on the torn cover of the Niagara puzzle box with a flow pen. "Sweet

broke the furnace again," she said to Leah. "He made it hot."
She stopped drawing and spun the cardboard flap through the
air like a disk toy.

Leah found Sweet watching boxers on television. He had his
shoulders hunched and his elbows raised off his knees to catch
blows. "Number one," he said when Leah came in. He smacked
the sofa cushion for her to sit down. He pressed a tab on the TV
remote control. "Look," he said, nodding at the television. In
the late movie, an eye on a snaking tentacle was searching
through an apartment complex. "You can have that," he said,
and pointed to a tumbler of liquid on the sofa arm. "Bourbon
and branch water on the rocks."

Leah got onto the sofa beside Sweet and started the drink.
During the next commercial Sweet sat forward and snuffed
through his nose. "After the war," he said, "I had a spray-painting
job." He held his hands out as if they were pistols. "Just for weekends, way, way down, one hundred feet in the hulls of ships they
were building. You were on a hairline." He pointed up and
looked at the ceiling. "Hanging there."

Leah looked up, too.

"That was lead paint," Sweet said. "To stick to steel, it must
be lead. You wore a respirator. But I'll tell you, most new men
fell. Because the lead got them. Leave a bucket of lead paint un-
sealed for eight hours"—he clenched his fist—"it goes rock
hard."

"Did you see men fall?" Leah said.

"I had a physical," Sweet said, "once every two weeks, and a
urine analysis. Some men, after a while, couldn't even make water. Plip, plip—pure lead. But I got paid for that work. Your
mother and I lived in Red Hook, on a man's front porch. She
was all right then, but she was going to have a baby."

"That was me," Leah said.

Sweet bagged a foam pillow behind his neck and sat looking at the frostwork on the opened windows. Snow was sailing in, spitting on the heated TV.

"Are you going ice-fishing with me tomorrow?" he said.

"No," Leah said. She put her fingers in her bangs. "Jack's coming by. He's decided to teach me Russian."

"I wish Jack could teach Bobby and Doug regular everyday English," Sweet said. "I've been sitting here listening to them cuss all night, not believing my ears." Sweet yawned with his mouth closed and pulled with his fingers at the white hairs on his throat. "Of course, Bobby's a little girl, really. She's got plenty of time to change."

"I guess so," Leah said. She finished her drink and made a sick face. "What'd you think of what Jack said? That I need to change."

"You? Oh, you never will. You're just your mother all over again," Sweet said. "You don't know friends from enemies and you'll never be able to. When I was taking her to the hospital the last time, do you know what she said? She looked around and saw the tracks she'd made in the snow and said, 'That's good.' And I said, 'What's good?' She said, 'The tracks. They show where I've gone.' And she was right, but not only that: if you ever looked at your mother, you noticed this. You could tell everything she'd been through. You could tell it on her face. Just like yours."

"Oh, great," Leah said.

"No, it's good," her father said. "At least for your mother and you."

25

Doctor's Sons

DICK WAS SITTING AT the kitchen table with his left hand resting flat, fingers spread, on a linen placemat decorated with Coast Guard flags. He was trimming his nails with a pinch clipper and crying. The mustache he had recently grown for his twenty-fifth birthday was wet with tears. He was embarrassed, and his cheeks and throat had the high color of a rash. Mrs. Sorenson, Dick's mother, sat across the kitchen table with a paperback book in her hand. She was humming along with the *Porgy and Bess* tape being piped from a tape deck in the family den.

Dick arched a finger and wiped away a streamer of tears from his cheekbone. He used his fork to break up the last strip of bacon on his breakfast plate. He looked out the kitchen window and said, "Here comes a pregnant girl." He clicked a fork tine on the windowpane.

Mrs. Sorenson stood up to get a better look at a pretty woman in white who was striding up the Sorensons' driveway. A fabric bag, stuffed with flyers, was slung on the woman's shoulder like a purse.

"About seven months pregnant, I would guess," Mrs. Sorenson said. "Is Spencer still out there?"

Dick nodded and shoved the window up a crack. "Here comes someone," he said to his brother, who was lying on his stomach in a nylon lounge chair on the blacktop just under the window. Spencer was wearing green swim trunks and dark glasses. His back was basted with oil. He flipped over in the chair and waved to the young pregnant woman.

Mrs. Sorenson put the window down. "I would imagine that's a volunteer who's canvassing for the school-bond issue," she said.

Dick was frowning. He watched his brother chat with the girl.

"She'll be sorry she ever came by," said Mrs. Sorenson, "once Spencer gets going."

Dick sighed aloud and appeared to have difficulty swallowing. His eyes spilled tears.

"Come on, now," Mrs. Sorenson said. She opened her book.

"I'm thinking about my wife," Dick said.

Mrs. Sorenson wet her index finger with her tongue and turned a page. "Which wife?" she said.

"Gladys, of course. She's living somewhere in the Oldsmobile you and Dad gave me. I told you already."

"This sounds hard," said Mrs. Sorenson, "but we gave it to both of you."

"But she's *living* in it," Dick said.

"Don't let your father hear you complain about that. He thinks there are worse places to live than in new Oldsmobiles."

"No one but me ever liked Gladys in her whole life," Dick said.

Mrs. Sorenson sang a little with "I Loves You, Porgy." "Oh, I apologize," she said, breaking off. "You'd probably appreciate a little quiet."

"No, I enjoy the music," Dick said.

"Well, it's beginning to bother *me*," Mrs. Sorenson said. She stood and touched Dick's shirt sleeve. "I like that grille pattern," she said.

"I'd better tell Spencer to come inside," Dick said, "so that girl can get the word to the voters." He picked a navel orange from a fruit bowl and bumped it several times on the window. Spencer shifted his position on the lounge chair and grinned broadly at Dick. The pregnant woman moved off, walking backward and making good-bye gestures. When she was gone, Dr. Sorenson appeared outdoors, trailing a garden hose, and squirted the blacktop around Spencer. Steam rose from the wetted drive.

"I'm going to stop that tape," Mrs. Sorenson said, leaving the kitchen through a swinging door. Dick took his plate to the sink and cleaned it with a damp lilac-colored sponge.

Spencer came through the outside door, slamming the screen, and sat in Dick's chair. His chest was wet with hose water, and he had stuck a blue paper sticker over his ribs. "Thumbs Up on Issue One," the sticker read.

"That girl I was talking to," Spencer said, "her husband's on the staff at White Cross with Dad. He's a neurosurgeon."

"I'm so glad," Dick said.

"I told her she's wasting her summer campaigning for a bond issue," Spencer said. "I told her the economy's collapsing and there'll be a global depression by 1990."

Mrs. Sorenson came back into the kitchen and found Dick sniffling. She bent over and put one arm around his waist. "You're so attractive, with those blond curls framing your face," she said.

"I'm so attractive," Dick said in a squeaky voice, mimicking his mother.

"Uh-oh—Dick's in a ditch," Spencer said. "Did you see the girl I was talking to?" he asked his mother. "Her husband's at White Cross with Dad."

"And I remember her from someplace else," Mrs. Sorenson said. "She's a patient of your father's. He'll be delivering that baby."

"None of us wants to think about that," Dick said.

"I told her what will happen with Eurodollars, and how the depression in 1990 will show that the 1930s depression was just one in a series," Spencer said.

Mrs. Sorenson was spraying the steel sinks with the dish rinser. "You look very tan and fit," she said to Spencer. "You seem to be having a good summer."

"I told that woman to bury her pocket change in her backyard," Spencer said. He took a pack of gum from the waistband of his swim trunks and slid a stick between his white teeth. "Come on, Dick," he said, getting up. He pulled his brother out of the kitchen by the arm.

Upstairs, in their bedroom, Spencer shoved Dick into a velour chair. "Put this on," he said, handing Dick a cordovan loafer.

Dick slid the shoe onto his bare foot. "It's too big," he said.

Kneeling in front of Dick, Spencer lifted the foot with the shoe onto his thigh. He laid a yellow scrap of soft cloth across the toe and began to shine it, buffing the leather.

"Did you just put a lot of polish on this shoe?" Dick said, shaking his foot loose. "Because look what it's doing." There was a ring of dark wax on the side of his ankle.

Spencer had his head turned. "Sh-h-h," he said. "Listen— Mom and Dad."

There was a baritone noise from Dr. Sorenson, and Mrs. Sorenson's tinkling response.

"What are they laughing about?" Spencer said.

"I wouldn't know," said Dick. "Probably not about us."

26

What I Hear

ONE HILL AFTER ANOTHER, this bumpy flight. My view is of the void. If anyone asked, I could make known my opinion of these seat covers. Or watch the beverage cart take forever. How does it fit, coming down the aisle? Eight inches—I'm measuring with my eyes. Four inches on each side.

Christian, asleep in the middle seat next to me, agreed to come along on this Alaska trip, travel up and back with me, on my dime. I can see the little tattoo inside his right forearm, from his Navy SEAL days: a face that looks like maybe Magellan above a map of some ocean or other. He's not quite my boyfriend. He's been divorced three years but remains in love with her. She's always on his mind: Anna.

I'm famished. I *bought* cashews, so where are they?

Christian comes out of his troubled sleep and says he feels rejuvenated. He doesn't realize his face is stained with tears.

The woman across the aisle is ripping perfume cards out of the free magazines. She's also ignoring her child, who's saying, "Mom, remember that girl? Mom, Mom. That girl, remember?" If I were the child, I'd stop that this minute and look out the window. Those weird little metal blades sticking up from the wing top. Over there will be Mt. McKinley. Or Denali. Whatever.

My snack from the cart is a bar of old banana cake, stuck to its cellophane; tough like a sponge. Where are my cashews? Why didn't I bring ninety-five dollars' worth of snacks?

Below us there are mountains now, glinting with sunfire, grouped around Anchorage.

"My bad mood's not about you," Christian says. That's probably true.

"Look," I begin, and he does—looks at me. "What about the time she—"

He waves his hand to stop me. In some ways, this entire flight has been something to forget.

On the bus ride to our hotel, Christian reads aloud some stuff from a folder. "'Edged by the fierce beauty of the Chugach and the waters of Cook Inlet, Anchorage is cosmopolitan but with the Alaskan wild always at its back.'"

"Plus it's eighty-two degrees and only June," I say. "Look, there's a Kinko's. Hey, an Eyewitness News truck. And—oop, a Cirrus machine."

We stop and let off some passengers, but Christian and I stay on, headed for our hotel: the Wallchart or the Woodwork. I can't get the name right. It's still daylight, of course—one of their days—but only for a few hours more. Christian asks me about Pammie, my daughter. It's funny: she's the whole reason I've come here but this is the first time either of us has mentioned her name.

Still the same daylight, but now it's another day. Christian looks groomed and handsome, and even seems glad to be here. He excuses himself and disappears—off, he says, to ask the way to Matanuska, the home of the softball-size radish. I have coffee and—I can't put it off—go to see Pammie.

Here in the tiny box of a house she never leaves. She wears a coat indoors, and cheap red boots. Her legs are bare, I notice. We don't really talk. She's busily scribbling notes in a college notebook while she watches the TV—a black-and-white '70s portable, older than she is. The picture is a muck of gray halftones. There's no black or white.

Pammie doesn't want me to replace the TV or buy her better red boots, or to say that everything else in her life is trash that should be hauled off to the dump. She wants me to stay seated, here on this futon chair, and get interested in this cartoon show. A *Heckle and Jeckle.* I try to. I do. And time goes by.

She got off track, it'll be a year ago this October. Since one night when she was sitting here, a perfectly normal, only a little bit messed-up junior-year anthropology major, holed up here studying for comps. A crazy man crashed in, nobody she knew. He smashed furniture, broke her eyeglasses, broke her wrist, broke her cheekbone, three of her teeth. Then he left, got away. The doctors did a great job; gave her a new face, if not quite hers.

"Am I bothering you?" I ask her. If I am, she doesn't say. Should I ask her again to open these crinkly presents I've brought? She's in something like pain when it comes to opening gifts, so I really have to think. Or I can be quiet. I don't need entertainment. That pretty hair barrette is sliding down. No, I won't touch it.

～

The taxi driver taking me back to the airport smiles around and asks, "Who am I?"

"I'm sorry?" I say.

"Guess my name," he says.

"Ah, let me see—" It could be anything. "Sidney?" I say. Wherever that guess came from, he's nodding.

"You saw my license," he says. "So, something harder. My birth sign."

"You're a Gemini" comes out of my mouth, and Sidney nods. He's not so happy this time. He says, "I bet you have a boyfriend who's informed about that stuff."

I spend the rest of the steamy ride trying to figure that one out. As we pull up at the Departing Flights curb, Sidney consults his wristwatch and says, "Fast." The cab putters off and I look around for Christian, who must have been surprised when he came back to the hotel and found my message telling him we were heading back so soon. Check out, I said. Meet you at the Delta counter. I'd turned chicken—anybody could see that.

It's half night, finally, though there's still a ghostly sun above the trees. A little thing, my guessing Sidney, but my elation over it is big.

⟋⟍

Hours we've been waiting at this gate. I've skipped sleep. Our night will be across the whole country of Canada. "You don't make me feel important," Christian says, slumped in his plastic scoop chair. I'm wondering, Does he want me to correct that? Now?

"We'll need soymilk," he says, and I don't ask or argue. His shoulders are sagging as he drifts on down the concourse. In the mint lighting there it all looks like a colorized film. He should lighten up. None of my mood is about him.

I get up and leave his plane ticket on top of his *Jimi Hendrix* magazine, but hidden under his cap, where he'll find it. He can sell the ticket or use it and leave. He has my number at home.

Beside the luggage lockers is a postal machine. I buy all the Mary Cassatt stamps it'll put out. Some Raoul Wallenbergs. The red Georgia O'Keeffe. My, what a pretty stamp. I feed in bill after bill on those. I'm going to be up here for a bit, not flying anywhere.

She should be afraid of a lot of people, but not afraid of me. It's like I can hear my parents calling, my mom saying, "Get up, honey. You've been asleep for a while. Honey. Honey bunch. You want to get up."

27

Smart

MOM SENT MY BROTHER, Jackie, over from Wheeling
to take care of me the last week of March, right before
I had the baby. I was living in D.C., alone, in five rooms of a sagging apartment house called the Augusta, on Wisconsin Avenue,
opposite the National Cathedral. The Augusta was a worn,
white building, and it shone behind me, cold and crooked in the
sun of a false spring. I was waiting on the sidewalk for Jackie's
car. Across the wide dangerous street, the cathedral's huge towers and many points glowered. I had been waiting for over two
hours, which was the longest I'd been out of my rooms for
months, including trips two blocks away to see my O.B.

I was living mostly in the study then. It was a dim room that
smelled of old drapes and waxed paneling and rusty radiator
heat. I spent my hours there in a resident chair that was covered
with some kind of bristly horsehair, like an old theater seat. The
chair had a cracked foot and leaned, perforce, into a corner. One
nice thing in the room, some people would think, was a little
window with diamond panes of blue and brown glass.

When I got up from the chair, it was just to change a record,
or twist my spine, or to nibble some of the food my neighbor,

Mrs. Sally Dixon, brought me. Mrs. Dixon was eighteen years old; terribly shy. She always said, "This is Mrs. Dixon" when she knocked on the door, so I never called her Sally. I liked that she didn't try to talk with me when she came—twice a week or so, all winter—to stock my cramped kitchen with cans and boxes. Before her visits, I always spent a lot of time on my appearance so she wouldn't worry about the baby. Still, I could see her distress whenever she actually *faced* me, to accept my grocery lists, or my money, or my thanks.

I wore socks usually, but no shoes, and, always—because it was the only covering that still fitted me—a cottony slip that had been my mom's: blue, size sixteen. I normally had some sweaters on over the slip. I had one expensive lamb's-wool cardigan. My hair was wrecked by pregnancy. It swelled in a cloud around my small face.

᭬

When Jackie arrived, he surprised me by being a pedestrian—by stepping out from behind a cluster of tourists on their way to the big church. I had expected him to drive up, in his West Virginia car.

He gave me an impatient kiss and began scolding. "Aw, don't tell me. You can't be on the level. You couldn't have stood outside here, waiting since four o'clock."

"I didn't know if you could find my place," I said.

"Hell, I *found* it forty minutes ago. But they don't want you to park your car in this city. I've been going up one way and down the other. Finally, I just got out, set the car loose, and told it, 'Every man for himself.' Is this your place here? Looks pretty good. You don't look very good."

He frowned as if I shouldn't have been in my own body.

I led him inside, and he gave me more of the same. He took one look at the ratty magazines, the plates and glasses in unhealthy stacks, the empty jar of Nescafé, the slumping rows of record albums. He said, "I'm sorry, Eleanor, but I'm mad."

He stalked out the apartment door. I followed him down through the little lobby, with its tiled floor and round mirrors, to the Augusta's front walkway. The sun had dimmed, and the temperature had dropped about ten degrees.

Jackie scuffed his shoes on the cement a while, and then he went into a shallow park that was between the Augusta and her taller, newer neighbor, the Frontenac. He tapped a few trees. He had a cigarette.

"That's the scariest damn church I've ever seen!" he called to me.

"It's the National," I said.

"I know it. Of course. I'm going for my luggage, Eleanor, and then I want to start straightening up that mess in there. Are you going to stand around on the sidewalk, pregnant?"

"I've got to be here in order to let you in," I said. "The front door locks itself once I go through."

❧

When he got a few pieces of his luggage safely inside, some of the irritation went out of him. He put me in my chair, and gave me the cap from the thermos he had used on his road trip. The cap was full of still-warm cocoa that Mom, back home, had made for us.

"Really," Jackie said, as he pushed around the furniture. He yanked the vacuum cleaner from the closet, and bullied it over the rugs in the study and hall and in the old living room, which I had fixed up for the baby. I opened a Modern Library edition of *Cousin Bette* and pretended to read it.

Jackie was in and out for the next few hours, until after dark. He reported to me every so often. "All right. There's a good hardware just two blocks from here, and now we've got decent light bulbs, at least, and some emergency candles.

"Get me up at eight o'clock tomorrow morning, Eleanor. I have to move my car from across the street, or I'll never move it again, because the police'll put a boot on it.

"You do have an alarm clock? Because we'll need it, and if you don't, the hardware store's open until six.

"There's a good pharmacy close. Closes at ten."

I heard him dragging open drawers, loading things into closets. "One more haul from the car," he said.

About nine that evening, he made his last trip in, with a purplish leather shaving kit that had been our father's, and, under his left arm, a cardboard six-pack of drinking glasses. "Look here. They were selling these at that grocery for three bucks," he said. "Tumblers."

When everything was put away, we went to inspect the room I had arranged for the baby. It was a green and yellow place, though I was banking on a girl. There were two pieces of Bambi furniture, and gowns and outfits still in gift boxes, and Fisher Price toys some relatives had sent. I had hung up an Animaland poster, and strung a fruit and flowers mobile over the crib. On the floor, there was a fierce, icy-looking polish that Jackie had produced with mop and wax.

"Tonight, I'm going to sleep like the dead," he said.

"Me, too. I've had it," I said.

I went to the dining room—a windowless nook at one end of the kitchen. I had had the movers wedge my tall bed into this area. It had been a lifelong habit of mine to sleep near the center of activity in a house. I wouldn't have felt safe in the back bedroom.

I was thirty-six—old for a first baby, I know. In nine months, I had gained forty pounds, and I'd been trying to cut back in the last weeks. I had a dream that first night Jackie was there. Apples, pears, and squash rolled by. I saw a table laid with a roast, glazed carrots, salty potatoes. A voice told me, "Eleanor! Eat these."

Jackie was up, drinking coffee and scrambling eggs, in what seemed to be the middle of the night. I lay on my back, in bed, in a little bit of pain. I watched him, framed by the kitchen portal, as he hunted for utensils, checked plates and glasses for stains, and chatted out loud. Every few minutes his panicky activity would stop, and he would stand and seem to dissolve into himself.

"I forgot what I was going to say," he whispered.

"What?" I said.

"Do you want to wake up? It's seven-thirty. I've got to go move my car. Oh, don't tell me it's raining."

"Probably. It's been so nice. We had weather in the high sixties. On one day, we—"

"Before you go on, I want to tell you this." Jackie had some coffee and then stepped out of the kitchen and sat at the foot of my bed. "When it's time for us to go, and you're ready for the baby, you should already have packed your nightwear, and so forth. You know—toothbrush, robe, slippers. Stay awake, Eleanor. I want to tell you this, and then I've got to get my car moved."

"O.K., I'm listening," I said. "I think today I'd like to sit on a bench outside and watch the rain."

"Smart," Jackie said.

I rose, yawning and stretching, and waddled to the record player. "I wish you'd have let me sleep," I said. "I haven't had *dream* sleep in about four weeks. The place looks nice, Jackie. Thank you a lot for cleaning."

"What do you want for breakfast? Tell me fast," he said. "Got to get sliding."

"Nothing," I said. I went to the shelf in the closet and got out a lap blanket.

"Well, if you don't eat, and you're not sleeping, you'll have a terrible baby. I'm here to make sure you take care of yourself."

"Look at me," I said, heading for my three-legged chair. "Could you lie down and sleep comfortably, do you think? Or eat? Imagine a big pointy rock turning in your stomach. Roaring up your throat."

"Hmph," Jackie said.

He was shaking his raincoat, getting ready to put it on.

✎

Jackie had his own disappointments. On the drive to D.C., he had got tar all over the flanks and bumpers of his new car. He had, he said, a mean sore throat. But his real depression came from the fact that he had somehow failed his comprehensive exams in clinical psychology at Marshall University. So, as a result, they weren't giving him his degree.

"Mom pressured me into coming here and nursemaiding you," he said. "She thought it was a way out for both of us."

We were in the study. Jackie was combing through the *Washington Post* for something to read. For Jackie, a newspaper had always meant more physical exercise than actual reading. He read standing, with the paper held high, and at his spread arms' length. He would rush through a section, his arms closing and opening, the paper beating like big wings. Whenever he paused, it was just long enough to cock his head and brood a few seconds over some column or picture, before his arms snapped again, and he moved ahead. He used the little intervals, when the paper was closed and his fingers were pinching off a new page, to raise his chin and stretch his neck—as if he were fighting a headache. He brushed through the financial section, discarded it, and started on the editorials.

"What's in there? Nothing?" I said.

"Nothing," he said.

❦

That was typical of Jackie—and of me. We weren't learners, really. We had spent our lives rushing through everything: music albums, books—though never a *whole* book from start to finish. We took in whatever we thought we could turn into conversation, from TV shows, movies. The only reason we liked to know a thing was so we'd have something to yammer about—not that we had anyone to share our talk with.

"Let's get a breath," Jackie said. "Can you walk? The walls are closing in on me."

We walked toward downtown. There was still some orangeish sun on the buildings, but the stores and cars were burning lights. In a chained-off, empty parking lot, beside a closed gas station, some rangy black men were playing basketball. One man, bearded and in a wool cap, dodged around two defenders and sprang and fired a shot at the brick wall of the gas station.

"They don't have a basket," Jackie said. "There's your metaphor for urban blight."

"This isn't really the blighted part of town," I said. "Those guys are probably ambassadors from the Zimbabwe Embassy."

"Probably," Jackie said, but he looked a little surprised. "Can I ask you something?"

"Normally when people ask if they can ask, I say no. But go ahead," I said.

"Well, Eleanor, what do you intend to do?"

I tapped my stomach. "When this is over, I'm going to crash-diet, drink real tea for a change, and I thought I'd hunt up a filing job, or maybe be a salesgirl at Saks."

"The point is, it's not going to be over," Jackie said. "Not at the hospital. Not for at least twenty years is this going to be over, and that's if you get most of the breaks. It makes my head swim. It'll probably *never* be over."

"Tell me something new," I said.

A jogger went by, hurdling some traffic cones, and started a couple of dogs barking. I was ready, right then, to have the baby. I wasn't sure of the date, and didn't want to be. I might have been overdue. The one night with Phil had been in early June.

"You're going to run very quickly through the rest of Dad's money, especially in this rook-joint city. I was just wondering how you plan to live? It's supposed to cost something like nine hundred thousand *dollars* to raise a kid these days."

"What do you want me to do?" I said.

"Not you," Jackie said. "Phil! Doesn't Phil ever say anything?"

"All the time," I said. "He says he'll do everything a human being can possibly do."

Jackie hissed and gestured at the buildings around us with both arms. "Oh, Eleanor, *think!*" he said. "Where *is* he?"

×

Phil was eleven years younger than I, and we'd been engaged to be married, had lived together for a long time before I broke things off. But we never were very close. Phil carried our courtship and cohabitation as he carried most every situation— with a lot of bluster and bluff. He had a broad, heavy accent that, for all I know, was faked. He said his sentences had "reverse spin." He was incapable of talking to people, it seemed, without moving toward them and actually taking them in his hands, or roping an arm over their shoulders, or, at least, resting a finger on their lapels. Constantly, and toward no end that I could see, he *lied*. If asked where he was from, he would say, "Originally? Pensacola," or, "*All* over. I'm an Army brat."

The one last time, in early June, happened after a pool party in Woodbury Hills, in Wheeling. I hadn't seen Phil for months, but I asked him to drive me to West Virginia for my mom's birthday. He was entertaining enough on the long, nervous trip across Maryland and Pennsylvania. He told me a lot of—I'm sure—*lies* about his tour of duty in Vietnam, to keep my mind off the big hills and the sixteen-wheelers that blew around us. At a rest stop in New Stanton he bought me a souvenir paper booklet about Amish cooking. He had raised a dark beard, which worked a wonder for his face, giving him a strong, sharp chin where he had had none, and setting off his black eyes.

The pool party we went to was given by the Zigglers: twins, who were classmates of Jackie's at Marshall U. They were beautiful lean girls, each with a fat brown braid that went between her shoulders. On the party day, their tan skin was oiled, and they wore matching orange bandeau bikinis and pearl earbobs.

I never removed the long blue football jersey I was wearing, but sunned my legs from a lounger, and watched Phil doing laps in the pool. His arms pointed in easy arcs, and his legs pounded the water without throwing up much splash.

He sat with me for a moment as he toweled off his hair and beard. He called to Jackie, "Hey, champ! Going to get yourself wet today?"

Jackie hadn't even brought a swimsuit. He was down on the Zigglers' lawn, where he had cornered a collie dog. He seemed to be holding the dog back with both arms, talking intently to it while he ruffled its ears and scratched the back of its neck.

Brenda Ziggler joined us. She looked pleasantly harassed by her hostess duties. She was streaming water, and there were wet highlights left on her torso and nice legs.

"Here's a guy who looks capable of building a grill fire for us," she said to Phil.

"Hey, I'm a *guest*," he said.

"Well, we can all just go hungry, I guess," Brenda said.

"I don't know where anything *is*," Phil said as he stroked his beard.

"Follow me," Brenda said, and Phil went along.

He was still excited, I could tell, on the ride back to my mom's house that evening. And though I knew that the glow he had, and the involuntary smile, were from being with the Zigglers and not me, just the same, he was something. I didn't even mind his built-up tennis shoes, or the silver saint on a chain around his neck.

In Mom's driveway, he sat on the hood of his car and spun his keys with one finger. When he spoke to me, I noticed a sweet grape Life Saver staining his tongue.

Jackie, who had been sullen in the back seat for the ride, went into the house alone. Phil and I decided to scare up a bar and get drunk.

I explained this whole episode to Jackie, a month or so later, over the phone.

"Fine," he said lifelessly.

"Okay. But it's a fact."

I heard him cough and clear his throat. "You don't *stay* pregnant at thirty-six," he said. He was in his typical bad mood, just off from interning at the County Mental Health Center. "A place," he once told me, "in what you might call a ghetto, uglier than any bowling alley, where they've never heard of air-conditioning."

He said how my baby could be born an idiot because of my age. "Not to mention who its father is," he said. He talked about postpartum depression and what it had done to our grandma.

I waited until he was through, and then I put down the telephone and went into my kitchen and kicked a utility pipe that was ticking there. When I came back, I said, "You can go to hell, Jackie. Let me speak to Mom."

🙰

Phil appeared one evening, two days before I went into labor. He had a small rocking chair and four cardboard boxes— "cases," he called them—of baby food in the trunk of his car. He improvised and said he had been away for a while, in Chicago, helping some brother-in-law set up a construction firm.

I let him inspect the baby's room, and then we toured the rest of the place. It was the first time Phil had been inside the Augusta, and he told me, in a critical tone, that he approved. He spotted Jackie, who was on the floor by the TV, shelling peanuts and watching *Wonder Woman.*

"Say, champ," Phil said. "Or is it Doctor Champ now?"

Jackie snapped a peanut and swore. He looked hurt when he turned back to *Wonder Woman,* and after a bit he pulled himself off the floor and retreated to the kitchen.

We heard him running the electric mixer for the next twenty minutes, and then I detected a cake baking. I excused myself and peeked in on Jackie. He was up on the counter, furiously thrashing a wooden spoon around a bowl of cake frosting that was pressed between his thighs.

"Will you please be willing to *eat* some of this?" he said.

I went back to the study, where the TV was still on, its picture rolling and flashing. Phil had gone out to his car and brought in a gray metal box from which he emptied two checkbooks, a ledger tablet, a sawed-down pencil, and some stock certificates. He was in my three-legged chair.

"Let's see," I said, but he waved me off. He put the pencil lengthwise in his mouth, and shuffled his papers for a while before he spoke.

I stuck on an old record by Lambert, Hendricks, and Ross.

"Man, *good!*" Jackie yelled from the kitchen.

Phil said, "Turn it down, will you, princess?"

He pressed forward in the chair, but couldn't seem to get started at what he wanted to say. He directed his small eyes at me and smiled without separating his lips. He beat his ledger tablet against his leg.

I said, "This is about the future, right?"

"Indeed," he said.

He began slowly, but then he got a little wound up. He talked about schools, coaches, music lessons—flute or piano? He was wondering aloud about a dental insurance plan when Jackie came in carrying a plate of cake and a coffee cup, which he had pushed against his stomach. He was watching the coffee, moving one step at a time. He got seated on the rug and looked at Phil, who had kept on talking, and was now nodding at Jackie.

Phil said, "A lot of my life, as you know, has been spent kicking around, spinning my tires, and going from job to job, which was great, because I learned a hell of a lot about *people*. I found out about people involved in war—sick people, some of them, and healthy. . . ."

"Redheaded people and nonredheads," Jackie said.

Phil went on. "This business with my brother-in-law in Chicago, for example. That got me squared around and I did him a lot of good, though I won't see a damn lot of money from it. But I did see how you *make* money," he said. "You make money with people, princess. And people take to me. They like me. And if being liked isn't the whole war, it sure as hell is one big battle in the campaign."

"Boy, this is good for a mix," Jackie interrupted. He pointed at the cake with his flatware.

Phil kept going. His speech was rushed and urgent-sounding. "I haven't got a lot of what they call liquid assets," he said. "But I can read people like you two would read a book, and anything I'd want to get serious about, my people-reading talent would make me a success.

"I've got some things lined up for now and some for later," he said. "Step One, though, is a vet friend of mine who's in shipping and receiving for a big auto-parts warehouse and who's going to get me a job as a dispatcher, which I could easily handle. That position opens up in a month or two, when the guy they got now retires."

"In a month or two," Jackie said. He rose and changed the Lambert, Hendricks, and Ross record for a Duke Ellington. He put the needle down on "Cottontail," then sat again behind his coffee cup and plate.

Phil stopped talking and stared at Jackie and then at the record player. "Weird," Phil said. He sort of shook his head and then went on some more. "Step Two is an idea I've had for a long time and which I hope to activate through a contact of mine at the Coca-Cola headquarters in Atlanta, Georgia. It's so simple it's genius. Dietary Popsicles. You got diet soda, which sells like mad, and you got fat people who suffer more than anyone else in the heat and who could eat a million of these Popsicles to cool down, and never gain an ounce. And it *works*. I know, because I put Tab and Fresca in my ice-cube trays, and they freeze and they still taste good."

"I hope you don't *buy* any of this," Jackie said to me. He lifted his coffee cup, and its cork coaster stuck to the cup bottom.

"Naw, naw," I said.

"You don't?" Phil said, and looked puzzled.

Jackie and I waggled our heads in the negative.

"You say I lie?" Phil said.

"No, Phil," Jackie said.

I sucked a breath. "It's just that people, they don't ever do what they don't want to do. And they can't ever be what they aren't already."

Jackie said, "The biggest favor you could do this baby, and its mom, is just to realize that."

≁

The sad thing was, it had been fun listening to Phil. There was great authority in his delivery. For an instant there I had wanted to *be* him, or at least his age, and have his ideas.

Anyway, his manner became rather formal and unnaturally polite. He suddenly offered to leave because of the "weekend traffic."

"All right," Jackie and I said in unison.

Phil stood, put a hand on his head, and smoothed the hair there. I noticed for the first time that day that he had shaved off his beard. He was wearing his pointed boots, beltless slacks, and a canary-colored Ban-Lon shirt. I remembered that these were not clothes he got into on Saturdays, as my dad might have. They were the clothes Phil *wore.* He loaded up his utility box and put it under his arm, and then he shook hands with Jackie.

"Thank you for the baby presents," I said.

Phil said, "I'll be around, almost certainly, tomorrow, princess, with a lot more stuff."

"Don't worry," I said.

We heard his car gunning off. Phil had tuned the engine to make a lot of noise.

Jackie paced for a minute or two, and then he said, "Thank God, thank God!"

"What?" I said.

"Nothing."

"No, tell me."

"All right, I will," Jackie said. "Thank God you didn't make Phil part of the family."

"Halt," I said. "Phil is *very* important to me. When he goes on like that, I don't really mind."

"Eleanor," Jackie said, "he's a wrong number. Something small and slimy that you throw back. God, what he says about your self-concept."

"What does he say?"

"Nothing, except that you're very, very bad off. I can't explain it if you don't already know."

"The psychologist," I said.

"Yeah, well," Jackie said. He started pacing again.

"Look, I *know* I'm not smart," I said. "I don't particularly *want* to be smart. That's the whole difference between us—*I* don't torture myself by going around with people who are smart."

"That's right. That's terrific," Jackie said before I hurried out of the room.

From my high bed, I had a side-window view of a corner of the big cathedral. The church looked black and threatening, but very meaningful, to me. I decided I'd never move out of the Augusta. Phil would probably continue to come by for a while. Maybe Jackie would stay. Mrs. Dixon would come by, and eventually maybe she and I would have a nice conversation—or a meal together. Or not. There'd be another Mrs. Dixon, surely, if mine tired out. There'd be another Phil.

28

Sisters

RAY SNAPPED A TOMATO from a plant and chewed into its side. His niece, Melissa, was sitting in a swing that hung on chains from the arm of a walnut tree. She wore gauzy cotton pants and a twisted scarf across her breasts. Her hair was cropped and pleat-curled.

"Hey," said Penny, Ray's wife. She came up the grass in rubber thongs, carrying a rolled-up news magazine. "If you're weeding, Ray, I can see milkweed and thistle and a dandelion and chickweed from here. I can see sumac."

"You see good," said Ray.

"I just had the nicest call from Sister Mary Clare," Penny said. "She'll be out to visit this evening."

"Oh, boy," Ray said. He spat a seed from the end of his tongue.

"Her name's Lily," Melissa said. "She's my sister and she's your niece, and we don't have to call her Mary Clare. We can call her Lily."

Penny stood in front of Melissa, obscuring Ray's view of the girl's top half—as if Ray hadn't been seeing it all morning.

"What time is Lily coming?" Melissa asked.

"Don't tell her," Ray said to Penny. "She'll disappear."

"Give me that!" Melissa said. She grabbed Penny's magazine and swatted at her uncle.

"Do you know a Dr. Streich?" Penny said, putting a hand on Melissa's bare shoulder to settle her down. "He was a professor at your university, and there's an article in that magazine about him."

"No," Melissa said. She righted herself in the swing.

"Well, I guess you might *not* know him," Penny said. "He hasn't been at your university for years, according to the article. He's a geologist."

"I don't know him," Melissa said.

Penny pulled a thread from a seam at her hip. "He's pictured above the article," she said.

"Blessed be Mary Clare," Ray said. "Blessed be her holy name."

Penny said, "I thought we'd all go out tonight."

"You thought we'd go to the Wednesday Spaghetti Dinner at St. Anne's," Ray said, "and show Lily to Father Mulby."

Penny knelt and brushed back some leaves on a head of white cabbage.

"I'd like to meet Father Mulby," Melissa said.

"You wouldn't," said Ray. "Frank Mulby was a penitentiary warden before he was a priest. He was a club boxer before that. Years ago."

Ray stuck the remainder of the tomato in his mouth and wiped the juice from his chin with the heel of his right hand. "Ride over to the fire station with me," he said to Melissa.

"Unh-unh, I don't feel like it." She got off the board seat and patted her bottom. "I don't see what Mulby's old jobs have to do with my wanting to meet him."

"Why do you want to meet him?" Penny said. She was looking up at Melissa, shading her eyes with her hand.

"To ask him something," Melissa said. "To clear something up."

❧

At the firehouse, two men in uniforms were playing pinochle and listening to Julie London over the radio.

"Gene. Dennis," said Ray.

"What are you here for, Ray?" Dennis said. "You aren't on today. Gene's on, I'm on, those three spades waxing the ladder truck are on." Dennis made a fan with his cards and pressed them on the tabletop.

"I'm supposed to be buying a bag of peat," Ray said. "Only I don't want to." He went around Dennis and yanked open a refrigerator. Under the egg shelf there was taped a picture of a girl in cherry-colored panty hose. "I'm avoiding something," he said. He pulled a Coca-Cola from a six-pack and shut the door. He sat down. "My niece is on the way. I'm avoiding her arrival."

"The good one?" Gene said.

"The good one's here already. I pushed her in the swing this morning until she got dizzy. This is the other one. The nun." Ray held the can off and pulled the aluminum tab.

"Don't bring her here," Gene said. "I do not need that."

"What*ever* you do," Dennis said.

"No, I wouldn't," said Ray.

"You can bring that Melissa again," Dennis said.

"I wouldn't do that, either. You all bored her." Ray drank from the can.

A short black man came up the steps, holding a chamois cloth. His shirt and pants were drenched.

"Charlie," Ray said, tucking his chin to swallow a belch. "Looking nice."

"They got me with the sprinklers," Charlie said. "They waited all morning to get me."

"Well, they'll do that," Dennis said.

"I know it," the black man said.

"Because they're bored," Ray said. He sat forward. "I ought to go set a fire and give them something to think about."

"I wish you would," Charlie said. He pulled off his shirt.

❧

"Why the hell is he at the lead?" Melissa said. She was looking at Father Mulby, who wore an ankle cast. They were in the big basement hall at St. Anne's, and the priest was carrying a cafeteria tray. Fifty or sixty people waited in line behind him to collect plates of spaghetti and bowls of salad.

"Lookit," Ray said, "you and Sister Mary Clare find a seat and have a talk. Penny and I'll fill some trays and bring them over."

"No, no," the nun said. "It feels good to stand. I've been sitting in a car all day."

"Besides, we couldn't think of anything to tell each other," Melissa said.

"Melissa, there's a lot I want to talk about with you."

"I'm sure."

"There is," Sister said.

"Hey," Ray said to Melissa, "just go grab us a good table if you want to sit down."

"I do," Melissa said. She left her place in line and followed Father Mulby, who had limped to the front of the room and was sitting down at one of the long tables there. She introduced herself and asked if she could join him.

"It's reserved," he said. "That seat's reserved for Father Phaeton. Just move over to that side, please." The priest indicated a chair across the table.

"O.K., O.K.," Melissa said. "When he gets here, I'll jump up." She sat down anyway. Her long hair lifted from around her throat and waved in the cool exhaust of a window fan.

Father Mulby glanced across the room and lit a Camel over his spaghetti. "I guess I can't start until everyone's in place," he said.

"That'll be an hour," Melissa said.

"Here's Father Phaeton," Mulby said.

Melissa changed sides. Ray and Sister Mary Clare joined them and sat down, with Melissa in between. Penny came last. She looked embarrassed to be carrying two trays, one loaded with silverware, napkins, and water glasses.

Ray passed the food and utensils around. "Someone will be bringing soft drinks," he said to Melissa.

"Coffee?" she asked.

"No," Father Mulby said. "We don't serve coffee anymore. The urns, and all."

"I'd like to be excommunicated," Melissa told him. "I want the thirteen candles dashed to the ground, or whatever, and I want a letter from Rome."

"I don't know," the old priest said. He forked some salad lettuce into his mouth. "If you kick your sister or push me out of this chair onto the floor, I can excommunicate you."

"What's this about, Father?" said Sister Mary Clare.

"Nothing," Ray said. "Just your sister."

Melissa leaned toward him and said, "Blah, blah, blah." She pushed her plate to one side. "I just have to hit Lily?" she asked Mulby.

"That would be plenty for me," he said.

Ray said, "Eat something, Melissa. Act your age."

"Don't mind me," she said, leaning over the table. She batted the priest's eating hand. "Is that good enough?"

"I'm afraid not," Mulby said.

Father Phaeton, a man with red hair and bad skin, asked Melissa to pass the Parmesan cheese.

"Ignore her, if you can, Father Mulby," Ray said. "I'm sure it's her blood week."

"And the salt cellar, too," Father Phaeton added.

Mulby jerked forward. His large hand closed down on Melissa's wrist. "It's not that," he said to Ray. "I can tell that about a woman by holding her hand, and it's not that."

❧

Penny was lying on the sofa at home. She had a folded washcloth across her forehead. Her eyes were pressed shut against the pain in her head, and tears ran over her cheekbones.

"It's not necessarily a migraine," Ray told her. He had drawn a wing chair up beside the sofa. "My head's pounding, too. Could've been the food."

"I don't think church food could hurt anybody, Ray," said Penny.

The nieces were sitting cross-legged on the rug. "Why not?" Sister Mary Clare said. "It's not blessed or anything. I've been woozy ever since we ate, myself."

"I just meant they're so clean at St. Anne's," Penny said. "And none of you are sick like I am. Don't try to convince yourselves you are."

"I'm not sick," Melissa said.

"You didn't eat a mouthful," Sister Mary Clare said. She exhaled and stood up.

"I wonder why you visit us every year, Melissa," Penny said.

"Do you mind it?" Melissa asked. "If you do—"

"She doesn't," Ray said.

"No," Penny said, "I don't mind. I just wonder if you girls could find something to do outside for a bit."

"Lily can push me in the swing," Melissa said. "O.K., Lily?"

Penny said, "You should have talked to Father Phaeton, Melissa. They say he's dissatisfied with the life."

"That would have been the thing," Ray said. He told his nieces, "Maybe I'll go out back with you, so Penny can get better."

Penny took his hand and squeezed it.

"Maybe I won't," he said. He turned the washcloth on his wife's brow.

\~

Sister Mary Clare stood in the moonlight by a tomato stake. She was fingering her rosary beads.

"Don't be doing that," Melissa said. She moved down to the end of the lawn, where it was bordered by a shallow stream. She bent over the water. In the moonlight, she saw a school of minnows swerve over a fold in the mud next to an old bike tire.

Sister Mary Clare followed Melissa and said, behind her, "I won't be seeing you again. I'm going into cloister."

Melissa leaned against a tall tree. She dug her thumbnail into a bead of sweet gum on the bark.

"And I'm taking a vow of silence," the nun said. "Do you think it's a bad idea?"

"I think it's a good idea, and probably what you want. I'm glad."

"If you care, I'm not very happy," Sister said.

"You were never happy," Melissa said. "The last time I saw you laughing was the day that swing broke. Remember that day?"

"Yes. Ray was in it when it went."

Melissa smiled. "He used to pay me a quarter to sit on his lap and comb his hair."

"I know," Sister said. "He still would."

Melissa hugged herself with her bare arms. "It won't matter before long. I'm getting old."

"So is Ray," Sister said. "But he's why you come here, I think."

"So what? There aren't many people I like, Lily."

"Me neither."

"Well, there you are," Melissa said. "The miracle is, I keep having such a good time. It almost seems wrong."

"You still do?"

"Every day," Melissa said, heading back for the stream. "Such a wonderful time."

29

Likely Lake

HIS DOORBELL RANG AND Buddy peered through the viewer at a woman in the courtyard. She had green eyes and straight black hair, cut sharply like a '50s Keely Smith. He knew her. She did bookkeeping or something for the law partners next door, especially at tax times. He also remembered her from his wife's yard sale, although that was a couple years ago and the wife was now his ex. She'd bought a jewelry case and a halogen lamp. He could picture her standing on the walk there—her nice legs and the spectator pumps she wore. She'd driven a white V.W. bug in those days. But it must have died because later he had noticed her arriving for work in cabs.

He had lent her twenty bucks, in fact. Connie was her name. Last June, maybe, when his garden was at its peak. He'd been out there positioning the sprinkler, first thing in the morning, when a cab swerved up and she was in back. She had rolled down her window and started explaining to him. She was coming in to work early but had ridden the whole way without realizing she'd brought an empty handbag. She *showed* it to him—a beige clutch. She even undid the clasp and held the bag out the window.

Now she waved a twenty as Buddy opened the door.

"That isn't necessary, Connie," he said.

She thanked him with a nod for remembering her name. She said, "Don't give me any argument." She came close and tucked the bill into his shirt pocket. "You see here?" she said. "This is already done."

"Well, I thank you," Buddy said. He stroked the pocket, smoothing the folded money flat. It was a blue cotton shirt he'd put on an hour earlier when he got home from having his hair cut.

She was still close and wearing wonderful perfume but he didn't think he should remark on that. He kept his eyes level and waited as if she were a customer and he a clerk. He said, "So, are you still in the neighborhood? I rarely see you."

"They haven't needed me." She pretended a pout. "Nobody's needed me." She stepped back. It was the first week of September, still mild. She wore a fitted navy dress with a white collar and had a red cardigan sweater over her arms. Her large shapely legs were in sheer stockings.

"We have one last problem," she said. She held up a finger.

He looked at her, his eyebrows lifted.

Her hand fell and she gazed off and spoke as if reading, as if her words were printed over in the sky there to the right. "I have a crush on you," she said. "Such a crush on you, Buddy. The worst, most ungodly crush."

"No, you don't. You couldn't."

"*The, worst, crush.*"

"Well," Buddy said. "Well dee well-dell-dell."

❧

He owned the house   a two story, low-country cottage. It was set on a lane that led into Indian Town and beyond that were the

roads and highways into North Pennsylvania. He sat on a divan
near a window in the living room now and, in the noon light,
looked through some magazines and at a book about birds.

He had a view from this window. Behind the house stood a
tall ravine and Buddy could see through its vines and trees to the
banks of Likely Lake.

His son had died after an accident there. Three years ago,
August. Matthew. When he was two days short of turning
twenty-one. His Jet Ski had hit a fishing boat that slid out of an
inlet. The August after that, Buddy's wife left him.

He had stopped going out—what his therapist referred to as
"isolating." He knocked the walls off his son's bedroom suite
and off the room where Ruthie used to sew and converted the
whole upper floor into a studio. He began bringing all his as-
signments home. He was a draftsman, the senior draftsman at
Qualitec, a firm of electromechanical engineers he had worked
with for years.

"Beware of getting out of touch," his therapist had warned.
"It happens gradually. It creeps over you by degrees. When
you're not interacting with people, you start losing the beat.
Then blammo. Suddenly, you're that guy in the yard."

"I'm who?" asked Buddy.

"The guy with the too-short pants," said the therapist.

✌

He would *dissuade* the Connie woman, Buddy told himself now
as he poked around in the kitchen. He yanked open a drawer and
considered its contents, extracted a vegetable peeler, put it back
in its place. He would dissuade her nicely. He didn't want to
make her feel like a bug. "Let her down easy," he said aloud and
both the cats spurted in to study him. Buddy had never learned

to tell the cats apart. They were everyday cats, middle-sized and yellow. Matt's girlfriend Shay had presented them as kittens, for a birthday present, the same week he died. The cats stayed indoors now and kept close to Buddy. He called one of them Bruce and the other Bruce's Brother.

He went into a utility closet off the kitchen now and rolled out a canister vacuum. He liked vacuuming. He liked jobs he could quickly complete. And he wanted things just so when Elise came over tonight. She had changed things for him in the months since they had met. Everything was different because of her.

One way to go with the Connie woman he was thinking, would be to parenthetically mention Elise. That might have its effect. Or a stronger method would be to say, "My girlfriend is the jealous type," or some such.

The cats padded along into the dining area and watched as Buddy positioned the vacuum and unwound its mile of electric cord. "Don't ever touch a plug like this," he told them. "It is hot, hot, hot."

⤚

Elise phoned from work around two. She was a group counselor at Cherry Trees, a psychiatric hospital over in the medical park. Buddy saw his therapist in another building on the grounds and he had met Elise there, in fact, in the parking area. It was on a snowy day last February when he'd forgotten and left his fog lights burning. She had used yellow jumper cables to rescue him. Buddy had invited her to go for coffee and the two of them had driven off in his black Mercury, zooming along the Old Post Highway to get the car battery juiced.

They ended up having lunch at a French place, where Elise put on horn-rimmed glasses and read aloud from the menu. Without the glasses, she reminded him of Jean Arthur—her figure, the freckles and bouncy, curly hair. Elise's French was awful and full of oinky sounds but Buddy liked her for trying it anyway. He liked her laugh, which went up and came down.

"Vincent escaped," she said now on the phone. "He broke out somehow. From right in the middle of a Life Challenges Meeting."

"I'm fortunate I don't know what that is," Buddy said.

"The problem for *me* is, with Vincent loose and Security looking for him, I can't take my people outside. Which means no Smoke Walk."

"Right, because you're the only one with a lighter. So that they have to trail along behind you."

"Well, they're not dogs. But they're getting mighty grumpy. And being critical of Vincent. They think he should be shot."

"Hard to know whose side to take," said Buddy.

"That it is," Elise said, and told him she had to go.

This flower garden was Buddy's first, but *gorgeous.* He no longer understood people who spoiled and killed plants. The therapist had suggested gardening, so one Saturday when Elise was free, she and Buddy went to Tristie's Arboretum and bought starter materials. She also helped shape the garden. They put in a design like a collar around the court and walk.

Buddy had watered, fed, and misted his flowers. With each day they bloomed, grew large, stood tall. "What more could I ask of you?" he asked them. "Nuts and fruit?"

He thought he might recruit Elise to help lay in winter pansies around the side porch if that didn't seem boring. She was good at a hundred things. She could play bridge and poker and shuffle cards. She could play the piano. She liked listening to jazz and she *knew* most of it. They'd dress up and go dancing at Sky Mountain or at the Allegheny Club, where there was an orchestra. Elise had beautiful evening clothes. She'd take him to all kinds of things—to midnight movies or a raunchy comedy club. Last spring they'd even taken a train trip to New Orleans for Jazz Fest.

From close by, Buddy heard a woman's voice and froze. It might be Connie's. He didn't feel up to another encounter with her just yet. She seemed interesting and he liked her. She certainly was a handsome woman. She had mentioned peeking out her office window, how she always found herself watching for him. That was flattering, but still. He'd felt jarred by it. What if he were just out on some stupid errand, grabbing the paper or the mail out of the box, if he hadn't shaved or his shirt was on sideways?

The voice came a second time. It was *not* Connie's. However, the next one might be, he warned himself. He shook off his gloves and poked his tools back in their wire caddy. It was four something. She probably got off work pretty soon.

As he scrubbed his hands, he rehearsed telling Elise the Connie story. Elise was coming over for dinner tonight after she finished her shift.

He started organizing the food he had bought earlier at the farmer's market. He got out a lemon and some lettuce in cello wrap, a net bag of radishes, a plum tomato. He heaped what he wanted of that into a wooden bowl; returned to the refrigerator and ripped a few sprigs of parsley. "Less like a picnic," he said to himself. He arranged a serving plate with slices of honey-baked ham; another with deviled egg halves and used the parsley for garnish. He knew he was not a great cook. With the exception of the jumbo shrimp he had grilled for Elise and her mom on July 4th. Those were delicious.

He carried the serving dishes into the dining room. It was too *soon* but he wanted to try the food to see how it looked set on the table. He got out a big linen tablecloth, gripped it by the ends, and flapped it hugely in the air to wave out the folds.

The cats somersaulted in. They leaped onto the sideboard. They stood poised and still and gazed at the platter of ham.

"Scary monster," Buddy told them, but sighed and dropped the tablecloth. He marched the ham back to the kitchen and hid it deep inside the refrigerator.

Elise knew a lot, in his opinion. She'd earned a degree in social psych and she was popular with the patients at Cherry Trees. Maybe he would skip complaining to her about Connie. That could only cause worry. He should be more circumspect. Why bother Elise?

He did call, but merely to ask how she was doing and to confirm their dinner plans. "I don't want anything," he said when she came to the phone.

"They sent Martha to the Time Out Room," Elise said. "The woman admitted last Saturday? You should see her now, though. Calm and quiet. Like she's had some realizations. Or been given back her doll."

"Who else is in your group?" Buddy asked. "I know you've told me."

"Well, it's evil and immoral that I did and I'll probably roast in hell for it. Donna, with the mysterious migraines. She's been here the longest. Next is Lorraine, the obsessive one who bought a hundred clear plastic tote bags. Barry, the E.R. nurse. He's tired, is all that's wrong with that man. And there's Doug, the pilot-error guy. Martha. Vincent. Oh, and the new girl. I love her! She reminds me of somebody. Kim Novak maybe."

"Then I love her too," Buddy said.

"Or she's one of the Gabors. With her collar turned up? Always dancing and singing with a scarf tied on her wrist, like this is a musical. I have to go, Buddy."

"I know you do," he said. "How'd they make out with Vincent? They captured him yet?"

"No, unfortunately. But he has been seen. Well, of course, he's been seen! At practically every patient's window. And in their closets. Or he's standing right beside them in the mirror."

"Don't make jokes," Buddy said.

"No, I have to," said Elise, and she clicked off.

✿

Buddy had the dinner table all prepared and he wanted to start the candles. He had read on the carton that the wicks would flame more evenly if lighted once in advance. He went hunting for stick matches, which weren't where they were supposed to be, in the cabinet over the stove. The sun was going down and he glanced through the sliding glass doors to the side porch. Connie was here, sitting in the swing, mechanically rocking an end of it. She held a cigarette and was staring ardently at the floor.

Buddy forgot himself for a second. He wasn't sure what to do. He crept out of the room, turned around, and came back.

"Nine one one," he said to the cats before he slid the door and took himself outside.

"So, what's shaking?" he asked. He made an unconcerned walk across the porch and to the railing. Half the sky had grown purple. There were red clouds twisted like a rope above the lake.

Connie went on gazing at the floorboards but stopped the swing with the heels of her shoes. They were snakeskin or lizard, very dark maroon. "Don't be mad," she said.

"I'm not," said Buddy.

"I like to sit in strange places, don't you? Especially if it's someone else's place. I play a little game of seeing what effect it has on them."

The curve of her throat when she looked up now was lovely. That surprised Buddy out of making a comment on the game.

"I wonder if it's ever occurred to you," she said. "These past two summers. The drought, right? You've heard about it on the news. You probably aren't aware that I live in Langley. My father and I. You always hear it called 'Scrap Pile' but it's Langley. It is poor and it's all wrecked. Of course, my father didn't guess that would *happen* when he inherited our house. This is only about eight miles—"

"Isn't that . . . Crabapple?" Buddy asked.

"No, it isn't. Crabapple's about twelve miles. Or was, it hardly exists anymore. But you wouldn't go there, so that's part of my point."

Buddy shuffled over and lowered himself next to her in the swing.

"When I'm coming to work?" She spoke straight into his face. "It gets greener. And greener. Until it's this lush—I don't know what. There's no drought here. You folks don't have a drought."

Buddy was nodding slowly. "I'm ashamed to admit it. . . ."

Connie exhaled smoke and now rearranged something in herself, as if she were closing one folder and opening the next. "I feel very embarrassed. About the confession I made to you earlier," she said.

"Oh," he said and laughed once. "It's not like I could mind."

"Horseshit." She rose in her seat and flicked her cigarette expertly across the porch into a huddle of Savannas shrubs.

"Connie, my girlfriend is a counselor over at Cherry Trees."

"What about it?" she asked and Buddy winced.

"Sorry," he said, as they both nodded and shrugged.

"You people." Her hand worked in the air. She clutched at nothing, let it go.

She said, "I am happy about this much. I've finally been at my job long enough that I've earned some time off for the things I enjoy. Such as travel."

"Where to?" Buddy asked.

"I'm thinking Belize," Connie said, and after a moment, "I've heard you don't really go anywhere. Mr. Secrest or someone said. No, it was he. He knew your wife. He said you hardly ever go out since your son died."

"That's mostly correct."

She said, "I didn't mean it as a criticism."

꙳

The phone began ringing and—certain the caller was Elise—Buddy apologized, scooted off the swing, and hurried inside.

"I'll never get out of here," Elise said. "I know it ruins our plans. There's no alternative."

"It doesn't matter. We'll do it tomorrow."

"Everyone's so spooked I wouldn't dare leave. And the nurses have them so doped up on sedatives. You should see this, Buddy. They could *hurt* themselves. It's like they're walking on shipboard."

He was smiling.

"It's because we're now told that Vincent is inside the hospital. So there's an all-out search," she said. "Anyway, I did one thing. I raced over to Blockbuster and rented them a movie—*The Matrix*, is what they voted for. That is helping. It's got them focused. All in their pajamas, all in the Tomorrow Room with their bed pillows, doubled up on the couches and lying over chairs."

"*I* want to do that. That sounds great!"

"No, you're not invited," said Elise.

She giggled at something on her end and said to Buddy, "You remember how I said they're always nicknaming the psychiatrists? I just heard, 'Here comes Dr. Post-It-Note accompanying Drs. Liar and Deaf.'"

"My therapist looks like Al Haig."

"That's . . . See, you don't belong here," Elise said.

"I'll call you later on," she told him.

From where he stood, he'd been viewing his dining room setup. His table had crystal, candlesticks, and thirty red chrysanthemums in a vase. He hadn't realized, until the line went dead, how very sharp was his disappointment.

He had stepped down off the porch to inspect the walkway where a couple slate tiles had strayed out of line. He was stooped over, prompting a piece back into place with his shoe. Here were weeds. Here were ants, too, crawling in a long, contorted file.

Connie watched him, smoking hard and unhappily, still in the swing. "I need to say a few things. About my feelings," she said.

He stuffed his hands in his pockets and rejoined her on the porch. He leaned on the far railing, facing her. They were quiet a moment. "I'm sorry. I'm an oaf," he said.

She answered that silently and with a brief, sarcastic smile.

He said, "I do want to hear."

She looked at the ceiling.

"O.K., I probably just don't understand then, Connie." He brought his hands from his pockets, bunched his fingers, and consulted them. "Is it that you have a kind of *fantasy* about me?"

"God, no!" she said and clicked her tongue. "It's actually a little more adult than that." She pronounced the word "*aah*-dult."

Her smile grew reproachful. "So you know all about my feelings."

"Oh, I don't think that."

She said, "Since you're Mister Perfect." She began fussing with the cultured pearl in her ear. "Bet you wish I'd kept my feelings to my own fuckin' self."

It was one of the unhappiest conversations Buddy could recall. "I really don't think any of that," he said.

Connie's long legs were folded now with her feet tucked to the side. She had the grace of someone who had been an athlete or a dancer. And she used her hands prettily, holding one in the other or touching the prim white collar on her dress. Her hair was fascinating—a gleaming black. But there was sorrow in her eyes, or so Buddy thought. They moved slowly, when they did move. Her gaze seldom shifted. Her eyes were heavy, and gave an impression of defeat.

He was thinking, patting his fingertips. He said, "I'll tell you a few things about myself. The morning Matt died, by the time I arrived at the ICU and could locate Ruthie, my wife, she was standing with her face to a wall, clenching her diaphragm like she'd run a marathon and couldn't breathe. So I tiptoed over and tapped her on the shoulder to show I was there. Only she didn't feel it or was too distressed. At any rate, she didn't acknowledge. I wasn't sure. I just stayed there waiting. Until, when she finally did turn she looked straight through me. So, what I did? I gave her this huge *tick-tock* wave. Like, heidy-ho."

He smoothed his hair a few times. "How much have I thought about that! It was just a bad moment probably, a slip-up, but it might've paved the way for this second thing, a situation I found myself in."

He said, "My son was riding his Jet Ski, I don't know what you heard about it."

Connie's head moved, no.

Buddy's head nodded. "On the lake. He crashed into a fishing boat that had a couple of high-school boys. No one else was killed, but damn near. I found it hard. Hard to stop picturing. Then this urge came that if I could talk to someone I didn't know very well. Have a plain conversation with no mention of my son. So, for some reason I chose a woman who's the floor rep at Zack's Print Shop. We'd exchanged a few words. I doubt if she remembered my name. I gave her some information, the first call. I told her their sign—for the rear parking whatchamajiggy—had fallen down. Then I started calling with everything you could name—a TV contest, or foreseeing a weather problem. Or call and make some joke about Zack. Ten, fifteen times a day. Sitting in a spindly chair there with the phone, not even comfortable. And my poor wife, having to overhear all of this, was just beside herself. As to why I kept harassing this woman. Who, finally, when it got too much, went downtown and filed a restraining order."

"Man!" Connie said.

"She did indeed," said Buddy.

He got up. The cats were yowling and hopping at the glass door. "I have to stop for a second and give them dinner. I'll be right back."

"Go," Connie said, "go," and signaled with a flick of her hand that she understood.

✎

While he was filling the dish with Science Diet, he caught her figure in the shadows, descending the porch stairs.

Buddy rocked on his shoes. Now a light switched on at the lawyers' place next door.

He watched as the cats chowed. He refreshed their water.

He stood in the center of the kitchen and waited, without going to a window, for the effect of a taxicab's headlights out on the lane.

ↄ

It was quiet where Elise was. She almost had to whisper. "This is eerie. All the patients' colored faces in the TV light? It's despicable that I'm always canceling on you. It's the worst thing I do. It's what destroyed every relationship I've had."

"Oh God, let that be true," Buddy said.

He was flicking a stub of paper around on the countertop, to no end. "Are you ever nervous around me?" he asked Elise.

"What?"

"Nervous *about* me, I mean. Because of the way I bothered that woman."

"Don't insult me," Elise said.

"Excuse me?"

"I'm a smart person. One of the smart ones. They insisted on textbooks where I went to school."

"Oh," he said.

There was a pause between them. Buddy paced up and back a step, holding the phone. The room was overly warm and the cats had taken to the cool of the floor tiles.

"I should go," Elise said. "I really have to pee. Plus they're right now carrying Vincent in on a stretcher. Directed toward the Time Out Room is my guess. Will you be O.K.? Do you feel O.K.?"

"Maybe I'll just keep that to my own fucking *self*," he said and grinned. "It's a joke you don't know. I'm sorry. I'll explain it to you some other time."

"They don't need me that bad. I'm free to talk," Elise said.

"No, I feel fine. The joke isn't even about me." His index finger traced around and around one of the blue tiles set in the countertop.

"Listen to me a second," she said. "Are you there? This is the last thing I want to say before I have to hang up. Grief is very mysterious, Buddy. It's very personal."

"'Bye for now," she said, and Buddy stayed a moment after he'd hung up the phone, his hand on the receiver, his arm outstretched.

꘏

He stood on the side porch. The night was warm and a full white moon dawdled over Likely Lake.

Across the lane at the Tishmans' a car was adjusting behind a line of cars—latecomers for the bridge party Carl and Suzanne hosted every other week. One of them or somebody appeared in the entryway, there to welcome in the tardy guest.

Buddy was thinking about other nights, when he and Elise had sat out here until late, telling each other stories and drinking rum. On his birthday, she had worn a sequined red dress. There were nights with his wife, their last sad year.

How silly, he thought, that Connie's confession had bothered him. He should have absorbed it. He should have taken her hand and held her hand, as a friend, or even clenched it, and said what a very long life it can seem.

30

Yours

A llison struggled away from her white Renault, limping with the weight of the last of the pumpkins. She found Clark in the twilight on the twig- and leaf-littered porch, behind the house. He wore a tan wool shawl. He was moving up and back in a cushioned glider, pushed by the ball of his slippered foot.

Allison lowered a big pumpkin and let it rest on the porch floor.

Clark was much older than she—seventy-eight to Allison's thirty-five. They had been married for four months. They were both quite tall, with long hands, and their faces looked something alike. Allison wore a natural-hair wig. It was a thick blonde hood around her face. She was dressed in bright-dyed denims today. She wore durable clothes, usually, for she volunteered afternoons at a children's day-care center.

She put one of the smaller pumpkins on Clark's long lap. "Now, nothing surreal," she told him. "Carve just a *regular* face. These are for kids."

In the foyer, on the Hepplewhite desk, Allison found the maid's chore list, with its cross-offs, which included Clark's supper. Allison went quickly through the day's mail: a garish coupon packet, a flyer advertising white wines at Jamestown Liquors, November's pay-TV program guide, and—the worst thing, the funniest—an already opened, extremely unkind letter from Clark's married daughter, up North. "You're an old fool," Allison read, and "You're being cruelly deceived." There was a gift check for twenty-five dollars, made out to Clark, enclosed—his birthday had just passed—but it was uncashable. It was signed "Jesus H. Christ."

Late, late into this night, Allison and Clark gutted and carved the pumpkins together, at an old table set out on the back porch. They worked over newspaper after soggy newspaper, using paring knives and spoons and a Swiss Army knife Clark liked for the exact shaping of teeth and eyes and nostrils. Clark had been a doctor—an internist—but he was also a Sunday watercolor painter. His four pumpkins were expressive and artful. Their carved features were suited to the sizes and shapes of the pumpkins. Two looked ferocious and jagged. One registered surprise. The last was serene and beaming.

Allison's four faces were less deftly drawn, with slits and areas of distortion. She had cut triangles for noses and eyes. The mouths she had made were all just wedges—two turned up and two turned down.

By one A.M., they were finished. Clark, who had bent his long torso forward to work, moved over to the glider again and looked out sleepily at nothing. All the neighbors' lights were out across the ravine. For the season and time, the Virginia night was warm. Most of the leaves had fallen and blown away already, and the trees stood unbothered. The moon was round, above them.

Allison cleaned up the mess.

"Your jack-o'-lanterns are much much better than mine," Clark said to her.

"Like hell," Allison said.

"Look at me," Clark said, and Allison did. She was holding a squishy bundle of newspapers. The papers reeked sweetly with the smell of pumpkin innards. "Yours are *far* better," he said.

"You're wrong. You'll see when they're lit," Allison said.

She went inside, came back with yellow vigil candles. It took her a while to get each candle settled into a pool of its own melted wax inside the jack-o'-lanterns, which were lined up in a row on the porch railing. Allison went along and relit each candle and fixed the pumpkin lids over the little flames. "See?" she said. They sat together a moment and looked at the orange faces.

"We're exhausted. It's good-night time," Allison said. "Don't blow out the candles. I'll put in new ones tomorrow."

In her bedroom, a few weeks earlier in her life than had been predicted, she began to die. "Don't look at me if my wig comes off," she told Clark. "Please." Her pulse cords were fluttering under his fingers. She raised her knees and kicked away the comforter. She said something to Clark about the garage being locked.

At the telephone, Clark had a clear view out back and down to the porch. He wanted to get drunk with his wife once more. He wanted to tell her, from the greater perspective he had, that to own only a little talent, like his, was an awful, plaguing thing; that being only a little special meant you expected too much, most of the time, and liked yourself too little. He wanted to assure her that she had missed nothing.

Clark was speaking into the phone now. He watched the jack-o'-lanterns. The jack-o'-lanterns watched him.